Spells

Spells

Michel de Ghelderode

TRANSLATED BY GEORGE MACLENNAN

WAKEFIELD PRESS
CAMBRIDGE, MASSACHUSETTS

Wakefield Press, P.O. Box 425645,
Cambridge, MA 02142

Originally published as *Sortilèges*, 1941 (Paris-Brussels,
Éditions L'Essor) and 1947 (Liège-Paris, Maréchal,
"édition définitive").

This book was set in Garamond Premier Pro
and Helvetica Neue LT Pro by Wakefield Press.
Printed and bound in the United States of America.

ISBN: 978-1-939663-20-7

Available through D.A.P./Distributed Art Publishers
155 Sixth Avenue, 2nd Floor
New York, New York 10013
Tel: (212) 627-1999
Fax: (212) 627-9484

10 9 8 7 6 5 4 3 2 1

CONTENTS

TRANSLATOR'S INTRODUCTION

Who are you then, Michel de Ghelderode?
—André Pieyre de Mandiargues

Recognized in Belgium and France as a distinguished twentieth-century dramatist, Michel de Ghelderode is relatively little known in the English-speaking world. A flurry of interest in him arose in the 1960s when two volumes of his plays were translated and some were performed. At that time, Artaud, Ionesco, and the theaters of cruelty and the absurd were in vogue; although Ghelderode, a lifelong citizen of Brussels, had few links with French avant-garde theater, the carnivalesque dimension of his plays and their rejection of realism made him seem like a close relative, and he benefited from the perceived kinship. But the Anglophone interest in his theater was short lived and is currently restricted to scholars and specialists.

Even more neglected are Ghelderode's stories. His major collection, *Spells*, was first published in 1941, and since then only one of its stories has appeared in English.[1] This is perhaps understandable: *Spells* is an isolated volume of short stories in the marginal genre of the fantastic and signed by a little recognized name. It has, however, achieved near classic status in Belgium and France, where it has been continuously in print for over half a century.

Spells has its own history, one that, perhaps, tells a particular story of its own. In the first edition Ghelderode gave an indicative date of 1939 at the end of the volume, but in the postwar second edition he altered this to 1919–1939, leaving readers to infer that the stories had gradually accumulated over the span of his writing life. This was assumed to be the case until Roland Beyen, examining Ghelderode's papers for his biographical study of the writer, found that they had in fact been written, in a few concentrated bursts, between February 1939 and April 1940.[2] This, given the sustained quality of the work, is an achievement that Ghelderode had reason to be proud of. So why the misleadingly changed dates? I would suggest that he wanted, retrospectively, to conceal the fact that

Spells was written when Belgium was under threat from Nazi Germany. In 1940, he had expressed pro-German sentiments in letters to friends; even more damagingly, he had, in the early 1940s, given a series of broadcasts on Nazi-controlled Radio-Bruxelles. These were largely nonpolitical but led, in 1945, to suspension from his regular employment on grounds of collaboration. His revision of *Spells* overlapped with his fight to clear his name.[3] Given these circumstances, he might have been mindful that two of the stories include indulgent references to the Spanish Habsburg conquest of Flanders; it was possible that, in 1947, Belgian readers might draw unwelcome parallels. The first edition, moreover, had featured a story that now threatened to become a major embarrassment. "Eliah the Painter," the only story that engages directly with modernity, is one of the blackest anti-Semitic fictions in twentieth-century literature. Unsurprisingly, it disappeared from the 1947 edition. At the same time a newly written preface by Franz Hellens was added, a straightforward literary resource no doubt, but, in reminding readers of Ghelderode's standing as a dramatist, it can also be seen as a prophylactic against any possible controversy.[4] The edition was then designated as definitive, a tacit disavowal of the wartime first edition.

The 1941 edition was birthed quickly but not happily. In addition to the onset of war, Ghelderode was experiencing isolation, neglect, and aggravated ill health—he even at times feared that his death was imminent. He had also developed a persecution complex, feeling himself vulnerable to various hostile forces.[5] Roland Beyen takes *Spells* as evidence of an acute psychological malaise: in his view the stories bear witness to an "increasing neurosis," indeed are "the fruits of a crisis."[6] Ghelderode was taking morphine to relieve his physical and nervous symptoms, and for Beyen this too informs the stories: "Their strangeness and their morbid and hallucinatory character might well be explained in part by narcotics."[7] Dreams and hallucinatory visions feature prominently: a number of the stories unfold on the open border between the fantastic and the oneiric, and an ambiguous overlap between dream states and reality determines the denouement of at least three of them.

But however relevant Ghelderode's ills might be, the confidence and technical control of his storytelling are never in doubt. The prose style is assured and flexible, able to shift between idiomatic directness and heightened eloquence. The stories are achieved on their own terms and there is little indication that the author was primarily a dramatist. With *Spells* he was in fact turning his back on the stage. "I've finally done with the theater," he wrote in January 1939: "I'm going in the direction of prose."[8] Hellens's 1947 preface sought to emphasize continuities between the plays and the stories, but this is misleading. While there is a shared antirealism, differences are no less significant. Ghelderode had previously stated that he wanted to pursue "a more inward art."[9] *Spells* bears this out; the voice of the stories is antitheatrical: subjective, interiorized, often introspective.

In addition to Ghelderode's imagination, the stories share his skill in shaping his themes into finished and often resonant narratives. *Spells* is haunted by nostalgia for the past, for its surviving traces in the city, above all in the old religious city: "I have always loved old churches. . . I cannot go past one of the churches of the past, one of our old chapels, without going inside."[10] The comment casts light on the mysticism of some of the stories: "What do I do in these holy places? What would I do other than tell the golden beads of dreams? And if you allow that meditation is a form of prayer, you will see me attentive to the call of angels, to the secret signal from a mystic country whither I shall go when the flame has left the ashes."[11] *Spells* is littered with neglected or decaying churches and cathedrals, church bells, domes, steeples, the grounds and cemeteries of old monasteries. These, along with the frequent presence of fog, contribute to a pervading unreality. In Ghelderode's unreal cities the uncanny lies close at hand: "Only the brute can deny that we are surrounded by the supernatural, that we lose our footing to the extent that reason advances in its sloping territories."[12] Miracles occur in at least four of the stories, for example in "Spells," where the alienated narrator is bent on suicide by drowning. This impulse transforms into a horrifying visitation, one that threatens not so much his life as his soul; at the crucial moment, however, he is saved by a mysterious guardian angel.

Spells is an emblematic title, one that was perhaps relevant to Ghelderode's state of mind at the time; Janus-like, the spell can either afford protection or threaten harm. Its dual nature, both holy and unholy, is glimpsed in "The Sick Garden" when the narrator attempts to recite a "prayer for the dead" with "Latin words as glorious as a magical incantation." Religion, in its supernatural guise, is fraught with such ambiguities; in "The Collector of Relics" a ciborium, a holy vessel serving in the "sacrificial" mass, becomes the focus of an uncanny spell; the sick garden, "a corrupt domain given over to the devil," is also "hallowed ground"—the site of a Carmelite graveyard.

An ambiguous commerce between the demonic and the angelic may provide one of the keys to unlock the mysteries of "the Sick Garden." "Spells" is Ghelderode's strangest, most original story; but "The Sick Garden" is no less remarkable. With a distinctive narrative that plays on both gothic and fairy-tale conventions, it has become his most celebrated work of fiction. André Pieyre de Mandiargues particularly congratulated Ghelderode on these two titles; their effect was, he said, "stunning."[13]

The narrator of "The Sick Garden" happens to visit a fairground where he wins a toy doll. This detail highlights a topic that was close to Ghelderode's heart, namely his fascination with masks and effigies:

> Even today I collect marionettes, dolls, puppets, little rag creatures that the children of today scorn—also dummies with lovely mortal faces of wax, models of hands,

adorable heads of young martyrs. [. . .] I welcome all these human shapes and reminders of human shapes to my home; I collect these image-beings as treasures. They are silent presences—I say they are presences, presumptions.

All these effigies thrill me by the fact of their somewhat magical nature, and even though flesh and blood actors can weary me and often disappoint me, marionettes, because of their natural reserve and silence, manage to console me. [. . .] Naturally I wasn't able to understand all this from my first playtime. [. . .] But even then I believed—and this strange belief is not yet dead in me—that objects were sensitive, living.[14]

This theme provides the title of Roland Beyen's critical biography—*Michel de Ghelderode ou la hantise du masque*—"the spell of the mask," a spell that extends to the author's name: "Martens was the face, Ghelderode the mask."[15] Beyen's book seeks to unmask and demystify its subject, but also acknowledges that "little by little Ghelderode came to coincide with his mask."[16]

The French word "masque" has three available levels of meaning, only one of which can be directly translated as "mask." Depending on context, it can denote a festival masker, and also, less obviously, the expression or features of the face. Ghelderode is able to play on these levels, creating puns and ambiguities that subtly merge man with masker, mask with face (an effect unfortunately lost in translation). More generally, *Spells* blurs the line between the flesh-and-blood human and its nonhuman replication in cardboard, wax, porcelain, or wood. In "The Public Scribe," the narrator visits a waxwork in a private museum. He feels a spiritual kinship with the effigy and the two become doubles as he breathes life into it. The theme is disconcertingly reversible; by a flip of the coin the human can be taken for something inanimate. In "Spells" the narrator is accosted by a street vendor, an old woman who urges him to buy a carnival mask. He says that he'll buy the one the woman is wearing. "I'm not wearing a mask," she barks, "it's my own face!" The episode is paradigmatic; characters in *Spells* are typically little more than narrative puppets. However, given the uncanny power of the Ghelderodian puppet, this isn't necessarily a handicap; when, in "The Collector of Relics," an antique dealer is viewed by the narrator in less than human terms, he becomes, as though in consequence, endowed with a mysterious potency and turns the tables on the narrator's attempt to manipulate and victimize him.

Voiced by dedicated solitaries, the narratives discount social or even human relationships. Companionship is found in the forms of a wax dummy, a dog, and a costumed devil. In "Stealing from Death," a drinking companion who makes professions of friendship turns out to be a jealous hypocrite. Women too are in short supply; Ghelderode, in a draft prospectus for a planned further collection of stories, promised that women would feature more centrally but, as it turned out, no such stories were written.

However, *Spells* is less somber than this account might suggest. While some of the stories pose enigmas or seem to ask for interpretation, others can be read straightforwardly in terms of genre, or as *jeux d'esprit*. "Stealing from Death" has the simplicity and morality of a folk tale; "You Were Hanged" is a wonderfully atmospheric spook story. "The Collector of Relics," "Rhotomago," and "The Devil in London" vary the tone with sarcastic humor, irony, and whimsicality. So, too, does "The Odor of Pine," though this story pushes its mordant humor to a grotesque extreme.

Spells was Ghelderode's only volume of *contes fantastiques*. In 1942 he started work on a further collection, but "The Odor of Pine," later incorporated in the 1947 edition, was the only story completed before the project was abandoned, leaving just a few fragments to which he never returned.[17] There were to be no further stories. Roland Beyen detects in Ghelderode's later plays an evolution "toward an art that feeds more and more on the personal obsessions of its creator."[18] This development culminates with *Spells*; Ghelderode himself wrote, "In my case the story has a confessional value, and whoever has properly read these tales knows my entire soul."[19] In *The Ostend Interviews* he declared that all the stories originated in incidents in his life, and while none of his varied narrators should be mistaken for Ghelderode himself, autobiographical details abound. A number of characters are based on people Ghelderode knew personally. In two of the stories we can deduce that the narrator is of an age with the author. Like several of his narrators and characters he kept dogs, cats, and a pet bird. The various ailments suffered by his narrators can be traced directly back to his condition in the late 1930s: he was asthmatic, depressive, neurasthenic, prostrated by hot weather, and took doses of morphine to alleviate his symptoms. The narrator of "The Devil in London" shares Ghelderode's own memory of the 1910 Brussels World Fair, part of which was destroyed in a fire. "Nuestra Señora de la Soledad" is an actual Hispanic Madonna that Ghelderode visited in l'église de la Chapelle, Brussels. Jacqueline Blancart-Cassou, a Ghelderode scholar, provides further details, outlining a generic narrator who doubles Ghelderode himself:

> Like Ghelderode he lives in Brussels; his street and the heavy door of his house can be found in "Fog," and, elsewhere, there are the churches of St.-Nicolas and the Riches-Claires. [. . .] The antiquarian Ladouce is none other than the antiquarian and man of letters Julien de la Doès. [. . .] Ghelderode said that he knew the innkeeper Jef. As for the servant Mortal Sin, she was actually in service with him and was called Mme. Lambert; it was, so it seems, her red-haired beauty, too much of a temptation, that earned her this nickname.[20]

While the cumulative effect of the collection derives from Ghelderode's imagination, its sense of conviction is rooted in his complicated personality, his experiences, emotions, and obsessions.

In 1932, already in a love-hate relationship with the theater, he had asked, "When can I write the tales and stories I dream of?"[21] His thoughts continued to dwell on the topic, for example in a letter of 1936; "I'm returning to the story which was the genre I chose at the start of my career."[22] By 1939, the seeds of *Spells* had evidently been germinating for some time, and the speed at which they were written suggests an unleashing of pent-up energies.[23] Did this creative surge then deplete his reserve of deeply felt story materials? After 1942, his creative powers, affected by ill health and wartime conditions, went into a steep decline from which they never recovered; but we might speculate that another reason why he abandoned further attempts at story-writing is that, as a writer driven by obsessions, he had already explored these so thoroughly.

The relationship between the stories and the life now became a closed circle. The situation of the scribe Pilatus in his museum uncannily foretold that of Ghelderode himself: a writer with pen frozen in hand, enclosed in an interior littered with curios and effigies that was, with supreme irony, destined to become itself a museum, the *Musée-bibliothèque Michel de Ghelderode*.

Ghelderode is a distinctive presence in European literature, but we should not hurry to claim literary respectability for his stories in *Spells*. Their ability to disturb and provoke the reader is a guarantee of their unrespectable *élan vital*.

ACKNOWLEDGMENTS

Thanks to Marc Lowenthal who initiated this edition and also checked the translations, advising usefully on a number of issues. Further thanks to Judith Feldmann for copyediting and more. *Spells* has benefited from their care and attention. Any remaining shortcomings are mine alone.

NOTES

1. "The Odor of Pine," translated by Kim Connell in his anthology, *The Belgian School of the Bizarre* (Madison, NJ: Fairleigh Dickinson University Press, 1998).
2. Roland Beyen, *Michel de Ghelderode ou la hantise du masque* (Brussels, 1971), p. 289. Beyen, the leading authority on Ghelderode, edited his collected correspondence in twelve volumes and curated, in Paris and Brussels, a major exhibition on Ghelderode's life and work.
3. In January 1945, Ghelderode, named as a collaborator, was suspended from his clerical job

in the Schaerbeek town hall archive. On appeal, the matter was eventually resolved in his favor, but he was left feeling badly wounded; he never returned to work, and in late 1946 took retirement with a pension on grounds of ill health. See Beyen, *Michel de Ghelderode ou la hantise*, pp. 293–298.

4. Hellens, a close friend and a respected writer, was active in Ghelderode's defense during his appeal against suspension. The preface is well intentioned but limited and careless.

5. "A feeling of fundamental insecurity [. . .] drove Ghelderode to see society as a vast espionage network directed in the first place against poets and against himself." Beyen, *Michel de Ghelderode ou la hantise*, p. 502.

6. Ibid., pp. 288–289.

7. Ibid., p. 289.

8. Ibid, p. 98.

9. Ibid., p. 279.

10. *Ghelderode: Seven Plays*, translated by George Hauger (New York: Hill & Wang, 1967), p. 6. Hauger includes a well-translated selection of extracts from *The Ostend Interviews*. These were originally radio interviews conducted by Roger Iglésis and Alain Trutat (1951); they were subsequently reworked by Ghelderode and published in 1956, still in the form of interviews but effectively a volume of personal reflections, full of insights into his life and work.

11. *Ghelderode: Seven Plays*, p. 6.

12. Ibid., p. 13.

13. Letter of December 1952 to Ghelderode, quoted in Beyen, *Michel de Ghelderode ou la comédie des apparences* (Paris: Centre Georges Pompidou, 1980), p. 216.

14. *Ghelderode: Seven Plays*, pp. 23–24.

15. Beyen, *Michel de Ghelderode ou la hantise*, p. 71.

16. Ibid., p. 368.

17. The intended title story, "Le dormeur de Bruges," exists as a ten-page fragment, tantalizingly unpublished.

18. Beyen, *Michel de Ghelderode ou la hantise*, p. 266.

19. Letter to Henri Vernes, quoted in the preface to the Marabout edition of *Sortilèges* (Presses de Gérard, 1962).

20. Blancart-Cassou, in *Michel de Ghelderode, dramaturge et conteur*, ed. Raymond Trousson (Brussels: Éditions de l'Université de Bruxelles, 1983), p. 138.

21. In Beyen, *Michel de Ghelderode ou la hantise*, p. 281, note 2.

22. Ibid., p. 278.

23. For example, the three most substantial stories, "The Sick Garden," "Spells," and "Eliah," were written respectively in twenty days, fourteen days, and ten days.

The
Public
Scribe

To the poet Marcel Wyseur

At that time I made my home in the Nazareth district. It was an all but abandoned area not far from the embankments of the old city walls and overgrown with vegetation, as though the nearby countryside had advanced into the town to reclaim its territory. You lost yourself there in a labyrinth of winding alleys between low buildings or interminable blind walls, mazes that made this decayed neighborhood into a vast, remarkably peaceful enclosure. Push open some worm-eaten door, and you came upon a field where sheep were grazing and orphans from a neighboring institute often chased about. The silence that reigned there was a true blessing, so much so that birds squabbling became a serious disturbance. And I wished for this mystic neighborhood to remain as it was, its roofs bowed under the weight of doves. Time barely existed there, and the bells that seemed to chime in the trees were indubitably mad.

I happened to leave my rooms at the close of day, my idle footsteps leading me toward a monastic-looking building that was still called the Beguinage. There were no more Beguines remaining behind these gables of rose-red brick, and the monumental entrance adjoining the aged building was rarely open. I possessed its heavy key, which conferred upon me the privilege of crossing the threshold of that house of yesteryear. I was also one of the few people to know that it sheltered a humble and endearing little museum of popular life and arts; a museum unknown to the majority, with no notices revealing it to passersby and to which I had free access, thanks to having assisted in its creation through some gifts and benevolent collaborations. The fact that I retained a key to the building spoke to the confidence placed in me by the founder—my smiling, white-haired friend Canon Dumercy. Although the finishing touches had long since been put to the museum, the Canon invented a thousand excuses for forever deferring the formal opening, seemingly fearful that the public would profane the pious refuge where his artless collections slumbered. I accepted the old man's arguments, which invariably concluded, "And anyway, my museum has its visitor, which is you ... That's good enough ..." Season after season I remained that exclusive visitor, something that never failed to flatter me. Wasn't I furnished with the key, not to a mystery, but to a place that was mysterious in the eyes of many people? That was enough to make me happy ...

Once past the main entrance you came across a square garden enclosed on three sides by the covered galleries of the Beguinage: an astonishing garden; a virgin forest where deep-rooted vegetation was inextricably entangled. Sundials or decapitated statues resting on some stub of granite emerged from grass gone wild. And an entire secret life swarmed in these vegetal masses whose proliferation threatened the stability of the enclosure's old walls. At the same time the garden retained a relative order thanks to the ironwork well that marked its center and the plumes of the four poplar trees grown tall at its corners.

Upon entering I was invariably greeted by sinister cries; a jay, crest bristling, stared at my arrival from the bottom of its cage, ready to attack. This impudent bird was better than a guard dog and alerted its master to my presence. Then Daniel, the warden, emerged from his lodge, a kind of outlying pavilion assigned to him for living quarters by his patron, the canon. He was a singular character and not easily defined, this courteous septuagenarian of whom it was said that as a fellow-seminarian he had been the intimate friend of the present bishop. His discreet and old-fashioned manners gave him a vaguely clerical appearance. I respected the old bachelor who practiced a philosophical renunciation, happy in the affection of a jay, smoking and dreaming in this garden where, when the sun failed to shine, there was no way of knowing the time of day. After what vicissitudes had he become warden, indeed the conservator of the Museum? Destiny knows what it's about, and in this case the fine old fellow seemed to have found his place, superannuated and dusty like the things he oversaw, and like them, precious and full of charm. In exchange for my deference Daniel thought well of me. "Make yourself at home! . . ." he announced ceremoniously on the occasion of each of my visits, and returned to his lodge, retreating backwards with little nods of his head.

I was without question at home in this bygone place, bathed in a light that was mellowed by stained glass windows, and whose shadows and calm no one could appreciate more than me. I wandered through the galleries and the rooms, knowing the sound made by each flagstone, what odors awaited me at each doorway. And in my heart how much I approved of the canon for keeping this house of memory closed! . . . The elderly child had been unconcerned with classifying the objects according to any method; he'd taken advantage of the existing décor to recreate interiors peopled by mannequins in costume. And in this way one visited the lacemakers or the weaver, after having visited the enchanting shop where schoolchildren spent their pocket money, or tumbled down to a dank cellar for puppet shows. What did I care that all this was dead . . . Night arrived surreptitiously and took me by surprise, seated at the hearth or bent over pious images. I regretted having to leave this home of remembrances and dreams. Daniel had taken in the jay's cage and I saw him through the window of his lodge, drowsing in the light of an oil flame. His head nodded, a mannequin just like those I was leaving behind, become a museum object under the round eye of the stopped clock whose weights touched the ground.

However, the most appealing representative of that community of effigies was not the warden. There was another person whom I took pleasure in visiting in the fading light and who, like Daniel, remained in place only through the good graces of the canon. He was called Pilatus, the name he had in fact borne when alive, soon to be a hundred years ago. To reach him you crossed a little interior courtyard behind the main body of buildings and at the end of which stood a deconsecrated chapel. A painted sign announced: *Public Scribe. Calligrapher. Letters, requests, and pleas for mercy. Visitors' books for companies, prose and verse for every occasion. Discretion honored* . . . How could one not be drawn to an individual who dwelt in a chapel, wrote poetry, and retained a sense of honor? No need to knock on the door or to enter in order to see him; all you had to do was to approach a lead-latticed side window. Pilatus was seated right beside it, at his table, clearly visible in the light. His age wasn't easily determined, but his russet coat and certain details of his dress said that he must have been born at the end of the eighteenth century. He no longer wore a wig like his fathers but he wore his gray hair long. And his triple-knotted black silk cravat lent him the appearance of some notary's clerk from the time when guineas were good gold and estates were feudal. But the good man's humble status and self-effacing attitude notwithstanding, he seemed to be of different descent. I found in him a fine air of priestliness, a distant resemblance to Daniel: the same clean-shaven face, with a hint of Voltaire, thin, discreet lips, qualities of listening attentively inscribed in the tilt of his head, and that glassy look that seemed to be full of thoughts, or else of dreams . . . A kindly little glimmer hid in the oval of that misty look, the indulgence of old souls who have seen everything and understood everything; the look of a father confessor. Why did I imagine that Pilatus too could have been a former seminarian who had turned aside from holy orders in times of trouble or through a nobly concealed passion? As for Canon Dumercy, he found this an appealing hypothesis and confirmed that the public scribe could have been worth more than his station in life. Hadn't he left Latin satires on the follies of his day in manuscript? And couldn't one read the names of Ovid and Horace in tarnished gilt on the faded bindings of the row of books lined up near his writing desk? But did the canon push his research any further forward? No, because between the dictionaries and almanacs he'd found a certain collection of *Gallant Letters* and brochures of the *Grimoire of Pope Honorius* genre, things that, in spite of the passing years, gave off a troubling whiff of the boudoir or a disquieting smell of the bonfire.

For a long time I was content to contemplate his presence from the outside, nose pressed to the glass, fearing to spoil the feeling of delight with which his presence filled me. The reflections of the setting sun helped me note the family of objects that bore witness to this prolonged existence. Beside the straw armchair occupied by the writer a vacant seat awaited the visitor, the woman or, more often, the young girl of whose sighs and tender sorrows he was going to glean. Yellowed leaves of paper were waiting within reach of his right hand, near the pens, the erasing knife, the candle, and the sealing wax. This hand, which I unreservedly admired, did credit to the sculptor who fashioned it. Elongated and as though transparent, it captivated me even more than the excellent man's lean face, not just any hand but the true right hand of the writer and scholar, more used to handling engravings or medallions. It summed up the tastes and character of the man, and, such as it appeared, adorned with a gold ring, I knew it would be incapable of writing down any ignoble thoughts. It remained suspended over the blank paper, holding the quill, ready to lift or lower it. But at the very moment that it seemed about to inscribe its calligraphy it also made a bizarre gesture, as though keeping an overexcited confidant from pressing in too closely, and again, as though to chase away inquisitive onlookers crowding the window. I was so impressed by this that I waited for weeks before daring to push open the door.

I'm not ashamed to admit that my first visit to Master Pilatus made me uneasy. I finally made my mind up one evening, having overcome my timidity and also my reluctance to intrude on a creature of so much unmoving dignity, who was so perfectly silent; but wasn't it his job to welcome visitors? Once inside the chapel, and after examining the furnishings, I greeted the gentleman no less seriously and sincerely than if he'd been real, and better still, I addressed him loudly, no doubt to compensate for the overly intense silence of the place.

"Master Pilatus, I'm honored . . . I esteem and admire you. No, I haven't come to ask you for anything, except permission to take my own good time in looking at you; I won't ask you to write me a love letter, business letter, or letter to a friend, even though my handwriting is clumsy and bad. I only want to sit by your side, as though I were a man like you, a man from a previous era still living on . . . I only want to sit in silence near you and to be still like you."

Soliciting his approval, it seemed to me that Pilatus smiled benignly for a fleeting moment, perceptible only to me. It was as though his brow lowered at the tail end of my phrase, by which I knew that he had consented to my request. And I sat cautiously down on the chair near the mannequin, intended for the unlettered, afraid to disturb the sleeping objects or even the mere air full of silvery dust. This Pilatus, was he no more than a dummy? In all logic I daresay he could be no more than that; but couldn't he aspire to appear as something more? The wax from which he'd been made was in fact a peculiar substance. And this face, these tinted wax hands, they expressed I don't know what disquieting authenticity . . . For a moment I had the stupid idea that I was sitting near a dead man, forgotten in this chapel whose door I was the first living creature to open after who knows how many years; that this dead man, miraculously preserved by the dryness of the atmosphere, was going to crumble to pieces at the slightest shock, or even from my breath. This shows how much I was a victim of the illusion and how much satisfaction I gained from pursuing it, even at the risk of troubled feelings like those that had overtaken me. This uneasiness persisted; I thought I might dispel it by engaging in a conversation whose burden I knew I would have to bear on my own.

"Master Pilatus, I revere you for practicing that honorable discretion advertised on the placard. Discretion is a difficult virtue; as for honor, it's a glorious sentiment whose name alone uplifts me. Ah, you're lucky to be protected by these walls, to not know anything about modern times! . . . The art of fine penmanship is gone; we only write with the help of machines or barbaric instruments. Better still, the worst imbeciles are literate or educated, even possess diplomas, though few people are able to read, write, or speak correctly, even in the smallest degree . . ."

I digressed in this way to maintain my composure, and Pilatus's smile reappeared, glinting in his pupils rather than traced on his lips. I observed him sideways, enough not to be mistaken. And I continued: "Last but not least, I like you because you protect so many secrets . . . But where are the lovers of yesteryear? . . . And the tears you bore witness to? . . . Nobody comes anymore to confide their hopes or their torments to you. Aren't you hurt by that abandonment? If yes, perhaps you'd accept someone coming to keep you company sometimes? I'll do so if it's agreeable to you, on days when I'm crushed by memories that I'd be able to get rid of if I could only write them down; you won't write them down, no point in that, but you'll be able to listen; that's where all your art, all your genius lies, in this gift for listening, for understanding . . ."

It seemed to me as though the old man nodded his head, consenting to my plea; perhaps an effect of the twilight shadows gaining on everything. My disquiet increased by several degrees, and suddenly came to a head. I felt that my visit had lasted long enough. And in this equivocal moment I found myself fearing that, through some galvanic force, the mannequin might come alive and make a gesture of farewell. Thus far had I been caught up in the illusion; thus far had the spell of the chiaroscuro acted on my nerves . . . I bowed before the man of wax, revealing nothing of the emotion I felt, and went away, too disturbed to feel ridiculous.

This ambiguous quality was absent from my subsequent visits. The ice was broken and Master Pilatus lost that air of abstraction that had made him uncanny. I now thought that when we first met my mistake lay in failing to appreciate the particular expression of the wax, of a creature made of wax. While still not accepting the evidence and admitting that Pilatus was artificial, my behavior toward him was less constrained and without further feelings of apprehension. I'd considered every aspect, explored every avenue; I intuited that that this "presence" accepted mine, and that to be understood by that subtle man I needn't necessarily speak, that by means of a certain telepathic sympathy, all he needed in order to hear was for me to meditate beside him, something I did all the more freely in that my confidant's discretion was dictated by honor. Did I have burdensome secrets to unload? By no means . . . But what I wished to confess would have been difficult to translate into the current idiom. I could easily envisage these things concerning my life but I couldn't easily tell them. What significance Pilatus found in them I don't know. To me, he never seemed inattentive or surprised. That was balm enough for my soul. And I owed an immense gratitude to the good man. I also brought him a faience Chinese grotesquerie, then a snuffbox that must have pleased him and remained on the table. A cordial relationship was established between us, to the point where I once risked placing my hand on his. He didn't remove it, although I felt that diaphanous hand shiver slightly, unused to human contact. The hand was neither cold nor dead, merely a little humid and cool. So we became friends. And I no longer saw anything unusual in the course of my twilight visits. I took great care not to disclose this new relationship. Once, however, I noted that the writing desk had been supplied with excellent black ink and that the goose quills had been trimmed. "It's my friend Daniel who has come across me in the chapel," I thought, "and wants to humor my whims... He's demonstrating his zeal, his devotion to the museum and to myself..." As I left the Beguinage one evening the warden accosted me and asked mischievously if I was satisfied with my companion. Yes, I replied, stopping to look at the little April stars in the poplar trees. When Daniel asked me again why I was sighing, I wasn't afraid to admit that I would like to have been Pilatus, eternally in silence: a man forgotten by other men, who knew how to write wonderfully well yet who never wrote anything, knowing that all is vanity.

This comedy that fooled no one but myself lasted through the springtime. May arrived and suddenly the world was invaded by a light that was so intense it left you blind. As with every reawakening of the sap, that renewal left me with fleeting dizzy spells and a kind of malaise similar to seasickness and that could be called sky sickness. It was in this debilitated state that I paid Pilatus a visit that I believed would be my last for a long time, having decided to remain resting at home until the season turned milder. I have a memory of that visit, during such an intensely mauve sunset that objects seemed to be radiant and nature itself magnetic. Thanks to this initial shock of the sun I'd passed the day in a state of lethargy, mulling over memories of my joyless childhood, and all these remembrances hovered around my heart, which was too feeble to rid me of them. I went into the Beguinage. Everything there was also mauve; mauve the lime-washed chapel and mauve the paper over which the public scribe held his hieratic hand. The chair came to my rescue; I let myself drop feebly onto it. I felt as old as Pilatus, and, just like him, awash with bitter pity, feeling like one returning from a long journey into the past. And in my sadness I let myself lean my head on my confidant's shoulder. I pulled myself together and, with the sweetness of the evening stealing through me, mutely recollected my dreams, my dreams become mauve with the evening. As I actively dreamed in this way, my breast, releasing its burden, was fully refreshed. I freed myself from my dreams; my childhood with all its cortège of Elysian shadows went away. Never was an hour more conducive to confession; never had Pilatus appeared more attentive, obedient to my inner story. Could it be that this old man too had been a child in times long gone? As my emotions left me they seemed to enter him, as though our two souls were in communion. His eye clouded over; I was afraid of seeing a tear sparkling there. But the drop that I expected to see rolling down the scribe's cheek formed in my own eye. And with unutterable happiness and a complete lack of surprise I found, through this new vision come to me, that my old friend was as alive as I was. At that moment his hand and nothing else was quick with life; his hand wrote slowly, resting on the page, and I heard the scratch of the quill. In all honesty it didn't occur to me that this could be some prodigy or happy illusion; the moment had been long preparing—my thoughts magically empowering this marvelous hand.

The summer was overwhelmingly hot. My lassitude worsened to the point where I no longer left my lodgings. The Nazareth district remained plunged in a burning haze and everything there slept, even the birds. It was a solar triumph, universal suffocation, splendid and terrible. The blinding hours were unending and passed in waiting for the all too brief nighttime. In my room, closed against currents from the outside, I suffered like the plants and the stones, poisoned by the azure violence and longing for a darkness that could only exist inside the hardened earth where springs trickle in the dark. My malaise followed the sun's progress and only ended when it set. In an attempt to react, and at the cost of absurd efforts, I pictured to myself fields of snow, icebergs drifting on freezing cold seas, rain-bearing clouds rushing in from the west. Physically exhausted, my head alone lived on, my thoughts gradually heating up with the atmosphere. And as the summer persisted I felt myself slowly dying of petrifaction. Just as dying people sometimes see their whole life unfold before their eyes, I saw again in a pitiless light every episode that made up my mediocre life, the most distant as well as the most recent. Although I had no serious faults of which to accuse myself, I was chained as a witness to this indictment that I brought against myself, punishing myself more effectively than any inquisitor, blaming myself for having never, in spite of my innate but ineffectual goodwill, been happy or brought happiness to anyone. I suffered from being unable to halt the feverish stampede of my thoughts, to the point of wanting a blackout or some congestive disorder to relieve me of consciousness. Ah! To stop thinking, or to expel from my head these thoughts spinning dizzyingly like a disc! . . . At twilight, however, the mad race slowed down, my brain became opaque, the fiery helmet that had imprisoned me gradually cooled. Only at this moment did I take the full measure of my collapse. I tried to tear myself away from my stupor and go out to meet the darkness. "I must get out," I repeated to myself, "get out . . . Go the chapel where Pilatus lives. Why are you deserting him? You're convinced now that he listens to you and understands. Go and confide to him the memories that have polluted you since dawn; he'll gather them up and you'll be rid of them. Even if he writes them down these papers will remain unknown; who will ever read them? . . . That way, tonight your head will be cleansed of its ferment and you'll make room for the obsessions that will visit you tomorrow . . . Go. If not, the sun's magnifying glass will burst your brain and when the scorching weather comes to an end you'll be sterile, mad, a stick of dry wood . . ." Each evening I tried in vain to tear myself away from this dwelling that was for me a torture chamber; I lacked the strength and, in the cowardly way that a man puts off a necessary visit to the doctor or the priest, I put off this outing till the next day. It was the twilight already acting on my soul, and with it came sleep, descending from the stars. My melancholy dissolved. And sleep, entering my rooms surreptitiously, just as it surely entered the man of wax's chamber, found me silent and still. And no doubt sleep thought that I was another man of wax, so thin, pale, and bodily wasted had I become.

The summer flowed by like lava. Not once did I go to visit Pilatus, although that visit, each day deferred, was a source of concern and remorse.

However, when the twilight approached, I prepared to go out, and above all I made myself mentally review the phantoms that had obsessed me, spelling out the essential points in painfully assembled phrases. It was up to Pilatus to divine the rest and develop this bizarre story from the theme I gave him. Wasn't that his job? Having done that, I stayed in place, finding it easier to remain in my armchair where sleep was about to come and overtake me. "Why," I soliloquized, "do I need to be physically present for my thoughts to reach my friend? What are the hundred meters that separate us? Can't I transport myself to my confidant in spirit? . . ." Having accepted this stratagem, I strongly and clearly imagined myself taking the usual route to visit Pilatus. I went into his little room and sat down by his side. And I relayed my thoughts to him; his mediumistic hand captured them, the hand that was soon busy and tracing arabesques on the paper. The euphoric proximity of sleep favored this delectable situation and insensibly leaving wakefulness behind, I was soon no more than a human semblance, hollowed out in the sidereal darkness. At midnight I sometimes emerged from my slumbers, finding myself sitting in my armchair, but tranquilly, as though I'd actually come back from a nocturnal walk. Thus it was that I often saw Pilatus without leaving home, my spirit effortlessly departing from and rejoining my body.

The cauldron of summer exploded at the end of August. Storms thundered uninterruptedly. In a few days, the air was cleared. The rain-washed town was able to breathe again. After that miserable seclusion I emerged from my lethargy and explored the sweet-smelling lanes of my district with all the joy of a schoolboy regaining his freedom. Like a man hastening to a rendez-vous I called straight away at the Beguinage. The rosy façade gave a delicately glazed impression; the gables were outlined against the ultramarine of space, like a scene painted by Vermeer of Delft, and the portal that I opened belonged to an ideal dwelling that I no longer felt worthy of entering. I had scarcely taken a few steps into the garden than the jay made a frightful racket. The bird was thrown into such a state of fury by the sight of me that I hurried away toward the buildings, afraid that it might kill itself against the bars of its cage. Meanwhile I had noticed that the warden wasn't in his lodge, busy as he must surely be in the museum. And I proceeded to the chapel where my old friend the public scribe awaited me. I feared his astonished look, full of reproach: "You here at last? . . ." But a surprise awaited me. Through the glass pane I no longer saw the man of wax seated at his table, where, however, nothing was changed. In his place, comfortably ensconced in the straw armchair and smoking his pipe, was a man of flesh and blood who looked at me with impish benevolence. I burst out laughing, recognizing Daniel.

"And Pilatus? . . ." I called as I entered the chapel.

The warden rose to his feet when I entered and, greeting me, pointed to a shadowy recess where a body lay covered with a canvas sheet. Dumbfounded, I could find nothing to say, but Daniel was able to read the word written in the movement of my lips:

"Dead? . . ."

He smiled and spoke. "Not dead but a little unwell . . . A victim of the sun! . . ."

And he jerked the canvas aside. Pilatus lay on his back, curled up, just as he must have fallen from his seat, knees in the air, his right hand clenched over his chest, so old and ridiculous that I could scarcely suppress a sudden sob. Still, I had enough self-control not to put into words the absurd images aroused in me by this sight, and, leaning over the mannequin, I looked for the cause of his undoing. His face showed a sickly hue and was lined with bitterness; the eyes, extinguished, were sunk into bruised circles; the right hand was contracted. That hand must have suffered. "Poor wretch!" I murmured silently, within myself, "it's I who ruined you in making you write. After having obligingly accepted my first confessions, out of pity, did you rebel against my thoughts taking possession of yours? Did you revolt against this force that held you spellbound from a distance, stronger than your own, until your hand dropped the twisted quill? . . . Forgive me . . . I didn't know what I was doing in thinking so single-mindedly about you, in transmitting to you the unhappy phantasmagorias that festered in my sorry brain . . ."

Daniel's keen voice brought me back to reality: "Come, sir, come, it's much too late in the day to be surprised! . . . Our Pilatus has lain like that in the three months since May, and not a word of complaint . . . Why all this concern?"

I looked at the warden with the look of a simpleton. The good man continued calmly, but keeping an eye me all the while: "As soon as the temperature rose—you'll remember when—I didn't wait for the canon's advice to move this waxwork away from the sun's voracious appetite; it's ruined plenty of objects this year . . . The hand can be remodeled; as for the face, cosmetics will do the job well enough. And before you know it Pilatus will have taken his rightful place again, now that the weather is fresher . . ."

I kept quiet, not daring to ask any questions; I didn't understand. However, with the warden showing a compassionate concern for me, I needed to say something. At last I spoke: "Me too! I've suffered this summer . . . How do I look to you Daniel, since you haven't seen me since the spring?"

This time it was my turn to see my interlocutor's dismay. Daniel appeared taken aback and threw me some odd looks. Disturbed, he was barely able to reply.

"Come now, sir, come . . ." Then approaching me he took my arm with more assurance: "Yes, you've been ill; I can see it . . . I've often been on the point of asking how you were getting on, but I didn't, not wanting to intrude on your solitude . . ." Interrupting himself, he examined me and, finding me calm though puzzled, explained further: "How could you forget that you came here all summer, almost every day, at dusk? . . . You came again the day before yesterday . . ."

I thought that his words came to me in a dream and I waved my hand in front of my face, to dispel a haze, or I don't know what reflection of the declining light. Daniel must have taken this gesture as an admission of the debilitating ill-health that left me at a loss to understand him, for he was full of solicitude.

"I know your habits so well that I wasn't concerned about your daily visits, but I was worried, seeing that your behavior was so odd, and felt it was my duty to keep an eye on you from a distance, not daring to say a word.

So I took a peek into the chapel, where I found you, sitting there instead of Pilatus, head in the clouds and, more often than not, with pen in hand, writing, even writing lots, since I found that the quills had to be trimmed again every morning. Sometimes you were still writing when it got dark. Then you went away like a ghost and without turning round, without a second's hesitation, quietly . . . And if I happened to wish you good evening you didn't reply, something that didn't bother me because I have such a high regard for men like you . . ."

"Yes! . . ." I was only able to stammer, "Ah! Yes . . ." And I contemplated that table where, so I'd been assured, I came to sit down so many times without knowing it, without ever having left my rooms . . . The need for fresh air drove me to the door, and the need too to get away from this place where mysteries held sway. Understanding that I wanted to leave, the warden picked up a bundle of papers from the table and handed it to me.

"Take your papers sir; I'm going to put everything to rights in here and we can both forget about the existence of these writings . . ."

What writings? I accepted the papers without asking for explanation. Daniel followed me like a shadow, all the way to the door. His somber face showed that he regretted this conversation, thinking that it had troubled or pained me. I had enough presence of mind to bid him a friendly farewell and I fled, into the saffron light of a huge moon on the rise . . .

The
Devil
in London

For Franz Hellens

Man's worst enemy after man himself is the microbe; and of all harmful microbes the most dangerous, the one against which there are only empirical remedies, is boredom! But the very worst boredom with which I had to contend was the English boredom that for several months I breathed in like a treacherous gas with the London air, the boredom that is apt to be emitted by a moralizing nation—if not a moral one—and by the most moralizing of all nations. No one will be surprised to learn that in London, the most imposing city on our planet, I was literally crushed by the reality of the boredom that the French call "spleen." All the same, I acknowledge that I'm indebted to it for a bizarre adventure that I'll tell without false modesty or pretended humility.

One dark, foggy morning I was wandering in some squalid commercial quarter, I no longer know which, a kind of evil-smelling depot or suffocating maze stretching alongside the mud of the Thames. It was drizzling rain. The fellow men I encountered showed faces that were either ill or criminal. Dare I describe as a stroll this aimless excursion along the slippery pavement in a fog that seemed to contain every plague known to history? But how else to deal with boredom? "Ah!" I sighed, "if only I had some friend in this monstrous city! . . ." Nevertheless, I congratulated myself on not having a friend and remaining so perfectly alone there. Other people's lives are of no interest to me and I assume that mine can't be of interest to anyone else. That's why I avoid ties with my peers, something that isn't difficult on English soil. But that morning, boredom, like the cold drizzle that it embodied, saturated me to such an extent that I ended up longing to witness some event: for example, a disastrous earthquake or a horrifically strong cyclone. It was a lot to ask. Strictly speaking a lesser accident would have satisfied me, a fine fire or an encounter with some character who was eccentric or even mad, some important person who had gone to the dogs, or a down-and-out prophet, someone with enough individuality to make me forget my own, so very negative, above all on that particular day.

To be sure, such encounters carry their own risks; the longed-for madman, prophet, or important person soon reveals his bourgeois mediocrity and, with time, the most charming of creatures becomes odious. So I resigned myself to solitary wandering, to the point of surfeit, to the point where I was ready to lose myself in some sepulchral museum or else in some bar smelling of dog-piss, which, taking everything into account, was more reasonable than going onto a bridge to meditate over the foul Thames, the least drinkable of rivers . . .

"Damn!" I soliloquized, "how the days God sends us drag themselves out! How tedious life is for anyone who hasn't the constitution of a sinner! How intolerable eternity is under any authority other than that of the devil! . . ." I had blasphemed and I knew it, and I was all the more guilty in that I hadn't befuddled my faculties with drink; it was only that I thought these impious ideas rather than uttering them, since it's written that one mustn't tempt the devil. But the danger of invoking him even in spirit promptly made itself felt! No word of a lie! At that very moment an adventure began for me that wouldn't have taken place if I hadn't rashly named the infernal power latent everywhere in the universe . . .

It happened in Sea-Dog Lane, a narrow passage between leprous buildings dating from the reign of Queen Bess. I was glued to the sticky pavement, unable to go any further, and left open-mouthed with surprise. The devil showed himself, albeit in a banal manner; but it was a case of one of those absurd, unexpected encounters like those that occur in the course of a light fever. I was in fact a little feverish in that damp weather, and yet it wasn't any disorder of my senses that revealed to me the zinc plaque fastened to a moldering door, that plaque on which, at the very moment I thought of him, I read the name of the devil: *Mephisto*! I wasn't delirious. I examined that narrow, wretched, red-painted house squeezed between others looking just as shabby. And what was it that the plaque informed me of? The entrance to a sordid and exclusively private club? A warehouse for commercial goods? The meeting-place of a mystagogic sect? Everything is possible, everything sprouts like fungus in the noxious surroundings, in the age-old mildew of the banks of the Thames! And nothing could shake my conviction that I found myself in front of the devil's residence, and that most popular of devils, Mephisto! . . .

I felt a sense of pleasure mingled with anxiety; just what a student feels standing before a house of ill fame. It was also a feeling of relief, of being on the verge of ridding myself of boredom. Didn't I have the right to find out about this Mephisto announced on the façade, and to discover if he was in legal possession of this prestigious name?

About the existence of the devil I have no doubts; my teachers lodged that belief in my head and up to now no rationalist has come along to prove that this belief, or this dogma, was a children's fable. Do I believe in the devil? Absolutely! And more firmly than in God and his saints. Hasn't he always spoken to my imagination? Hasn't he always resided in my brain? Doesn't he galvanize me in the same way as the hero of a drama or a story? I was now dying to see and hear him, always supposing that he was available and that I wasn't confronted with an impostor. And already my hand was seeking the doorbell; but doorbell there was none, no more than there was a lock. Only the devil could present such an impossible door, and that black door was in no way designed to gain my confidence: I truly found myself in an antechamber or a consulate of Hell!

How was it to be opened, that hermetic door? What burglar could I call on? As though its timbers had heard my complaint, it opened all by itself onto a dark corridor, so dark that I stepped back, alerted by my old Christian instinct and reciting to myself Dante's line: "All ye who enter here . . . ," but I don't know what force impelled me, or rather sucked me toward that corridor, that mouth of nonbeing, similar to the throat of the Leviathan. Without exactly knowing what I was doing, at the same time delighted to be doing something so foolhardy, I advanced into the interior darkness while the door closed behind me, cutting off all retreat along with the objective world, its police, moral laws, rules and regulations. The only remaining course was to trust to the devil, which I did, though fearfully.

"Excuse me, Mephisto? . . ." I whimpered.

"This way, sir! . . ." a disagreeable voice croaked.

I spoke again with more presence of mind, though still in shock from the surprise: "It's the devil, isn't it, and not a substitute, that's to say the devil himself? . . ."

"Just so, sir," the voice assured me, "the devil himself and not a pantomime devil."

An invisible right hand took me by the arm and pulled me. Where did it pull me? Clearly I was still in London, but if we more or less know the "surface" of cities, what do we know about their underground, down toward the depths of the globe? So I went stumbling along, pulled gently and insistently. And suddenly, a veil was torn, a curtain slid on its rings, and I was pushed into a fairly large room, bathed in a light that was filtered by an awning. The hand of my guide led me over to a comfortable armchair, the only object that furnished the room, and condescended to tip me over, so that I fell onto its cushioned seat.

"And the devil? . . ." I cried.

The grating voice drew away: "He won't be long, sir! . . ."

And I didn't have time to see what my guide was, quick and fluid as a draft of air.

How to express my bewilderment and my divided state of mind? I was afraid and I was relaxed! I wanted to find myself elsewhere and I was afraid of my adventure stopping short! And though I was full of confused thoughts I had enough native wit to mentally address myself to Providence: "Lord above! I'm not asking for your help in this rather ridiculous situation that I've managed to contrive; but I'd beg you to maybe order your angels to pull me out of here and put me down in the street if it so happens that the devil I'm waiting for is an Englishman. Let him, by all means, compromise me, undo me, claw me, mark me, stamp me with his seal; I accept any harm that might result as advance payment for my faults; I'm ready to endure everything, whether physical or metaphysical; yes, I'll put up with everything the devil inflicts, every pratfall, but not if he preaches me a sermon, starts moralizing, stuffs my pocket with little Bibles or temperance leaflets! . . ."

I exaggerated, of course, for I had a better opinion of the devil, banished by definition and temperament from the world of conformity; but I was exercised by the thought that he might take me for an imbecile. While waiting for him to appear I turned my attention to the surroundings. I found myself in a sort of sculptor's studio, lit by a tinted glass window. The rather modest distribution of natural light left the room hazy, and the gray hangings that hid the walls accentuated that impression of floating. In front of me, the far end was entirely taken up by a stage whose purple curtain remained closed. And in that solitude, nothing, apart from a persistent whiff of the stable-yard; no ornaments or signs, no emblems announcing that I was situated outside Space and Time, on the premises of the Damned One, or one of his delegates. I won't deny that I was somewhat disappointed by such arid surroundings, for who isn't sensitive to decorum, to what reveals the character of one's host? But I told myself that the poverty of the place could be deliberate and no more than a subterfuge aiming to discourage intruders. So much the better for me! I didn't have much time to indulge these glum sentiments: three loud blows, reverberating solemnly from a gong, enfolded me in their musical waves and their effect was to obliterate my reason, to suddenly put me into the happy and expectant frame of mind one feels at the start of a performance. And it was a performance that started, oh my blessed eyes! . . .

The stage curtain lifted silently, revealing the cube of a stage set, the rear of which was closed by black cloths covered with silver designs, comets, arabesques, shinbones and funeral tears, whatever was needed to enthrall children and their nursemaids. My breath stopped in my mouth; without a puff of smoke or the roll of a drum, the devil had just leaped onto the stage, supple, silent, and as discreet as a cat: hop-la! He was dressed all in scarlet from the tip of his toes to the cock-feather in his cap; scarlet his body stocking clinging to a bony torso; scarlet the tights wound round his thighs and scrawny calves; scarlet his lordly cloak; scarlet his gloves. He rose to his full height and swayed in the manner of a ruby-red flame or a poppy on its stalk . . . I saw that for makeup he wore a musketeer-style moustache and goatee beard. And two crystalline pupils glowed in his thin, flour-white face, two aquamarines that enlarged or diminished at will.

This apparition made me cry out: "Mephisto!..."

The devil rested his fine eyes on me and, hand on heart, greeted me ceremoniously. I got up from my armchair and returned the courtesy. But already the devil, executing a brisk jump, traced in the air incantatory gestures that caused the black backcloths to dissolve. And I was able to admire a second, deeper stage whose décor represented an enchanted grotto under a light that was so intensely red it made my eyes blink. And Mephisto, in scarlet, was as though evaporated in that combustion. I could only see his pale features and the play of his ungloved hands, interminable hands that caught the light on account of the big rings that adorned them. But the devil resumed form and substance when he moved away from the grotto. Leaning toward the proscenium, what did he want from me now? Flourishing a top hat, he addressed me in a melodious voice: "Do you like rabbit stew?..."

If I liked rabbit stew? As much as tricks with white magic! No sooner had I approved the menu than Mephisto adroitly extracted a pretty little white rabbit from the hat. Standing up, I applauded: "Bravo! Bravissimo!..." But this outburst of enthusiasm produced an unexpected result. The devil froze and stared attentively at me, letting the rabbit hop into the wings and escape; then he exited in turn. The grotto went dark and the curtain fell. I'd broken the spell! And I found myself once more in this drab space for evangelical meetings, with no luminous illusions or enchanted perspectives, having thoughtlessly ruined a wonderful chance of escaping from deadly boredom. My disappointment was about to turn to anger—against myself be it understood!—and at that juncture I was wondering what was going to happen when the devil appeared for a second time, emerging from an entrance, this time in the studio, relocated from the stage setting. He no longer sported moustache or goatee. I was impressed by his pale features, his easy demeanor, his weary and melancholy gaze; before me I found a man of breeding, refined and endowed with a certain beauty, though no longer young. As I greeted him, he spoke to me in a low voice without the least trace of rancor:

"You wouldn't be Mr. Dryocle, would you? The representative of the Performer's Union and the Lyric Federation?"

"I don't have that honor . . ." I replied, somewhat confused . . . "I'm no one special, and I apologize . . ."

Mephisto gestured affably: "I'm just as happy that you aren't that representative . . ." And he stared at me benevolently.

I thought at last of introducing myself: "I'm . . ."

"Delighted to make . . ."

"Merely a passerby . . ."

The devil shook my hand and spoke slowly and persuasively:

"My dear stranger, this misunderstanding doesn't bother me in the least. I was expecting a business agent who was coming to propose a tour of the halls, a tour that I've no wish to undertake at the moment; and destiny sends me a passerby who appreciates my art! I thank destiny and the passerby. The fact is, do you see? I'm bored . . ."

These words filled me with delight. I hastened to explain myself: "Exactly so maestro! No one appreciates your art more than I do. I recognized you as a superlative performer, which was the reason for my impetuous but sincere enthusiasm. Now, if you happen to be suffering from boredom, it's the same boredom that's led me to tempt the devil, to seek out the devil. The occasion was heaven sent since his name appeared on a door and that door opened all on its own! Clearly you aren't the devil . . ."

The man in scarlet cut me short: "What do you know about it?"

There was a silence. I was left shamefaced, and to make amends for that second gaffe I launched into makeshift explanations: "I mean to say that you are him without actually being him, for you have that academic look about you that the devil would take exception to, while your know-how exceeds the laws of science, witness that rabbit . . ."

I felt like an idiot, but the devil was kind enough not to listen to my equivocations; he was lost in thought . . . Hearing my voice come to a halt, he threw me a distracted look and continued, not without malice:

"And if I were the devil? Would you like me to be him, *in spite of* my theatrical cast-offs? It's a matter of faith, dear passerby. For now that you aren't the business agent that I was afraid of, I have plenty time to be the devil that you'd like to meet. A simple compact, after all . . ."

I bowed by way of agreement. The devil that he really was from now on continued with his proposal.

"Your desire for the devil shows that you're a man of character. Accept his hospitality. Forget his costume. I won't sing the misadventures of the *Flea* and I know that you won't ask me how I go about pulling a rabbit from a hat. You're an honest man, altogether different from the kind of people I detest, impudent journalists, show-business impresarios, and a plague of occultists."

"A passerby . . ." I repeated humbly, captivated by so much cordial civility.

Several minutes later we were seated in an intimate and comfortable domestic library where, aside from music hall posters, there was no trace of anything diabolical. Far from it, this devil was the most human of men, a collector of fine editions, a lover of flowers, and a friend to birds. The only things he liked were animals and the objects of the contemplative life; he also liked tobacco and mature spirits. Decanters of Dutch gin lined themselves up within reach of our hands, something that wasn't the least welcome of his magic tricks; but I had the good sense not to applaud again.

The hours flowed by in a conversation whose interest was unflagging, my host being an eloquent talker; and our dialogue pursued such fanciful paths that we pushed far into the night without having seen its arrival. It must be said that the alcohol provided internal illumination and that we both had a bent for twilight indolence. At length someone entered the room carrying an oil lamp shaded with a globe of rose colored glass; it was the devil's housekeeper, a kind of wizened Chinawoman and, no doubt, the mysterious creature who had received me in the morning. That intrusion wasn't enough to return us to the real world, though we consented to nibble at the anchovies that the witch had brought us. And for a long time we stayed buried in a rosy penumbra, near the lamp that glowed like a newborn star. The devil had caught the white rabbit and held it on his knees, caressing the animal's ears. He was lost in thought. And I contemplated his reverie.

I contemplated this face lit up by dream, this face of a thinker, noble in its design, pure in its outline. This man was made of superior stuff and inspired respect. Not one of his statements sounded a banal note, not one of his thoughts that didn't bear the imprint of individual reflection. His speech at moments took on a certain note of solemnity, but without ever departing from simplicity, the muted tone of the confessional. Only a very wise man, free from the usual prejudices, would be able to adopt this manner, a being like Montaigne who has lived long enough to see everything and its contrary. Sincerely admiring this distinguished devil who had a touch of the prelate, I was unmindful of the hour and the century, no longer noticing the carnival costume of that man of genius whose very silence was expressive; I admired him in all good faith, with all the remaining ingenuousness of my soul, and under the dominion of his feline eyes that strayed hither and thither without ever coming to rest. Sometimes his eyes lit on me and a green gleam flashed, a phosphorescent signal that I failed to understand. What did he think of me, the devil, and how did he judge me? There could be no doubt that it was my person that he was considering. And suddenly the devil started to guffaw, laughing so hard that I thought he was drunk. But before I was able to question him, he spoke to me in a playful lilt:

"Dear friend, yes, dear friend, I can no longer call you dear stranger, even though I haven't seen your personal dossier. I've already seen you; I knew you, and oddly enough I've been able to recognize you through a detail. You've been staring at me, lulled into a trance, and your wits must be all at sea. I've noticed your gesture, the one you're making right now, the gesture of an enthralled child!"

Caught in flagrante, so to speak, I hastily removed my right hand from my mouth, ashamed of having fallen unawares into that puerile posture. How long had I been with my right hand buried in my mouth? The devil was still laughing and my embarrassment seemed to add to his enjoyment. Finally he resumed speaking.

"I saw you thirty years ago. It was in a continental capital where a World's Fair was being held, the one that went up in flames; and it was in a music hall, a big winter pavilion or maybe a summer one for all I remember, where I was billed at the end of the program. I was wearing this costume, I had this famous name, just like today. And you, a little boy, about ten years old, you were standing in the first box of the proscenium, on the right; and my conjuring seized your attention to the point where you'd buried the fingers of your right hand in your mouth. I noticed that. From time to time a very beautiful blonde woman wearing a large floral hat pulled your hand out of your mouth and scolded you affectionately; but this call to order was lost on you. I was pleased with a spectator of your quality and I worked with a will . . ."

The devil fell silent. As for me, I was under the spell of emotions that I couldn't easily hide. It didn't occur to me that the devil could deceive me through some skill in mind reading. In any event he didn't leave me time for thought. He went on:

"So, I was coming to the end of my act and I was going to make a well-disposed spectator disappear in a golden coffin, and, you have to believe me, not a stooge. I turned to the public in the pit, the same as on every evening, requesting someone small who trusted Mephisto to come on stage. No one responded. Then, wanting to reward the little boy for his attention and thinking that the occasion might please him, I went over to his box and held out friendly arms: 'Would you like to? . . .'"

I got to my feet in a state of great agitation, deeply moved by this terrible memory, and completed the story:

"I howled at the top of my voice, I fled toward the exit pursued by my mother, followed by the applause and jokes of the entire house, who thought I was a plant. The devil wanted to take me! Help! . . ."

In my excitement I heard the clamor and I felt ready to flee again. But the devil—this very same devil—took me by the hands, and his laughter won me over! I laughed so as not to cry.

"Oh Mephisto, you're telling the truth!" I murmured . . . "I was eleven years old, and this drama (which it really was for me) took place in Brussels, in nineteen hundred and ten . . ."

In spite of my best efforts, a tear rolled down my cheek. Mephisto embraced me in his arms.

"Don't weep for your childhood, for you're still that same child, a child grown old just like I myself am a devil grown old. The important thing is that you still believe in the devil! . . ."

The dear old man lowered his head, no doubt so that I couldn't see his eyes. His voice trembled a little when he spoke again.

"Do you know what you did this morning when you stopped in front of my door? And in seeking to meet the devil weren't you acting at the behest of a mysterious power, not at all an infernal one? There's no such thing as chance and there's nothing in life that lacks meaning. But I can't do anything for you, and I'm not sorry about that, seeing as you aren't asking for anything. What with all my knowledge, I earn my daily bread by pulling white rabbits and flags out of top hats. But all the same I'm pleased to have freed you from the perils of boredom, that same boredom that chased you through the streets; to have rekindled that spark of feeling in your body sore with the rain . . . Perhaps you'll now recover your taste for life, a life that's worth what it's worth, which is a great deal, when, at my age, one feels that it's receding into the distance . . ."

The devil had nothing more to say to me and the lamp was burning low. It was time to go. Taking me by the hand Mephisto carefully led me back the way I had come and, on the threshold, said once more: "I'll see you again, but where? In some music hall? . . ."

His laugh didn't ring true.

"Maybe in hell!" he finished by saying, "and what does hell matter to us, so long as friendship is permitted there! . . ."

The door closed.

It was nighttime and cold. The rain still drizzled. I shivered. The cold took hold of my soul as well as my flesh. I cried out in the foul alleyway: "Hell? Why, this is hell! It's this monstrous city, its everyday existence. And the damned? They're my hideous fellow men and me too in their sordid flock! . . ."

I walked on miserably, and from somewhere in the fog a slow midnight tolled, to which the horns of the boats on the waters replied. Ah! How cold it was in this stinking limbo! . . . And what a desire for light and fire in my heart! . . . What was there for me besides the mad hope of finding once more "that other hell," far from the world, where devils like Mephisto reign over sensitive, instantly awestruck children; a hell full of grottoes and curtains, where white rabbits trot over red fields, where blonde phantoms with floral bonnets come into view, vanished figures who pass by with the majesty of archangels? . . .

The
Sick
Garden

ILLUSTRATIONS BY JACQUES GORUS

To the storyteller Jean Stiénon du Pré

(Extracts from a Journal)

June 1917. In the end, what we most ardently desire almost always comes to pass; but such is the heart's perpetual dissatisfaction that we fail to recognize it, or else that which comes to pass no longer corresponds to the dream we had of it. When as a child I ran about in this derelict quarter of my city, abandoned by the noble or upper class families who built it, now deteriorating and overrun by the general populace, who could have foretold that one day I would take up residence in that vast, lengthways-facing house with the forbidding exterior, an enigmatic house that my inflamed imagination has never ceased to revisit? At that time it was, as it still is today, a proud-looking private residence, wedged between others built in the same classical French style—an austere, closed façade whose five windows seemed blocked up behind their locked shutters and whose main entrance, heavy and forbidding as the entrance to a tomb, never opened. This patrician dwelling already had an air of abandonment thirty years ago when I went down the street daily on my way to the nearby friar's school; the blackened stones spoke so absolutely of hermetic closure, like an old, tarnished face that the years can no longer alter, that it was difficult to conceive of any other possibility. Nevertheless I couldn't bring myself to believe that the décor hid nothing but emptiness, that some kind of destiny wasn't concealed behind this dead screen. I knew that there were beings who didn't show themselves and who, for personal reasons, preferred to exist outside of society. Could there be any better retreat for them than a house like this one? Each day as the fancy took me I would concoct a fresh notion. Between the crazed millionaire collecting forbidden books or imprisoning a woebegone niece, and the senile actress ruminating on her glory days or inhaling faded bouquets, there was room, by virtue of their very mystery or peculiarity, for every kind of bizarre and fascinating character; the exiled prince, the counterfeiter, the disgraced general—who knows?—and all this without taking into account the thousand others sprung from the romantic literature I read. In winter, in dark days when the streetlamps were lit, my imagination became more dramatic and suggested to me that the house was the scene of a crime, a crime that was now forgotten but which in its day must have made people shudder. Such horrors came readily to me and not for all the money in the world would I have dared to cross the threshold of this residence that was surely guarded by menacing or melancholy phantoms lurking in the shadows. I'm going to cross that enchanted threshold now, for here I am, a tenant of the ground floor of the apartment block. I've rented this locale without even paying it a visit, much as one buys a memento. A child wouldn't have behaved any differently. But have I ever ceased to be a dreamer? And the years that have piled up on my shoulders, have they taught me anything other than to bury myself more obstinately than ever in my dreams? . . .

My meeting with the owner is worth the telling. I found the gentleman, who didn't live far away, in a filthy kitchen. He's a suspicious septuagenarian whose servile manner betrayed an old manservant who must have inherited the property or who had purchased it not long since. Learning that I wanted to rent the ground floor he observed me sardonically, his bird-like eye gleaming with curiosity. And the interview got under way.

"How do you know that there's anything available to rent? . . ."

I'd been able to make this out from the scraps of a poster stuck to the door. The old man sighed.

"You're really the first since . . ." He seemed to journey back in Time . . . "since the late Baron de Ruescas, whom I served." And, without pausing, "Do you want it for warehousing goods? . . . It's no use for anything else in the state . . ." When I naïvely confessed that I wanted to live there, the old gentleman seemed alarmed, and I thought that he was going to show me the door. He restrained himself and gave me a pitying look. Speaking gently, as though to someone whom it would be wiser not to contradict outright, he gave me a description of the place, no doubt aiming to discourage me.

"It's a barracks . . . One single room out of seven fit to be lived in. It isn't healthy. Can't be heated. No woman would be willing to look after the property . . . Anyway I don't carry out repairs. The ceiling could fall down on your head, the floor could collapse . . . The risk is yours alone . . . And then the building is due to be condemned, like the rest of this district . . . As for the garden . . ."

I interrupted the old fellow's recital of woes. "Exactly. I know that there are huge gardens, trees, behind these buildings. That's what brings me here."

The old man looked disconcerted. "Yes, of course, the garden, very big, deep. As unhealthy as all the rest, it's no good . . ."

Wanting to bring matters to a close, I replied, "That makes no odds. It's for my dog . . ."

Taken aback, the old man wagged his head. "There's a dog? A big one? A guard dog? Well, if it's for the dog . . ."

Feeble though it was, my final argument took effect. No doubt the proprietor liked the idea of obtaining a measure of security for his dilapidated property. He confided that the upper floor was occupied by a respectable lady whom I would never see but who, living all on her own, sometimes felt afraid. Having told me this while prattling on about other things, he accepted the deposit and, answering to conscientiousness, gave me the keys, a whole bunch of them, most of which were no longer able to open doors.

The rent is moderate! The old gentleman isn't greedy, as one might have expected; he's suspicious and fearful. He must have taken me for an eccentric, maybe even a madman . . .

With a wealth of keys, I'm the happy master of a domain, Rue des Dames Anglaises. This street is still fine looking in its decline; it's busy enough, but goes quiet in the evening and is rendered pure by its gardens. So I'll be able to live in an old-fashioned, provincial spot while in the middle of a present-day city. What's more I'll be on my own without being alone, for I enjoy the friendship of a dog—and what a dog! Someone whose opinion I regret not having asked. Will the premises meet with his approval? It's my one concern, though I'm sure he'll get used to them. Mylord—that's his name—has an air of distinction, that of a lord to be exact, with his black perruque and his drooping mustachios. The building has the same air of distinction, notwithstanding its disrepair. Mylord is scornful of mere circumstance. Phlegmatic, abstract, reserved, and a proper thoroughbred, he doesn't argue the odds, he either accepts or refuses, leaving displays of feeling and attitude to ordinary dogs. As I've said, this is a dog with character. The simplest thing would be to give him the news straight, without preamble; "Mylord, from now on, you know, we'll be living in the Hotel de Ruescas ..."

15 June. I moved in a short while ago. This was quite easy for us because I travel light in life, with few belongings; a divan to sleep on, an armchair, a little table, with the better part of my baggage consisting of nonessentials; books and a collection of prints. My dog seems satisfied. I can be satisfied too, buried in this enormous cube of silence and shadow that forms the mansion, with nothing to remind me of the outside world or the century. There's no electric lighting here, no dead, unmoving, and intrusive light. I find nothing so agreeable as the light of wax tapers. Did I say that moving in was easy? Yes, but if I'm physically at home here, my spirit is still hovering mistrustfully on the threshold, awaiting the moment when it can confidently occupy this disquieting abode. Mylord must be in exactly the same state of mind, seeming to have settled in but always on the alert, eyes half-closed, nostrils twitching. We understand each other and don't let it show. It's wiser to wait, to let the imponderable take its course; either the building will subjugate us to its mysterious laws, or else it's we two—for I repeat that there are two of us—who will impose our will on it. Once more I'm aware that it seems to gird itself against us who are intruders, and no doubt it'll be a long time before it accepts us. In the first few days there was the tragedy of the keys, and of locks that refused to yield. Certain doors won't open or let themselves be forced open. After all these years a building, having reached a certain age, will no longer accommodate change; logically, it only remains to knock it down. In any event I have no interest in the various obscure rooms that make up my apartment, preferring to live in the only one that receives light, opening mainly onto the garden—the only one, as the proprietor informed me, that's habitable. The others are the preserve of shadows. As for the cellars and caverns, I never venture down there; it's the lower world—of which I'm afraid.

The entrance makes a tremendous impression. One expects to see the apparition of some hoary retainer, manifestly deaf and rigged out in ceremonial livery. It's a large marble lobby with a wrought iron door at the far end, giving access to the gardens that can be discerned through the glass panes; opening to the left is a hallway where a massive oak staircase ascends toward the upper floor; innumerable funerary panels hang from the walls recounting the obituary annals of the de Ruescas family, and these heraldic mementos enliven the pale walls of the vestibule—paradoxically—like illuminated images with their fabulous animals and chimerical emblems. Having thought that I'd have to brush away cobwebs and step over heaps of rubbish I immediately noticed that the lobby and stairway were to some extent kept clean. Who tidies these locations? There's no need for me to concern myself. Numerous doors remain, each with its own particular creaking noise. When knocked on they resound with the hollow resonance of a coffin.

My room must have served as a salon, south-facing and receiving daylight through three high windows. The double door opens onto an insecure flight of steps down which one descends to the garden. The ceiling is molded with cherubs and garlands in gray stucco. The interior walls have retained their period tapestries, charmingly faded, and the Louis XVI chimneypiece imparts an overall tone of distinction, even though loose and thick with dirt. The parquet flooring seems to be ebony. Everything is badly dilapidated but still tenable, and even if this interior speaks of decay it's by no means a ruin. The doors have conserved their mirrors, imprisoned in

patterned squares of worn gilt wood. These misty mirrors trap the light and bathe the room in a secondary and spectral luminosity, enchanting to my gaze. I'm forgetting the chandelier, left behind by the previous tenants, or rather the skeleton of a chandelier, like bronze roots down which trickle a few crystal teardrops.

Above all there's the garden, source of my delight and my disquiet. On its account I forget about the house. Like a fragment of virgin forest enclosed within thick walls, this garden mesmerizes me; I spend hours staring at it uncomprehendingly, with no thought of setting foot in it. It seems impenetrable, a riddle that won't let itself be solved. It's all bush—already ablaze with springtime—crowned by trees, chestnuts and lindens, and seems bathed in a perpetual half-light. So abandoned is this sloping ground that rises toward the far end, more than sixty meters from the steps, that one is confronted by a wall of vegetation where trails can be traced in place of paths that have disappeared. I find this territory wild and unfriendly to man.

This vegetation grown monstrous with age is a spectacle that isn't without instilling a sense of uneasiness, even of fear, not because of the animal life that must shelter there, but because it expresses an unrelenting force. The ivy, the wisteria, the Virginia creeper are octopuses in combat, suffocating the shrubs and pushing at the walls. This uneasiness—to tell the truth, this fear—doesn't come from imagining that the vegetation, suddenly pruritic, might overspill the garden and, like a groundswell, invade the house and its rooms—its unnatural luxuriance remains at a distance from my windows, arrested by a paved walk, bordered by a ramp that is low but serves to mark the boundary of a yard; my unease derives rather from the thought that this green mass can and necessarily *does* conceal a mystery. It's a forbidden zone—I can sense it—and in the same way that certain faces remain closed, this garden declares itself hostile, keeps itself apart. It doesn't only protect itself with meshes of branches and bundles of thorns; worse than that, it's protected by its expression, yes, that's the right word; it seems to be sick, and, in spite of the ample breezes circulating in the neighborhood and the generous spread of sunlight, its contents remain wan, pallid, if it's possible that an explosive growth of vegetation can appear listless.

No, the garden is not anarchically left to its own devices as a consequence of neglect; it has a high fever, or, more accurately, it's gone mad—no less . . .

The walls are sick too; canting outward, they wind through the district like fortifications, propped up with buttresses, showing red wounds of naked brick. I know that, in the past, monasteries congregated in this neighborhood; these gardens found everywhere, these enclosures run wild and losing their identity, these are the remains of monastic properties. It's peaceful in this vast space that's now been wiped clean and parceled up by urban planners—as they're called—those wreckers of old cities. The buildings that flank my house seem to be uninhabited, and their gardens are as big and as unruly as mine. Farther away, I sometimes hear the noise of children at a school, and, in the distance, the clinking of a forge. There's also, somewhere, a cock with a magnificent crow that sounds the dawn reveille.

I thought that my dog would go bounding into the wild undergrowth; after all, wasn't that his terrain, just the thing for absorbing a whole canine existence? But no! Mylord considered it all from the steps, then went down, very dubious, muzzle quivering. He deigned to venture as far as the balustrade, a little step at a time, came back, returned, came back for good—disappointed or disgusted, I'll never know. Since then and up to the moment of writing, he hasn't been further than the yard, satisfied with inspecting the garden from on high and afar. Clearly it's a tempting hive of activity; but Mylord knows how to wait and camouflage his natural instincts. Or, if he isn't playacting, then doesn't he, like me, even more than me who's merely a man, perceive the peculiarity of this enclosed space? What is it that he tirelessly noses? What does he sense that I can't? All day long he stays stretched out on the steps as though on the lookout, one eye closed, the other watching . . .

What might disturb a dog or a sensitive human needn't necessarily be anything out of the ordinary. A certain refinement or decadence of the senses is enough to identify something that would go unremarked by the average person; secret noises, mysterious odors. I know what it is that preoccupies my comrade. The building creaks at night—and one gets used to it. The odors remain more difficult to define. The house has its very own, every nuance of mold; it's unwell too—the house—and while still robust has slightly gone to rot, in the same way that very old folk anticipate a demise that's late in arriving. But it seems to me that on certain days the smell is more pronounced, as though its condition is worsened by changes in the weather. Rank infirmary smells? I'm not far from thinking that this distressing staleness comes from the garden; the stink emanates from there and I don't want to admit it. Is the garden slowly decomposing with the passing seasons? There must be some kind of quarantine hospital in the vicinity, I'm sure of it. The garden is all humus, able to secrete nothing but rotting vegetation. But at twilight, I discern furtive phosphorescent lights at ground level in the undergrowth, which can only be seen at the moment they're extinguished . . .

End of June . . . Keeping a journal like mine is one more act of vanity among so many others, the action of the lunatic that, I accept, people take me for. I've imposed this task upon myself freely, out of a concern for order and knowing that the trivial facts recorded here will no longer interest me when I read them later. No matter! Habits, compulsions help a man to live . . . If uncommon events were to occur in my days and nights here, I won't confess to them, I won't ever write them down. I've now lived in the Ruescas mansion for a fortnight. I'm not especially satisfied and not dissatisfied either. I feel at peace and that's good enough; so many walls, so many empty spaces separate me from the city, from my contemporaries. When I have to go out I come back nearly poisoned by petrol fumes from the traffic. And though I don't inhale the scent of flowers here at home, or even any natural smells, I breathe freely, grown used to the pharmaceutical smells emanating from house and garden. I'm acclimatizing myself, but my dog isn't. He remains alert. His canine nature is at work. There's enough here to puzzle him, this lethargic garden where things move about unpredictably. But Mylord's curiosity is matched only by his prudence; he hasn't yet ventured beyond the paved yard. Very often I find dead shrews. This isn't the work of my dog, who's above such small quarry. I can testify that Mylord is at peace with any animal who doesn't provoke him; if he sometimes likes to go roving he doesn't enjoy hunting, and seems to say, "I'm a decorative animal; what more do you want?..." I know, nevertheless, that he can be dangerous when he chooses, yet even when angry it seems to me that he stays within limits. He would certainly come to my defense if I were in danger and he displays a fearsome set of fangs. And what is he doing all day long if not standing guard? I notice too an absence of birds. And yet they're there, I hear them somewhere in the surroundings; however, their cries echo with alarm. Are they afraid of the dog, the best creature in the world? I've found dead birds on my doorstep, in the grass. Is it really the garden that's caused their death? Lots of questions remain unanswered for those who don't know how to wait. Already I know who cleans the pavement, the lobby, and the stairway; the proprietor! Does he want to please someone? Not me, that's for sure!... I caught him at it one Saturday morning, outfitted with clogs and an apron. He handles brushes and pails noiselessly and as though ashamed. Is the old manservant nostalgic for the days when he served in this house that's now become his property? I don't find that so very silly. Here below everyone does what he likes best to do. The old gentleman is just as humble and apprehensive as ever. I greeted him without seeming to take any interest in his little game. I could have asked him questions; I never enquire—it's the best way of eventually finding out what one wants to know...

Will I eventually get to know the respectable lady living on the upper floor? I've yet to meet her. However, there are lace curtains in the windows, and I've sometimes come across traces of a presence—but a phantom presence. She must be an old person with bones that have gone brittle, an early riser who only leaves her rooms at daybreak. Sometimes I've fancied that someone was talking overhead, and even that a voice, whether that of an old person or a child I couldn't tell, was muttering a perpetual dirge, a litany. Perhaps it's the old house rambling, enduring its senile nights... The hallway bell has never rung. Does it work? There are no visitors, there will be none. That's one of the ingredients of my tranquility, not to say my happiness.

○

2 July. Tonight has been marked by a fright that still holds me in its grip. The evening was fine and warm, all the stars lit high in the sky; but as the hour grew late a fog rose up from the ground, a milky haze that covered the garden and didn't rise above the height of the walls, leaving the stars and the trees visible. The fog carried with it the rank smell I'd already encountered. Deciding that it was unhealthy I closed the door and the windows. Lying back on my divan by the light of a candle, I opened a book intended less to distract me than to send me to sleep while Mylord remained sitting in the armchair, facing the window, looking obstinately out, though there was nothing to see other than the fireflies on the screen of the fog. I must have fallen asleep. At the very moment that the candle flame, guttering out, cracked the sconce, I was awoken by furious barks. Mylord jumped on me then leaped toward the windows, and his barks re-echoed in the room, the uproar of ten dogs in the dark. It was then that I froze in fright. Outside, against the window, someone was staring in at me; someone was staring, unconcerned by the dog's fury, and all I could see were the terrifying, hypnotic eyes; two riveting pupils that seemed demonic to me, that could only be belong to a Demon. I cried out a conjuration, for how else can one protect oneself against that?... Then suddenly the eyes were extinguished. The dog stopped barking but remained in a posture of attack until dawn, growling within himself. The fright gradually ebbed from my body in a cold sweat. What would have happened if I'd left my door open? Those stories of vampires who batten on you and suck your blood are as old as time! Obviously no one believes in them any more. Nor do I. Nevertheless from now on I'll take care to close the windows and doors. I'll paper over the windows. Wouldn't it be wise too to have some means of defense at hand, for example holy water, no less vital than a firearm—for we would be truly naïve to think that our worst enemies are only our fellow men, only belong to the human race, and that their activities must necessarily be ones we can see or foresee...

○

7 July. At last I've met the respectable lady. She's purposely avoided me, and all I knew about her was the rustle of a flight, the draft of a backward retreat. She's right to react this way; every new face carries its own riddle; every new encounter entails a risk. As I went out very early this morning the entrance door swung open: it was the lady coming back from mass, her book clasped to her. The meeting was unavoidable. Backing up against the wall, the lady faced me as though offended by the occasion. I greeted her with elaborate courtesy, introducing myself by name. She replied with a nod of the head. I didn't pick up any of the few words fallen from her lips, some distance away. Then the lady slipped off to the staircase, lithe and upright, as though disembodied in her gray clothes. She wore a kind of headdress that gave her the look of a nurse or a nun in lay garments. What impression did she leave behind her? Tall and thin; and her age? Thirty or sixty? Above all I remember a face that gave nothing away; lips thin and willfully sealed, green and evasive eyes, their dullness concealing an oblique gaze that subjects you to an inquisitorial scrutiny. Respectable, this lady; I write "lady" and not "woman": I was unable to conclude that I found a woman in front of me. I suspect that our relationship will never amount to more than greetings in the lobby. The lady is at home in this mansion from another time just as much as I am. Perhaps she's judged me favorably, finding me unmodern to a fault . . . Eventually it occurs to me that the creature carries about herself the smell of the house, that she's succumbed to mildew, or is it her breath? Does she, like the house whose gray color she shares, harbor this persistent perfume, this whiff of nothingness? To tell the truth, she struck me as macabre. And yet there's nothing to suggest that the creature is baleful or carrying the bacillus of Ill Omen.

13 July. I owe another discovery to my dog. Since the bad night of the 3rd, Mylord has redoubled his vigilance. At midday—clear the decks for action. My dog has suddenly found his voice again, his clarion call at its most arresting; he howls magnificently, never out of breath; his vaulting leaps are wonders to behold and his persistent jumping doesn't tire him. Better yet, it's my dog fleshed out, rejuvenated, his flair and instinct renewed, all on account of the garden. I've written "at midday clear the decks . . ." What was it that he'd finally discovered? Nothing, no one; but he didn't stop jumping at the left-hand wall, bouncing up and down like a virile dancer facing combat. Then, with difficulty, I saw what the dog had already seen: the enemy! A cat perched impassively on the ridge tiles, holding its assailant's gaze and from time to time retreating imperceptibly. War was declared, the dog at last identifying its enemy, the bird killer, source of the garden's mysterious crackling noises. The cat could be in no doubt that access to the house and the yard—at the very least—would be forbidden from now on. It estimated the distance that effectively separated it from the aggressor and retreated only as much as was required, taking itself for master of the situation. It looked at me and looked at the dog, determining the ties that linked man and beast. I neither encouraged nor discouraged Mylord; he was free to act, and secretly I would have been glad to see him break the feline's neck, not that I don't like cats, but this one horrified me. It was extraordinarily big, nearly hairless, and seemingly tainted by a leprous condition that left its skin morbidly shaded with reds, browns, the creams of the wall with which, through mimicry, it merged. Evidently a garden like this one could offer asylum only to animals like this, returned to a feral state. Yet the sight of its physical condition wasn't the source of the horror that it inspired in me, the incrustations and pustules rather inclined me to pity; my feeling derived from the fiendish expression of the skull, a flat head, almost that of a serpent, pierced by blood-shot pupils, momentarily dilated, then vanishing in a white pus. Now I knew what had visited on the night of the 3rd, the supposed vampire: this cat, cruelty incarnate—what am I saying—Evil incarnate! I'm not mistaken about this, neither is my dog, but the monster—I can't call it anything else—understood that its designs were now thwarted. I left it with the run of the garden, as monstrous and diseased as itself; it would not cross its frontier. Defeated by the baying of the dog, the cat retreated like a swaggering delinquent, full of implied threat and occasionally turning back in provocation. Mylord was victorious, his eyes triumphant, his mouth moist. Suddenly inspired, I christened this apparition with which I sensed I would have to deal. I've named it Tetanus . . .

17 July. Man can get used to anything, even the worst—I've no doubts about that; people have been seen living near a decomposing corpse. The garden is a corpse in its own way, one that I've grown used to. I've grown used to the cat, another corpse, although its appearances never fail to unnerve me. It's part of a landscape to which it's well suited and to which it seems to belong. Mylord's mouth sounds a fanfare at the sight of it, but that's all; cat and dog maintain their positions. Tetanus appears to take no interest in me; its scorn for my dog and me must be boundless. It doesn't see me and doesn't want to see me. It examines the upper floor often and at length. By contrast I never tire of studying this pellagra-ridden beast which is, so to speak, stitched into a gummy skin, with nothing on its spine but a crest of bristling hairs. It inspires horror as much through its expression of cruelty as through its look of animal rot; the horror bound to be felt by anyone venturing into a jungle where beasts surviving from prehistory roam at large. This cat looks venomous to me. It possesses a death's head in model form: earless, its cranium as though flayed, its fangs bare of lips. And doesn't it look like something that's just been disinterred and retains the color of the soil? I've thought of killing it, though I don't feel capable of shooting a beast, even a dangerous one; but I'm sure that this cat wouldn't die in any ordinary way, and better to live in wary accord with this monster that I can only know from its outward appearance. To tell the truth, I prefer not to speculate on what dwells beneath that skin! . . .

24 July. I notice that Tetanus doesn't appear every day, as I'd first thought; for reasons unknown to me it comes only on certain days. Stationed on the wall, it observes the interior of the garden, the impenetrable mass into which it alone is able to plunge. Its manner of appearing and disappearing remains a mystery. Magically and at will it can take on the color of reddish leaves or become like an old brick. Or am I suffering from optical illusions? I have little if any doubt that the cat is bewitched, is even itself a witch. But I've reached the point of wondering whether the garden isn't unholy ground. Places like that exist, places over which hangs an ancestral curse. But the district consisted of nothing but religious establishments, and if I'm to believe one of my friends—an archivist with whom I've corresponded on the subject—the mansion I'm living in must have been erected on the old cemetery of the barefoot Carmelite friars, between the boundary wall and the street, therefore hallowed ground. But it's known that before the decrees of Joseph II—and even after that—the fathers were willing, at a price, to bury the bodies of outcasts, heretics, and the excommunicated . . .

27 July. Early this morning I saw the respectable lady whom I call the lady in gray. Formalities ensued. The lady, afraid of being bitten, pressed herself against the corridor wall, looking at my dog. Mylord, who was in the best of humors, inspected this specimen.

"Don't be afraid, madam, this a well-educated dog; as far as I know he's only got one enemy, the cat . . ."

At which the lady seemed to shudder; her voice reached my ears.

"Oh! The cat? . . . Yes! . . ."

I read on the creature's face the same horror that I felt, but it was a mere flicker on a face that remained impassive. And the lady deigned to address a smile to the dog, even gesturing a caress, from a distance . . .

30 July. The summer progresses implacably. Vegetal life burgeons. Eden after the fall must have been like this garden, a corrupt domain given over to the Devil alone; a place of excess, just the way the Devil likes it, either utterly arid or else furiously fruitful. What herbs, known to necromancers, produce this humus? And why does the vegetation remain moist and clammy, as though what circulated in its veins was not sap but rather the charnel putrefaction that it sucks up from this burial ground. I fancy that the roots reach down through ribcages; I dream, not without a perverse turn of mind, of everything that the ground might contain that will never be cleared away. Am I to remain haunted by the cemetery? Everything brings me back to it; that iodine smell that induces morbid thoughts and is wrung from everything: stones, plants, myself; the nocturnal phosphorescence; these laments, these complaints, as though a service was being held somewhere in the depths of night. That might just be the case, or else I'm deluding myself. Already yesterday evening I experienced a brief alarm. Twilight was falling; the sky was dark blue. I was on the flight of steps, my dog close by. Something moved in the undergrowth. Mylord growled, then lunged toward . . . what? I couldn't tell. A short figure bolted out from the vegetation and fled limping toward the building, swallowed up by the corridor. We rushed over, my dog and me, for the hallucination was shared by both of us. Nothing! But that figure? I had been able to make out a cloak and hood, yes, a sort of dwarfish monk. It came from the garden, therefore from the cemetery . . . And went where? The big corridor door was bolted. There's a service entrance in the wall that seems to lead to the cellars, or somewhere else, I don't know; but we launched ourselves forward so rapidly that this door couldn't have been opened and closed in that instant. What, then? To tell the truth it's an event that amuses me as much as it disturbs me. I'm not afraid of the dead, not *all* the dead, and I believe what my mother taught me, namely that, above all, it's the living we should be afraid of . . .

1 August. I'm having lots of dreams. After all, haven't I perfected the art of sleeping while awake, eyes open and standing upright, so that my feet are hardly ever planted in reality? Tetanus no longer concerns me; I leave it to its walls, which it won't abandon. I'm much taken by the thought that this phantasmagorical cat could be the degenerate offspring of some dragon kept in chains by gothic dread in a portal or a shattered stained glass window, and I'd be more than a little proud to live in a disused cemetery guarded by a serpent. Those acquainted with me know that I appreciate everything that is lit by the smile of Folly. No, Tetanus is only a subsidiary figure that I leave the dog to monitor. I dream of the little twilight monk broken out from a sepulcher, and who, for good reasons, I wasn't able to overtake . . . What concerns me is the narrow door that I hesitate to open and that, I suppose, leads to the cellars, or rather to the underground, ancient basements predating the present building. It's well known that underground passages proliferated wherever there were monasteries. The spirit of adventure would tempt me to explore, except that I'm afraid, an insurmountable fear going back to my childhood; I received too many threats from parents and priests back then and my life is founded on fear. Besides, where would these noxious corridors lead me? To other burial grounds, to some monastic oubliette, to a bone-filled pit, to a wall? He, the little fleeing monk, the odd little fugitive monk, knows where. But imagination runs even faster than phantoms, and I wonder if I haven't confected a sinister and baroque story in this regard, the embodiment, dressed up in my clothes, of one of the antique dead who goes about the town . . . Such stories must exist in literature, which also has its lower depths . . .

○

3 August. Normality has its limits, abnormality has none. I'm writing this commonplace at the end of a lethargic day, one that wasn't without upsets for me. Another discovery, and not the least peculiar one in this house where ghosts circulate in the air like germs. However, it merely concerns a reality linked with other realities; but reality can take on forms that no one dares to conceive. Whoever describes or paints it thus risks being taken for a dreamer, if not mad. But, like a ship's log, a closed book to anyone who doesn't know and love the ocean, this journal recounts nothing but events that are absolutely true. I set down here in writing that I've seen the little monk in a sultry clearing, in broad day. Toward ten o'clock, coming back home from the vegetable market where I'd gone to buy fruit for my meal, I found Mylord standing upright on the outside steps, stock-still, straining toward the garden and seeming ready to attack. The heat was intense.

"Come in out of the sun, black dog; you're going to catch fire! . . ."

The dog, its attention held, was no longer listening to me; on the wall, Tetanus, hideous as ever, was indulging in a peculiar display that compelled my attention just as much as it had gripped Mylord. The cat, leaning out over the garden, stared unblinkingly into its depths, interested in something that only it could see; then, interrupting its surveillance, it crept forward a little, halting further on, and then continuing its feline progress, keeping pace with something that moved. But could the watcher be in any doubt that it was being watched in turn and that its slightest movements provoked imperceptible nervous starts in the dog—quivering with a tension that was on the point of being unleashed? This scene made me uneasy and I didn't dare to either move or intervene in this animal contest. At a certain moment the cat reared abruptly, as though about to spring onto some prey in the garden; but just when the bushes moved it thought better of it. This vegetable rustling ceased and Tetanus, no doubt deciding that the matter wouldn't end well, headed off toward the far end, looking disdainful, as though there was no longer anything to be concerned about. All the same, its departure in no way lessened the intensity of the moment either for the dog or for me, both of us sensing the presence of a living being, invisible and concealed, just a few steps away from us. We were evidently being watched. I didn't want to either return to the front room or go down into the yard for fear of breaking this unprecedented tension, this painful suspension of both spirit and breath . . . I relied on my dog whose wisdom I couldn't but admire. I'll never forget what happened next; the cat gone, Mylord goes into action, slowly descending the steps. It's his turn to see what the cat saw and what I still can't. To my surprise, he doesn't growl; it's enough for him to position himself in front of one of the trails that lead into the bushes; he waits . . . And suddenly his bark changes key; he snorts, seizes a dark stain, and, digging in, works at dragging the thing he's caught in his jaws. I hurry down the steps then pull back in surprise. My dog has caught hold of the little monk! I'm thunderstruck; I can't see very well; at that moment the light is so glaring that I can almost believe that I'm in a mirage. The little monk? Yes, the dog has fixed its teeth in the habit and is pulling furiously. The person is struggling in the bushes. I can only perceive it as an abstract form, like I saw at twilight. It's made of flesh and blood, it can be grasped and held. It's alive insofar as it struggles and whimpers— and how pitifully—in a high-pitched tone that would have made me laugh in the way that the tears of a clown make me laugh, if at this point I wasn't overcome with astonishment; the little monk captured! A phantom? No. I couldn't describe as human the creature that was staggering in front of me, waving its arms like someone drowning. Its stature was abnormally small. It was covered from top to toe by a reddish habit; its head remained imprisoned within the hood of the habit, or in a kind of cowl that left in view a waxen face that had once belonged to a man, but no longer, remodeled by the fingers of agony. I could scarcely see its hands; two chicken feet one might have said, twitching spasmodically. For the space of several seconds that seemed to stretch out interminably, Time being suspended by encounters like this, I contemplated this animated cadaver, this semblance of a being that death had patiently compressed, returning it, ironically, to the stature of an abortion; but I remember that the monk made a number of convulsive gestures, defensive rather than aggressive, and wielded in his hand a yellow coated tibia as he might have wielded a weapon. What happened then? The dog released the cloak. And the little cadaver, leaning over to the right as though about to fall, pivoted around on itself. At that moment a sharp cry broke the silence and the monk stiffened, dropping his bone. The lady in gray—did she jump down from the upper floor or emerge from the wall?—rushed across the yard toward the apparition without paying me the slightest heed and abruptly led him toward the corridor, or rather dragged him, for in her imperious grasp the creature huddled into a ball in the manner of insects afraid of being crushed. So rapid was this intervention that the lady in gray left me with the vision of a furious angel bearing down on a soul in flight. So, was it her I saw there, that dignified lady, full of clerical reserve and who seemed disembodied? That wasn't the least of the things that surprised me. But why had she taken this reluctant cadaver into the building instead of consigning him to the charnel pit of the garden, and what was she going to do with him? Torture him as punishment? I suspected as much, then was sure of it when, without quitting the yard, I heard lamentable cries, lamentable . . . As for the astonishment I read in my dog's eyes following that scene that was as farcical as it was tragic, I won't try to describe it . . .

Same day. Evening. I spent my afternoon reconstructing the events of the morning. I don't understand anything, neither does Mylord, who sometimes looks at me as though to say, "What about that!..." There's nothing to understand, and anyway, why always this need to understand, at least immediately?... I reconstructed the event, getting nowhere. What is it? Some old person for sure, a little old man or a little old woman, though I'm inclined to think a monk, on account of the costume. Ah! Those senile, watery eyes, and the mouth twisted in a sorry grimace, the lower jaw loose—that yawning mouth where a few stumps of teeth were decaying. Then the hands . . . No. It's an anatomical specimen, an exhibit for a museum of horrors, for it arouses horror, not the kind that makes you cry out, but the kind that leaves you dumbstruck. Then that tibia, brandished like a toy rattle or a scepter; I'd kicked it over to the hole from where it came. Well done, dog; but what strange hunting parties these, and for once you've caught a tidbit!... To think that this male or female gnome lives in the apartment above us! Enough for infinite wonderment, and no more sleeping without nightmares peering down at us. Alas, come this evening, all the uncertainty has been cleared up, much to my regret! The lady in gray came. She knocked at my door, and Fatality in person could not have come knocking in any other way, brooking no delay in answering. Disdaining my invitation to come in, she remained in the corridor. She spoke in her confessional voice and her face looked to me like it was sculpted in boxwood, forever unreadable, the words she uttered barely troubling her lips. Her words? Just as often silences accompanied by whispered words. And this is what I understood her to say:

"Excuse the child . . . I've forbidden her the garden. She's ill and hasn't understood how much of a nuisance she is. I've punished her . . . You won't see her again . . ."

I crashed back down to earth and everything I'd been imagining on behalf of my ghost collapsed in a moment; the monk was a child, the old man was a little girl, the cadaver was alive—relatively speaking, and unwell, how very much so!... I was devastated ... Suddenly I was overwhelmed by pity, a pity of which I could find no trace on the woman's mask of piety. This creature had the nerve to punish an invalid, a monster, for this child was a monster, offspring of what kind of sacrilegious fornication, burdened with what age-old malediction? Rather it seemed to me that the real monster was the lady in gray, whose eyes this evening burned with an unhealthy fire, no doubt a remnant of the pleasure she took in mistreating the invalid. My thoughts were in such turmoil that I was afraid that a momentary lapse of reason might make me act out of character; in short, I felt an urge to hit this woman, or to ask maliciously if she was the mother of a child who was guilty of being ugly, retarded, and unwell. She divined this secret impulse, for she made a retreat down the corridor. Having quickly regained my sang-froid I replied to the tenant's disclosure as politely as I was able.

"Madam, I'm very sorry about this incident, and above all that you had to punish an innocent child . . ." I emphasized these last words. "Considering that she's unwell I think it's a good idea for her to go into the garden. My dog will soon get used to her, and even protect her. As for me, I only want to be of assistance . . ."

The lady in gray vanished, absorbed by the shadows of the staircase, after having nodded her head at me in what might have been agreement or thanks, I don't know. Right now I'm left in the dark, lost in thought. The sight of the most beautiful children has always saddened me, I don't know why; but when a child is sickly, misfortunate, or carries with it the signs of mortality, then that hurts me so much I flinch. That's the hurt I feel tonight. For the first time since I came to stay at the Hotel de Ruescas I would like to be somewhere else. Come on, Mylord, let's go out . . .

15 August. The tropical heat continues unabated. The vegetation fumes from dawn to dusk; at midday, it seems to flow like greenish lava while the smell of the dissection room gains steadily in strength, emanating from the ground. Finally it's like a narcotic. Has my sense of smell degenerated to the point of indifference? This triumphant high summer keeps me in a state of permanent nostalgia, lines me with lead; the overly intense light covers me like a winding sheet and no help is provided by the pockets of shadow in rooms that I enter only out of boredom. Never have I felt so close to the void, to that nothingness that the sick garden remains for me. It overpowers me; I'm tied to it and its features set my nerves on edge. The vegetation threatens me like a high wave towering over me; one day I'll be rolled up in it, along with the flints and the bones . . . My willpower slackens under the action of the heat. One can't be too careful about the places where one chooses to live . . .

If I haven't written any more in this journal in recent days, it's owing to lassitude, and also because my mind, when still capable of activity, hasn't ceased to dwell on the little girl. I can get used to the house, to the garden, to the postmortem smells, to the hideousness of Tetanus, to the reminders of the dead buried here; but I can't get used to the presence of the little monster. Seeing her causes me no revulsion, but I remain distressed, and this feeling increases each time the child enters the yard. She comes frequently, alarmed, and promptly fleeing into the thickets where she spends hours, even whole days. Lots of things remain troublingly unexplained. Why, in this heat, is she covered by that thick cloak, and above all why the cowl that confines her head to such macabre effect? No doubt her head must be deformed. Under the cloak can be glimpsed a ragged silk skirt that reaches her feet. Why, if not to hide a deformity of her legs? Other questions come to mind. Does the girl have a name? How old is she? And then again, can she talk? No. Her twisted mouth can only utter inarticulate sounds—I've tried—I'm sure that not even the simplest words are understood by that rudimentary brain. My relationship with the child couldn't be more basic; by contrast, my dog has gotten further than me. As I'd foreseen, child and dog very quickly grew close. Now Mylord accompanies the girl into the bushes; he only emerges from them when she does, as covered in stains as she is. I've noticed certain details; the girl talks to the dog through movements of her chin or her hands; then too she often leans on his back, and Mylord always accompanies her on her right-hand side. Here I can't but admire the animal's intelligence. I hadn't noticed that the little invalid was often on the point of falling, always to the right; the dog noticed that before I did. Still in this class of observations, she progresses crabwise, invariably butting against a wall; the dog requires her to walk straight. Mylord protects the child. I'm delighted. But the lady in gray, who no doubt spies on us from the upper floor window, does she feel any satisfaction? Besides, the dog must have ideas of its own. If he accompanies his friend, it's because he realizes that she's in danger, and that detail too had escaped my attention. Danger lies in wait on the wall; I'd eventually come to disregard Tetanus, with its demonic eyes. Mylord hasn't forgotten. Finally I need to note here that the horrible cat only shows itself when the child turns up. As I say, the dog has ideas of its own. Me, I have a heap of ideas about all this, ones that would alarm me if my thoughts didn't glaze over in the solar oven, and I end up not thinking of anything—except for the physical ordeal of the little girl, a mass of lard and soft skeleton under a heavy cloak, and who seems miraculously insensible.

18 August. The child has a name. Ode or Oda, a name from long ago, little used today. I know this because I heard the lady in gray calling her with this word from the upper floor window. As the little girl crossed the yard this morning I spoke her name; she looked at me attentively; her face convulsed and I understood that she was trying to smile. Then I asked her what she was hiding under her cloak. She opened her hand. It was a dead bird.

"What are you going to do with it? . . ."

She pointed to the end of the garden, the graveyard. Presently her hands will be dirty with soil, the bird buried. Ah! These painful games . . .

Sunday. August. I went to a fair near the outer boulevards. The crowd moved resignedly in a cloud of dust under the cruel sun. The fair stank of fuel oil. In my day, fairs smelled of manure. I didn't see anything worth my attention, except for a tent where fairground marvels were being exhibited and where painted canvases announced extraordinary human monsters, secured at great cost. A tubercular fairground barker spat out his patter and that all too familiar smell which is the essence of hospitals—iodine, form-aldehyde, ether, I don't know what—seeped out from inside. Nobody was prepared to enter. A peevish woman at the till looked at the crowd with an expression of anger and contempt. Was I dreaming? This woman resembled the lady in gray like a sister, an observation that didn't fail to unsettle me. On hearing the tubercular showman announcing that, for promotional purposes, he was going to parade some of the exhibits in broad day, I went away, afraid of some frightful revelation. In order to forget this depressing spectacle I took hold of some darts that a stall-keeper offered me. I threw them at the target without bothering to aim. The stall-keeper let out a shout, crying that I had won the first prize. I could take my pick, a doll or a parakeet. I chose the doll, which came in a box. With its delicate porcelain head and genuine hair it was no ordinary doll.

Monday. Back from the fair yesterday evening I spent some time with the doll. It's nothing but an effigy but its likeness to the human form affected me. The fixed smile on the porcelain head is heart-rending. When I tilt the thing it emits a moan, a shrill little cry, "Ma! . . ." Mylord finds this entertaining; not me. What, I wonder, can be done to heal and console people? No sooner come into the world than they're crying! . . . At noon today I gave the doll to Ode. Her amazement, or rather her fright at the object, and the look she threw toward the upper floor window! . . . Before she would accept it the dog had to pretend that he wanted to make off with the gift. The little girl then disappeared into the garden, like a thief.

End of August. I'm unwell. The dog too. We aren't eating, or at least not very much. The heat is torrid. I can't remember such a long, monotonous summer. The sun hides behind screens of cloud—the color of pewter—but it only gets yet more stifling. Everything seems tainted or spoiling, starting with the garden whose mulch must be dully smoldering. The vegetation is pallid. The stones are sweating. I suffered a brief fit of tears, for no reason; it's a sign of the depression that has laid me low, and the cost of my solitude. Any form of response is out of the question; I'll have to wait until the skies are milder. If I were to flee from the house now, I would feel like a coward running away from a perilous situation, imaginary no doubt but one of which I have a clear foreboding—while at the same time I don't feel threatened myself, save by dehydration, yes, by wasting away . . . So here I am, reduced to despair by excess heat, excess light. What will hell be if not a place of exorbitant light, without a hint of shadow, where you can feel yourself going mad while remaining pitilessly sane? . . . I take note of a sequence of odd details and derive a gloomy satisfaction from reading these as portents. A little while ago the music of the anvil ceased in the neighborhood. I no longer hear the dawn cockcrow. At night my dog dreams and snorts. But there's nothing wrong with him, though he's getting thinner, just like I am. While I tell him my dreams, he can't tell me his, except with his eyes. I sense the fear he feels in his dreams, also that he needs to fight. Then there's the cat, more abject and more persistent than ever. It seems to emerge from boiling fat, hairless and scorched; it's putrid . . . What then? I don't know anymore. One of the funerary panels has fallen down from the wall; the boards lie in the corridor. Finally there's Ode who persists in living in the garden, in the full blaze of day, covered up like an Eskimo. I haven't seen the doll again. Mylord, who dozes frequently, only leaves his couch for Ode. The animal has never been more vigilant, though it's clear how much it's costing him. I can see too how much the child needs his help. Her face is turning yellow, the skin is wrinkling. She looks a hundred years old. She remains dazed, saliva running down from her lower jaw, and it's painful to watch her trying to keep her balance. The dog is devoted to his task, a true canine Samaritan. Alas! The signs of death are in the air . . . The little girl makes painful progress, crab-wise, stumbling against the walls, as though blind. If she takes hold of something she lets it drop. The malady that seized her in the cradle and that has twisted her—that malady has revived. It must be located in her poor hydrocephalic head. Yes! The signs of death . . . I've seen them. A little while ago the child emerged from the garden. A black spider ran across her cloak. I pointed it out. The little one didn't feel the spider that climbed up toward her neck, reached her cheek and was going to enter her gaping mouth. I was able to crush it in time, on the flabby flesh. The child didn't flinch, felt nothing, understood nothing. She must have thought that I was punishing her. On the wall, Tetanus observed us with both its blood-filled eyes. This is the point we've reached. There's nothing to do but wait. I note that I've suffered a kind of dizzy spell; I saw snow, stretches of white, ridges of ice. Now I'm obsessed by that vision. If I had snow or pieces of ice I'd put that snow or ice on the little girl's head. No doubt the lady in gray would stop me. For some evenings past I've been hearing a monotonous voice coming from the upper floor. It's reciting litanies . . .

5 October. I have to force myself to pick up my pen again, for more than ever I feel that writing in this notebook is futile. Soon I'll close it for good, and if I still set down some incidents in these final pages it's more to rid myself of their memory than to preserve them. I'll lose the notebook and with it the memory of the things I've lived through . . . A long month has elapsed. Early mornings are cool; already nights are drawing in more quickly. Autumn is underway and the garden, in shedding its foliage, reveals its bare frame after the pyrotechnics and extravagance of summer. Its substance is fissuring, subsiding. It's slowly dissolving under the rains, returning to the spongy soil. This time the sick garden is dying. The district is dying too, its fate decided by a first blow of the pickaxe. My garden, my cemetery, is living out its last days; it won't see another spring. I'm living this out alongside it, full of melancholy, alone in the mansion and as though cut off from the present century. During the day I hear the gleeful cries of the street urchins throwing stones in the vicinity, breaking windows. I say alone because the lady in gray has abandoned the premises, just a few days ago. She departed like a mouse—a gray departure one dusty morning, carried out with the help of the proprietor, thoroughly disconsolate and more subservient than ever. The creature knocked on my door and thanked me for what I had done for her. I bowed and she left, unsmiling, as though headed for eternity.

Little Ode herself has certainly departed for eternity; I know this though no one has said anything to me. She's dead and I rejoice in having learned this from her own lips. Believe me when I say that she's visited me several times in my sleep, or at least her soul has—the soul of the monstrosity that she was. No bigger than a statuette. On one occasion she said, "Thank you, sir. I should have been a pretty woman in this world, one who could have been loved, and, even more, could have given love, and who should have raised children in a big garden, among dogs and birds. God decided otherwise. I'll grow up and become beautiful in Heaven where I am now. I have a head of hair now, I'm blonde, and I no longer stumble against anything..."

Yes, believe it or not she came another time and spoke to Mylord. My dog saw her just like I did. As for the other one, the cat, I daren't write that it's dead, for Demons can't die. It's been cast into hell; but such as it was, it won't come be coming back any more, not in its abominable form. May Heaven hear me . . .

How to tell the story of the drama, this drama whose approach I'd felt and that only occurred in the one moment I'd stopped thinking about it? It was the end of August. I was sleeping—I felt drowsy in the afternoons— and everything was the color of ashes. The drama must have been harrowing, like a murder. It might have been three o'clock. I was roused abruptly from my couch by four successive cries, so imperious, so formally tragic, that I too shouted out from the depths of my bowels. I'm breaking into a sweat as I write these lines. What was it that had happened, that I had long foreseen and had allowed to take place? My dog leaped up in a prodigious bound, howling as though possessed. An atrocious caterwauling responded to his howls. The upper floor window opened with a crash and a shrill cry for help rang out, while from the garden came an infantile wailing, starting with a moan and rising to the most harrowing rattle. It was then that I cried out loud. The little invalid emerged from the foliage, the terrifying cat, as big as her, clamped to her—to her head—and gripping its prey like a wrestler, its foul jaws on the child's face. Oh, that coupling! . . . Tetanus would not emerge victorious from this malign combat, for, besides the little one who defended herself in gouging the aggressor with her fingers, the dog intervened—splendidly, dare I say—and knowing the power of his enemy.

His initial lunge knocked both the child and its foe to the ground. Separated in a moment, the cat quickly righted itself, seeking to dodge the dog, but Mylord, quicker still, seized Tetanus by the small of the back. I heard bones cracking. The killer, mortally wounded but driven by an incredible surge of strength, jumped onto the wall. It climbed up the ivy, dragging the dog with it in a desperate ascent—the dog whose teeth remained fastened in his victim. Mylord didn't let go until Tetanus reached the ridge of the wall, only then falling back heavily, covered with saliva. And I saw the cat, dislocated and staggering, silent, but its maw frothed with pink foam, dragging itself along the wall to the far end of the garden, where it suddenly attempted, as it seemed, to mend its broken carcass. But it collapsed, shaken by spasms, and rolled into the undergrowth. Meanwhile Ode lay in the yard, her feet and her fists beating the flagstones in an epileptic tattoo. She looked like a Maybug. Before I could pick her up, the lady in gray dashed out and, without a word, took decisive hold of the child. The creature was as coolly self-possessed as ever. As she lifted the little one, the hood slipped off. And I knew then that the little girl was bald—completely bald—and the last earthly image I had of my protégé was this big, shiny, domed egg. Afterward I left Mylord in the yard, which he refused to quit. Under the spell of his exploit he barely recognized me. I made sure that he wasn't hurt, but no more. I had to go, the lady in gray having asked me from her upper floor window to inform the proprietor of the incident. The old man seemed upset by my story. Without a word he followed me, leaving me on the threshold of the mansion. He returned a little later, accompanied by a famished-looking individual who seemed to be a doctor—the pauper's doctor, so to speak. Two nuns followed behind. This group rushed into the mansion and climbed the stairs. Going back into my apartment I heard the child moaning above me and it was, uninterruptedly, the moaning of the doll, "Ma! . . . ma! . . ." For a long hour I listened to the moans. Then it seemed to me that prayers were said in unison. At last the building was roused by footsteps. I opened my door to offer help once more. Everything had been taken care of. The nuns carried Ode asleep and wrapped up in ticking. The doctor followed, face all shiny. Outside, the proprietor was waiting beside a cab. I sought out Mylord in the garden; he still wasn't his usual self. He refused to drink anything. Perhaps he was waiting for the return of the cat.

"The cat's dead and gone," I said. "You're a dog in a million."

No response; panting, he persisted in remaining on guard—while the twilight drew in, sinister and starless, some shafts of heat throbbing from time to time in the encroaching pallor.

The night that followed . . . To tell it the way I lived it would be impossible; it would be a tale told by a lunatic. I'll try, objectively . . . Darkness having fallen, the dog was ready to come in. I closed the door and the windows that opened onto the garden, the smell, under the stifling sky, acting on me like a poison after the afternoon's drama. I suffer from some kind of rash; and I scratch myself continually. My room is poorly lit; I only have three candles; I'd really like a hundred of them, burning away; but would that be sufficient to dispel this crypt-like atmosphere? . . . Mylord has collapsed by my feet, overcome with fatigue. But he isn't sleeping, as I'd like him to be; he remains distraught, the pupils of his eyes dilated. As for me, in my confused state of mind I'm trying to string together the prayer for the dead, Latin words as glorious as a magical incantation. I'm trying to pray for the child about whom I no longer know anything except that, somewhere, she's dying. The words won't cohere; the rash prevents me from praying. Then the wake commences, the hair-raising wake . . . At first it was far away, coming from the end of the world, a moan, "Ma! . . ." Was it the child that I heard through space? For a long time, at intervals, the moan grated in the nocturnal silence—"Ma! Ma!"—Was it the lament of the doll, abandoned in the garden? . . . Toward midnight I understood. Mylord had heard it too. He stood up, feeling each moan as a piercing shudder. And the moans got louder, coming closer, without my being able to discover from whence they came. Were they coming from the walls, from the cellars, from the ceiling, from outside? Mylord was trembling, his head hung down, his eyes expressing a nameless terror. These moans came from somewhere lower than the ground, further away than our world; they were coming from hell. Tetanus was expiring. It was coming back, the evil beast, to torment us with its mortal agony; and I held my forehead, and I blocked my ears, and I talked at the top of my voice, and I sang so that Mylord would no longer hear these moans; and I walked about, and I checked that the doors were closed, and I stroked the dog and looked at the clock . . . It was one o'clock in the morning, then two . . . Ah! my dog, like a guilty man who hears his murdered victim through the long night of remorse. His victim—or at least its voice—crept toward us, burrowing through the ground, closer and closer. Beside myself with anxiety, I sought to leave the apartment and carry my beast into the street, to escape the obsession at any price; but when I tried to pick him up Mylord went to bite me. He no longer knew me. I covered him with a blanket and so he stayed, lying there, his jaws opening and shutting, racked by the most violent of spasms; my dog was dying. The Demon was taking its revenge. Toward three o'clock, the Demon was still moaning; toward four o'clock, it howled from close by, so near that I thought it was in the room, so that I sought some means of defending myself, and so I started to howl feverishly, like it was howling, in order to drown it out. And I shouted at the top of my voice, "Ma! . . . Ma! . . ." Finally Mylord came out from under his blanket and took some steps toward the garden. He let out an almost human sob. And the Demon uttered an interminable rattle—the very last—that finished like a sinister burst of laughter. It was over. My dog fell on his side. Dawn was breaking. Having thrown open the door, fresh air invaded the crypt, my room. It was raining outside. My dog, struck down with a fit, spat out his life, gulping, lying flat amidst a spreading pool of urine. He suffered a final spasm and vomited bile. Would he rejoin the Demon in perdition? I had closed my eyes. When I opened them again, Mylord was looking at me. He was safe, he recognized me. I carried him out onto the steps, where he lay under the kindly rain, gradually recovering consciousness. Nearby a bell that I'd never heard before started to peal, strangely, with little chimes.

2 November. I waited until All Soul's Day before exploring the old cemetery, stripped bare by the autumn gales. Not without some difficulty, slipping on heaps of dead leaves, struggling through networks of sharp, cutting branches. In a kind of vast ditch at the far end I discovered piled-up fragments of tombstones, all very old, that must have come from the Carmelite monastery. This debris isn't without eloquence. I didn't linger to decipher the broken inscriptions: *Hoc monumentum . . . qui obiit anno domini . . .* and I murmured: *Requiescant in pace . . .* For this was the only thing that could reasonably be said on this day and in this place. While I counted the headstones—there were about twenty, most of which bore coats of arms—Mylord vanished into a masonry entrance that led to some cavern or underground space. Broken steps could be seen, descending under the ground. I had to call him for a long time, fearing that the dog wouldn't reappear. The rains had flooded the passageway from which Mylord emerged soaked. Where does this underground passage go? What might it contain? Tetanus and his agony come to mind. The mortally wounded cat—whose remains I haven't found in the garden, where he nevertheless fell—could only have taken refuge underground. The tunnel must go in the direction of the building, the cellars; this will be how the cat came to die under my room. Now the dog is having fun; he scrapes with his paws, he digs holes in the humus. What is it that he's found? I burst out laughing; Mylord looks at me adorned with a false beard. It's a clump of hair that's sticking to his muzzle. Disgusting creature! Giddily, he continues his work; clods of earth fly toward me. This time the find seems significant; my heart thumps. It's an exhumation, the doll unearthed, Ode's doll, in a state of decay. She's dead, she too, for everything dies. But in death she is scalped, the little girl no doubt having pitiably wanted it to resemble her . . .

15 November. The owner has come to inform me that the formal notification of compulsory purchase has been delivered; the state is taking possession of the mansion. Demolition comes closer with each passing day. Already, entire stretches of landscape on the other side of the district have fallen, and the space of the sky is expanding. The old man looked drunk to me, with sadness perhaps. His lips trembled. He rambled on all by himself, and what could he recount, without my understanding a word, if not the history, the annals of the great and noble house that was going to expire, and whose death he himself would not survive. Now was the moment to question the old man, but I was afraid of adding to his emotions. Slowly he made the rounds of the corridor, the rooms, the garden, as though to make his farewells, then departed, taciturn, and so pallid that I imagined I was seeing the departure of a phantom evicted from his haunts, carrying his secrets with him . . .

24 December. I've received a notice requiring me to quit the premises by such and such a date. The end has come. Mechanical diggers are carrying out their menacing maneuvers at the bottom of the street. I'm the last inhabitant of the neighborhood. The Ruescas mansion has held out until now; old, decrepit, scarred, it resisted with its every sinew, too proud to accept its downfall. But now it knows, as I do, that the time to surrender has come. It has capitulated. All of a sudden, it's disintegrating. I'll leave tomorrow, but the demolition men won't have to fight this house; it'll be no more than a cadaver, ready to crumble to dust . . .

25 December. On my last night I stayed up, holding a vigil under the benign light of the candles. The weather was mild. I drank wine and sang the carol *Christus natus est*! . . . Toward midnight all the bells in the city made a fervent reply. This morning, it's like a miracle. Snow has fallen, thick on the ground. Oh how peaceful! . . . My black dog gambols crazily in the yard. The sick garden is dead—it's wrapped in its shroud. Memories, may they melt away with these Heavenly crystals. I make my farewells—I throw the last drops of wine on the immemorial snow . . .

The
Collector of
Relics

It's always been there, that dim shop on the Rue de l'Impératrice; it must have seen the light of day at the same time as the street itself, which, however, is very old. My father already knew it sixty years ago when he haunted the lower depths of the university. Until recently a certain Ladouce stored his second-hand wares there. This little building seems fated to shelter only antique dealers, those often bizarre individuals, and to be forever a kind of cavern where the collector goes in fear of the accumulated debris of centuries collapsing on his puny person. Will we ever see a second-hand bookseller or a fruiterer set up shop there? I dare say not. And that's all to the good, because what is there more appealing than an antique shop window, a museum corner open to the gaze of the passerby? I'm one of those kinds of pedestrians who willingly stop there. Since my salad days as a student I've never missed the opportunity of standing in front of Mr. Ladouce's window display. Not a week goes by when I don't still linger there. But I've never gone inside.

Lately, however, I've found myself tempted to cross the threshold. To buy what? I don't want to think about it. Everything and nothing. Well might I examine the odd objects piled up in the window display, peer into the shop's shadows where antiques without name or date are heaped on shelves in a Rembrandtesque light, but there's nothing I'd want to take home with me that I'd give more than ten sous for. I gaze at Mr. Ladouce, or rather I contemplate him, the ornament of this collection of junk, the caretaker of this wrecker's cave. For a long time I observed him without realizing the attraction that this nondescript creature held for me. Is it the attraction of the void? Now I know it. And I'm aware of what I'm doing when I direct my steps toward the Rue de l'Impératrice where I've got nothing to lose; I'm off to admire Mr. Ladouce, object, animal, or rare individual I ask myself, and who isn't for sale.

In fact, this dealer in antiques is nothing special to look at. His flat, round face cut by a half-moon mouth, his porcelain eyes, his inconspicuous nose all belong to some lunar fish. His clothes aren't worth remarking on, either. And it's precisely this perfect lack of personality that intrigues me and, I admit, irritates me too. As far back as I can remember I've seen the gentleman sitting in an armchair, facing the street, sleeping with wide-open eyes. What does he do, comfortably seated like that? Wait for customers? He doesn't always bother himself if you knock on the door, which is usually closed and bolted. Is he dreaming? Nothing goes on in the porcelain eyes, whether sadness or gladness, much less the fierce light of interest. He's indifferent, the embodiment of indifference. What drama or what catastrophe could wrest that seated creature from his futile meditations? A fire in the shop? Not even that . . . What's more, after some thought I've found the key to the mystery: the man lacks a destiny! He's content to exist, legally and expecting nothing at all, the very image of his pointless and obsolete merchandise. That's all that was needed to provoke my puzzled curiosity. And I can't help but worry about my own obstinacy in spying on this abstraction, this prodigy of impersonality, this dead mirror that reflects nothing, not even whoever stares rudely through the grimy window. Mightn't this Mr. Ladouce be a corpse forgotten in that shop where dead things are preserved? No, seeing as he moves. And I ended up finding it intolerable that one of my contemporaries was inexistent to this extent, and therefore happy . . .

Not long ago I decided to visit the shop, as much to disturb his vacuous gaze as to try to discover his reason for being, or rather, not being. The antique dealer consented to leave his armchair when I entered. He spoke in a drab voice.

"Monsieur has seen something? . . . Everything can be found here. It's full from cellar to attic . . ."

"A waste of time, that's plain to see . . ." I said.

The dealer seemed to emerge from his somnolence and his glance quickened. So, some feeling existed in the man, however rudimentary; professional pride? It was the least that could be expected. And his voice acquired an edge.

"I don't know who you are sir, but you're by no means the first passing client . . ." And he gave my words back to me: "That's plain to see . . . Very well, if you want to test me, ask me for an object that's impossible to find, even preposterous. I have it."

I liked this challenge. "I'm looking for a little siren," I replied.

"I have the very thing! . . ."

And Ladouce disappeared into the back of the shop, opening onto a second shop that gave access to a third, and soon came back grasping a glass casket in which a horrible dried codfish with a supposedly human head grimaced.

I winced. "I asked for a siren," I cried, "not a freak from a fairground! You've got the wrong man. I'm no idiot, not me! Your siren here who escaped from a frying pan has never sung mariners to a watery grave! . . ."

This sally provoked no reaction. The antique dealer put down his mummy and smiled, that's to say the half-moon of his mouth extended to his ears.

"I see that monsieur is a poet! . . ."

"Ho ho!" I went.

"Or else monsieur visits antique dealers because he's bored . . . I understand that . . ."

This was my chance to exert more pressure.

"And you Monsieur Ladouce," I riposted, "do you never get bored day in and day out, in this armchair, in this moldy shop that you never seem to leave?"

"Never! . . ." came the disarming response, the porcelain pupils reflecting a genuine innocence.

After a moment's silence, I went on: "I don't doubt it. But don't you have dreams, nightmares, surrounded by all these strange objects that have been alive. They might carry magic spells, with consequences for your moral well-being..."

The man seemed not to grasp the meaning of my words, or pretended not to, and, still imperturbable, repeated, "Never!..."

To all intents and purposes the conversation was over. The dealer waited for me to go. Finally I said, "I get the impression that you don't want to make a sale, or is that the impression that all antique dealers want to give their customers?..."

Ladouce almost didn't reply, but changed his mind. "I like to sell. Not small stuff, not the thousand miserable nothings that surround us. This snuffbox, twenty francs. That Phoenician statue, ten. This extinguisher, a hundred sous. Mere rubbish, sir! When I sell, what I call selling, it's a thing of beauty, a marvel. And expensive! No, no more dross, rather, a museum piece of the kind I have in my treasure trove. That wouldn't interest you sir, because you don't want to buy..."

"What do you know about it?..." I retorted. And I went out annoyed.

As I headed off I saw that the antique dealer had already returned to his armchair, exhausted from having had to physically *exist* for a few moments.

For several days I thought about ways of playing a trick on this Ladouce, who'd had the last word. I decided to contaminate his mediocre existence like I would pollute insipidly clear water by throwing acid into it. Not finding out how, I put my trust in chance and returned to the Rue de l'Impératrice. It seemed as though the dealer had decided not to leave his armchair for the undesirable customer that I'd shown myself to be, but out of civility he gave no sign of how unwelcome my new visit was. Without any preamble, he harangued me as soon as I entered the shop, so as to let me know that he wouldn't be my dupe.

"Monsieur has come back? So my shop isn't altogether without appeal? Monsieur has something in mind; this time he knows what he wants. To each his own fad: weapons for some, clocks for others. Whatever it takes to satisfy even the most eccentric collectors, I have it. The first time round, a client hesitates to admit his tastes, he hides them like a vice. Good God, why? . . . I have a client who looks for guillotine blades. Then, would monsieur like to tell me what kind . . . Or he doesn't know, he wants to take his time to rummage through the establishment. He's welcome to make himself at home . . ."

This monologue was adroit and constituted on the part of the creature a courteous invite to go hang myself. However I hid my surprise at discovering how astute the antique dealer was, and I replied to him coolly:

"I collect relics . . ."

"I have that . . ." And the dealer left his armchair. A few minutes later he thrust a carved frame under my nose, enclosing a velvet panel to which were attached relics and scraps of parchment.

I burst out laughing. "These chicken bones, these locks from beards and these certificates in dog Latin? . . . Come off it . . . The Jews in Rome manufacture this stuff . . ."

The gentleman bowed with good grace, then exclaimed, "Wait, I have a pewter reliquary, it holds the tibia of I can't remember which saint . . ."

The reliquary wasn't without interest, but as for the fossilized bone inside it, the dealer admitted without batting an eyelid that he himself had scavenged it from the detritus of an old graveyard. I pretended to be disappointed. Were we going to carry on with this comedy and was I going to miss the chance of making a fool of this clown? I was in no doubt that today he wanted to sell me something, for he seemed livelier and keen to keep me there.

"Since your tastes run to the religious genre, I could show you better, more genuine things, that I'd only be able to sell in Paris or in London. But the prices, I warn you . . ."

I shrugged my shoulders and followed the dealer to a recess at the back of the third shop, where, in a subdued light, undoubtedly authentic objects of real beauty lay sleeping; a Brabant reredos, an alabaster pew, brass lecterns, illuminated books of hours, monstrances, and other marvels that it pained me to see dumped in this squalid backroom, in the possession of this dealer in bric-a-brac. Mr. Ladouce took my silence for admiration.

"Here we are at last, no?" he murmured.

"At last," I said. "This is worth our while . . ."

And the inventory proceeded in silence. The dealer's porcelain eye watched me obstinately. Was he dealing with a connoisseur backed by ample funds or one of the countless penniless halfwits who haunt superannuated premises? He couldn't know because he anticipated that my manner of purchasing or avoiding purchase would allow him to identify me. At length I spied a beautifully worked vermilion ciborium of Mosan origin, of undeniable quality. I took hold of it with all the respect of a priest celebrating mass. The dealer, seeing in my gesture the hand that both took possession and would sign the check, burst into a sales patter that I scarcely heard.

"That? A masterpiece! This ciborium is known, cataloged; it's been exhibited . . . That? Unique! . . . I don't want to spoil Monsieur's pleasure, but it's eight thousand, after having been valued at fifteen at the Seligman sale . . . Eight thousand! . . ."

The sum flung at me like a challenge didn't give me a moment's pause, and putting down the ciborium I took out my checkbook. It was then that the indomitable Ladouce who, until now, had acted the part of the professional so well, ceased to be what he seemed. At the sight of my checkbook the gentleman turned purple. He sputtered. He made little nervous gestures with his paws, as though to fend off. At first I thought that he'd suddenly been possessed by the demon of lucre and that in the excitement of a major transaction en route to being concluded he had taken leave of his senses. But no, his little gestures pushed away the offered sum, the eight thousand.

"Impossible," he stammered, "not like that! . . ."

As I looked at him enquiringly he pulled himself together and became almost intelligible.

"Understand me, dear sir, it's too easy, selling like that. It makes me unhappy. I won't sell the ciborium now. You come in, look, pay and then go away? No! . . . You don't argue, you don't haggle, you don't treat me as though I were a forger, and you behave like I was a rag and bone merchant who doesn't know what he has or what he's selling? . . . Impossible! . . . Unless you come back ten or tenfold times to rip that treasure from my hoard, unless you insult me, unless you harass me night and day, then nothing doing!..."

This time my man showed his colors and I had him just where I'd wanted. Completely deadpan, I interrupted his revelatory protestations.

"Just a minute, Monsieur Ladouce. You're mistaken. I'm not delusional, not the poet you take me for . . . I'll buy, but . . ."

And after a long pause for thought, I stared him in the eye.

"But on one condition only. Your ciborium is worth fifteen thousand, costs eight, and I'll offer ten thousand for it. Only . . ." And I interrupted myself again, seeing with satisfaction that the dealer's forehead, beaded with sweat, had turned from red to white. "Only, this sublime vessel that has shone between the unsullied hands of so many holy priests before being looted from some abbey by rioting peasants, I'll only take it, word of honor, and at a cost of ten big banknotes, if you deliver it to me full of Hosts!..."

Ladouce seemed to hesitate and stared at me, stricken with an infinite stupor. I didn't back down on that extraordinary demand and I spoke more enthusiastically, as though carried away: "Consecrated Hosts, not those white wafers sold to sextons; infallible Hosts that contain the body and blood of the Son of God by virtue of the rite of Consecration, do you hear? It doesn't matter where you find them, morality has got nothing to do with this business. You have everything, you can find anything, and I believe you. There's no shortage of churches, of tabernacles . . . And don't try to fool me! I can see what you're thinking. How would I be able to distinguish unconsecrated Hosts from Hosts consecrated at the sacrificial Mass? How naïve!..."

And my laughter must have sounded lunatic, for the antique dealer retreated to the wall. Speaking normally, as though restored to sobriety, I concluded: "It's quite simple; if your Hosts aren't consecrated, they won't bleed when I stab them with a dagger during a ceremony of profanation ..."

And I headed back toward the shop. Ladouce had seized the ciborium and clutched it against his breast. He wanted to speak, but nothing escaped his trembling lips. And I made my way out, calling out, not like a gloating madman but like a businessman sure of success: "Ten thousand! . . . I'll come back a week from now."

The dealer didn't show me out.

Some days passed during which I relived those comical moments, sure of having poisoned the animal serenity of Mr. Ladouce, forever sedentary, sleeping without dreams . . . I felt supremely happy, but not yet perfectly so. Had the antique dealer refused to have anything more to do with this peculiar client who was asking too much of him? It was possible, and that would have been wise of him. However, I preferred to think of him as spellbound, as much by the lure of profit as the temptation of making a sale under these difficult circumstances. While waiting I avoided the Rue de l'Impératrice, and, for once abandoning the old backstreets that I was fond of, directed my walks toward the city center. It was just as well I did so, because luck, whose machinations one can never admire enough, showed me that the adventure was by no means going to end with a whimper.

The sixth day after that visit, toward the close of afternoon, I was striding along the Boulevard du Hainaut. In the fairly thick crowd an individual caught my attention. It was Mr. Ladouce some distance ahead, garbed in a greenish bowler hat that covered his ears and a wretched overcoat fluttering in the breeze. He seemed preoccupied and from time to time looked mistrustfully behind him. His steps were occasionally hesitant. Then he set off again, knowing where he needed to be. So, the gentleman had consented to vacate his armchair? What were his intentions, what was he up to? Anxiously I followed in his footsteps and was more satisfied than surprised when I saw him take the street that led to the church of the Riches-Claires. He turned round several times, again without seeing me as I'd left a gap between us. After having examined the exterior of the church he vanished into the doorway, fulfilling my fondest wishes. The man was obeying me! My suggestion was at work in his criminal soul. The antique dealer had been transformed into a thief, or at the very least an apprentice thief! Of course the church of the Riches-Claires, though near the center, remained little frequented when services were not being held. The dealer could well find himself all alone there. But to burgle the tabernacle! . . . And I took care not to go any farther along the street and watch for his exit. This was sign enough for me. I'd succeeded in bestowing a destiny on an individual who lacked one. Perhaps the next day he would be arrested and surrendered to the courts. He wouldn't be sent to prison, that was too much to ask, but there was no doubt that he would be committed to an asylum; whoever stole Hosts while forgetting to empty the poor box wasn't a wrongdoer but a sick man. A sacrilege, proclaimed the Church, which in less clement times would have roasted him on a slow fire, my dear Ladouce who took so much trouble, who provided me with so many emotions! . . .

I took myself off to the antique dealer on the day after the next, a delay that I had determined. Need I say that the Rue de l'Impératrice seemed to me covered with a magic carpet and that venturing there was like moving through a dream, with the ease of a genie? The reality proved to be even more agreeable than I'd hoped; the shop-window shutter was closed and the door's wooden face confronted me in utter hostility. I rang and knocked in vain; there was no life inside. Was Ladouce shutting himself in so as to defend himself against me? Was he barricading his den to discourage me? Or had he left for Paris or London, in order to free himself from his obsession? It could only be, I decided, that Ladouce was in prison. And I pictured him sitting in a cell, his porcelain eyes questioning the void and seeking to make sense of the destiny that had befallen him. That vision left me unmoved and I hurried to buy the evening newspapers. There I only read of uninteresting goings-on, filthy larcenies, murders, abductions, and rapes. Of Ladouce, not a trace. Unless, at the request of the clergy, the sacrilegious theft hadn't been revealed so as to avoid the danger of contagion, as happens when a lunatic runs amok.

The most restless man in the world, that's who I was in the days that followed. I trembled at the thought that my victim had been able to avoid compromising himself. Afraid of that, I returned to the shop. It had reopened. Behind the shop window someone was dozing in the armchair; someone new, a bearded little old man with a Hebrew nose. Who was he? A partner? And Ladouce, where was he? I pushed the door open. The old man answered my questions affably. He didn't know where the antique dealer was. He himself was resuming business, and was hoping that the clientele would stay faithful . . .

However, I had to see Mr. Ladouce, and some little while after that it was luck that once more pushed me in his direction. I was going down the Rue de Loxum when curiosity drew me to an antique shop window, a really high-class one at that, with only a few objects on discreet display, but all of the highest quality. To my utter amazement I recognized things I'd already seen; an excellent triptych in the manner of Bernard van Orley, a portrait attributable to Pourbus, and a battle scene of chevalier Breydel's, really exceptional stuff! The Mosan ciborium, the illustrious ciborium, lay on ruby-red velvet, tastefully and advantageously placed between a Virgin of the Burgundy School and a Byzantine ivory! It shone with a mystical glow in a glass case. It was only then that I raised my eyes and read on the plate glass: *Ladouce, antiquarian, successor to Cahun, Established 1842.* I came down to earth with a bump. But since I'd rediscovered both my ciborium and my victim I was determined to demand explanations, apologies even. In an interior that was truly deluxe, a smart young lady received me with hauteur, her lips set in a smirk.

"That ciborium?" I said.

With a nuance of disdain the assistant replied: "The ciborium? Sold to the Portland Museum in the USA."

"What was the price?" I persisted, "because that item was very nearly mine . . ."

The mademoiselle condescended to reply to me. "I'm not allowed to reveal that, monsieur, but no doubt you can see what's what. This ciborium is the same one that was stolen in 1369 by the Jew Jonathas, you know, the celebrated crime committed under Duke Wenceslas, following which the Hosts, which had been stabbed with daggers, were collected up by the collegiate, where they still are, in the reliquary called the Saint Sacrament of the Miracle. This is confirmed by documents, including a letter from the late Monseigneur de Méan who owned the ciborium . . ."

I'd stopped listening to the damsel's recital. At the back of the shop, in a retired little salon, a man was sleeping with open eyes, stretched out in an upholstered armchair. I bowed respectfully to the man who owned such treasures. But Mr. Ladouce didn't deign to acknowledge me.

Rhotomago

To the poet Henri Vandeputte

Among the bizarre and recondite objects that litter my room can be found a rather pretty antique Bohemian glass jar sealed with parchment, filled with emerald-green water. It contains some kind of menacing insect, vivid red, all claws and antennae and also made of glass. On looking more closely, a human form can be seen delineated in the insect, its claws and antennae giving it a diabolical appearance. The jar holds a little devil. And, a long time ago, to ensure that there could be no mistake, the profession and civil status of the devil contained therein were handwritten in faded ink on the parchment that confines it: *I'm called Rhotomago, I go up, I go down, and I foretell Madame's future*! . . .

That this minuscule character is a devil I don't doubt; that pressure applied to the parchment makes the Cartesian devil or bottle imp go up and down I've confirmed many times; but that Rhotomago can foretell the future I find difficult to believe . . . And if he happened to tell women's fortunes it could only have been in exchange for a coin in a fairground booth, through the trickery of a fortune-teller! . . . The impostor! . . . Who would dare boast of reading the future and interpreting the signs that declare it? However, I grant that Rhotomago might know rather more than men, so ignorant in their rationality. But I've never asked him about the future, this gentle, lucid, and translucent devil; I've been satisfied with making him go up and down in his colored water, amused by this game just as much as I'm charmed by the light imprisoned in the depths of the jar. What has the future ever meant to me, whose heart has no desires and who knows how to imitate Mima, my cat, by living entirely in the hour that flows through the hourglass, in perfect peace and quiet! The truth is that if I enjoy manipulating the bottle imp it's to distract Mima, sitting in front of the jar, her gold-flecked pupils going up and down with the little red devil . . .

Yesterday, on an overcast and interminable Sunday, I had proof that Rhotomago is an impostor; this windswept Sunday, full of the screeching of weathervanes, and also of so many gales that the heavy curtains in my room seemed to be haunted, and the bizarre and arcane objects that surround me were so irritated by these treacherous drafts that they emitted alarming noises! My cat Mima prowled restlessly, jumping from one piece of furniture to another and mounting guard against these invisible intruders, fluid currents that I imagined as forming spirals, traceries, or Arabic letters—which shows how erratically inclined was my already drifting mood. Sleep, who had me in her sights, wasn't long in coming and my first dream (for I never fail to dream) was of finding myself on a very decrepit old wooden ship that was undertaking its final voyage. Around me a tempest was howling, so violently that I decided to stop sailing and return home; something I did through a simple effort of will, waking up in my armchair, still accompanied by the persistent storm outside, sustaining its orchestral crescendos.

One dream chasing after another, I wasted no time in returning to dreamland while at the same time keeping a foot in the real world; that's to say I dreamed of something normal and actual, finding myself positively in my room and sitting in my armchair, letting all the winds blow themselves hoarse and the world turn on its blessed axis. As for my dream, properly speaking it unfolded before my eyes, a few feet away, in the calm light of the lamp.

Mima had settled herself on the table facing the jar, and, with the incomparable disdain that cats show in the face of any criticism, had applied herself to making the bottle imp float up and down by pressing her right paw on the parchment membrane, exerting various pressures on it, exactly as I had done . . . From the depth of the shadows where I lay sprawled I clearly saw the little devil traveling in his bulging vessel that, well lit, seemed like an emerald moon or some phosphorescent fruit whose mysterious glow plunged me into a pleasant lethargy.

"Mima," I murmured, "I'm trusting you with the jar and its devil. Enjoy yourself, but only one velvet paw goes on the membrane; that bottle imp dates back to the end of the eighteenth century . . ."

The cat deigned to twitch her ears in my direction and continued to amuse herself while I pursued my own journey into the unfathomable, dreaming that for once I was sleeping without dreaming!

This pleasure didn't last long. I was roused to consciousness by a dismal moan, so dismal and imploring that I thought I was being solicited by a soul in purgatory.

"Please God," I cried, "that Boreas hasn't blown my door open."

Confirming that I was still on level ground in the exact dimensions of my room, and that my brain wasn't mounted on a pivot like the neighboring weathervanes and at the mercy, like them, of the winds, I saw a really extraordinary scene playing out on the table: Mima the cat, bristling all over, was delivering rapid blows of her paw to the jar, retreating, attacking again and giving little cries of alarm; in-between times she turned toward me, seeming to say, "Where are you? And can't you see what's happening? . . ." Before anything else I saw that my pretty Bohemian glass jar was going to pay the price of this spectacle and I rushed toward the table, from which Mima promptly absented herself. And as I leaned over the jar, the reason for the drama became clear.

The bottle imp, contradicting all the laws of physics, was singularly animated; of its own volition and without any pressure applied it ascended, descended, turned round, somersaulted and launched itself with particular obstinacy toward the parchment membrane, as though wanting to pierce it with its threatening horns. The emerald water bubbled, the membrane resonated like a drum, and, relatively speaking, it was a real storm in a bottle.

Not at all alarmed by this exceptional turn of events, delighted even, I decided to treat the angry little devil like I would treat a living being. I addressed it: "Rhotomago, is it meteorological disturbances that have upset you so much, or do you really and truly want to get out? . . ."

The imp heard me. He started banging his horns against the glass partition, so vehemently that without further delay I proceeded to give him his freedom, or the illusion of such. A penknife sliced through the cords and wax seals and the parchment sprang free from the mouth of the jar. The water foamed. A whistling noise sounded. And I no longer saw the bottle imp because I had to close my eyes against the flare of a purple-colored flame.

Surprised, I studied the ceiling where the little blown-glass devil had no doubt shattered, but I awaited the shower of fragments in vain. He could also have bounced over my head and got lost in the carpet. And how to find the little gentleman without squashing him underfoot in a room that was so littered and so poorly lit?

"Rhotomago, little imp?" I sang soothingly, "Where have you got to? . . ."

Receiving no reply, I then appealed to Mima who had taken refuge on the bookshelf, and whose pupils gleamed slyly in those high shadows.

"Mima, I appeal to your wisdom. Since nothing escapes your gaze, can you tell me where this hot-headed bottle imp, or what remains of him, might be lying? . . ."

The animal abruptly turned her sharp muzzle away and purred loudly in the oddest way. I knew the rascal well enough to see that she was laughing uninhibitedly, seized by an intense pleasure. A laughing cat? To say that these felines don't laugh is to misunderstand them! They often laugh, and generally at their owners. Faced with her mockery I shouted vehemently, "Wretch! . . . I'm the victim of a conspiracy, and you, cat, you're that devil's partner! . . . How could I have forgotten that devils and cats share the same abominable origins! . . . that devils often change into cats and the other way round, and that in all times and places cats have had a bad name. You're nothing but a shabby witch, and by shamming anger with the jar you only wanted to fool me, make me lose my head . . . But I'll find him, that accomplice of yours! . . ."

Relieved by this flood of abuse, I turned up the wick of the lamp, whose crystal globe gave off a silvery aura, and laid myself flat on my belly on the carpet, nose to the floor, hunting with my hands. That was the moment when, raising my eyes, I found Rhotomago, and not where I expected to find him. The devil was sitting very comfortably in my philosopher's armchair, that noble seat of meditation that no one else is ever allowed to occupy. I should have been choking with rage and indignation, but so compelling was the sight of Messire Rhotomago that I remained sidereally calm.

The bottle imp, who could only have measured five centimeters at the most in his jar, had suddenly shot up and acquired the dimensions of a newborn child. By what infernal stratagem? It wasn't the moment to ask him . . . And my surprise increased with each tick of the clock, for, second by second, as a result of simultaneously inhaling and exhaling, the rogue was swelling and visibly gaining volume. Soon he was the size of a small boy, then an adolescent, then a young man, still skinny, then an adult . . . However, he was still made of glass and completely transparent, still in the hybrid form of an insect-devil, with some reminders of human anatomy. I wasn't altogether sure if I should be grateful to Destiny for allowing me to witness this ambiguous miracle, for without further ado Rhotomago had already completed his development, finally acquiring the stature of a drum major and completely filling my big armchair.

It seemed to me then that, besides horns, antennae, and tubular excrescences, he was equipped with arms, legs, and a piriform head with sketched-in eyes, mouth, and nose. Thus constituted, he shone red, slightly moist all over, seemingly filled with vapor on the inside, and his transparent skin so stretched that I expected to see him rise to the ceiling, like a gas-filled balloon. Was this invertebrate made of glass or an unknown substance, micaceous? I hadn't forgotten that I was dealing with an unnatural being, and I established the essential point, the vital principle with which this object found itself abnormally endowed, or the appearance of life, whose inspiration was very easily guessed in the present case! . . . Confronted with this dubious phenomenon I felt no fear, only the uneasiness that a healthy mind feels before something perverse, and also a feeling of irritation. It annoyed me to see the bottle imp assuming such importance without my permission, while, contrarily, I was afraid of seeing him burst like the frog in the fable, whose vanity inflated it beyond its proper measure. Meanwhile, succumbing to my mania for seeking the causes of everything, I convinced myself that this procedure remained within the laws of physics and that Rhotomago had only acquired body, if I dare say so, by trapping in his tubes and antennae the currents of air circulating in my room.

"There's no need to be astonished! . . ." I scoffed, getting up, "It's nothing but a soap bubble, or not even that . . . A skin, a devil's envelope, and not a devil, ha, ha! . . . This Rhotomago here doesn't exist! . . ."

Although I'd only whispered this opinion, the reply arrived promptly: frightful whistlings needled my ears and I found myself enveloped in a warm vapor shooting toward me from the imp's tubes, doing the work of valves. I then perceived flutes, trills, roulades. And a sweet, sharp, castrato voice finally announced, "Good evening, my dear sir, good evening! . . ."

Readily accepting this mark of education, I gave a courteous greeting to the personage, who nodded his spiny, cactus-like top. And I said to him, "Good evening Mr. Rhotomago! It really is an honor . . . You know, I never receive visitors, but I confess the presence of such a beautifully colored devil isn't at all unwelcome . . ."

Rhotomago seemed to be moved by my cordial welcome and, his voice, taking on the timbre of an oboe, babbled, "Thank you, kind sir, thank you . . . You've provided me with air, the air to which I've aspired. Here I am full to bursting, full of that delicious air, even though your room smells of damp and cat pee. But I have air; thanks yet again! . . . Let me enjoy this for a little while . . . Then we'll talk . . ."

I observed a fitting silence, leaving the poor devil to his delectation. And my thoughts ran to conjectures; wasn't this Rhotomago going to develop a liking for his situation of little devil grown big and furnished with air to breathe? Wouldn't he want to stay on with me and share my life? . . . Certainly he showed himself to be well educated, but what do we know about devils, about their morals, their passions? . . . And what if in daily life this benign-seeming companion took off his mask and showed his true nature? . . . Might he not in fact belong to the species that I fear most in the world—the moralists? . . . Then I'd have to think about committing a crime . . .

Thus my imagination galloped away and I was seeing myself exposed to the reprisals of the Demon, that Demon who rules over the lesser demons, when Rhotomago roused me from my anxious thoughts:

"Dear sir or dear friend, you've been kind to the poor bottle imp that I was, wasting the days away in his juice. In return I want to make myself agreeable and show my appreciation. I have a little bit of light to shine, not floods, but a little bit . . . What do you want from me? . . ."

"Nothing," I promptly replied, "I expect nothing except from myself, and neither my fellow men nor enlightened devils can offer me anything! . . ."

Rhotomago was dismayed by this rude response and his glass shape darkened . . . He wasn't short of self-importance, this fine sir! And the mellifluous tone in which he sought to couch his proposals wasn't best suited to win me over! . . . But he'd already rallied himself: "Be careful," he insinuated, "I'm Rhotomago who goes up, goes down, and foretells the future! . . . The future! I know the future! . . . Can my disclosures really be a matter of indifference? You would be the first mortal to scorn them and you would be an utter fool! . . ."

I cut this discourse short with a sharp exclamation: "The future? My future? . . . What does it matter to me! . . . Keep your foggy and very relative prophecies to yourself . . . I know what little satisfactions and irritations will make up the thread of my life, and as for knowing the hour and circumstances of my inevitable decease, I don't give a damn! . . ."

The devil had gone pale, that's to say his surface broke out in unhealthy looking white streaks. He had difficulty breathing. I didn't give him time to recover, seizing the chance to quarrel and to send him . . . to the devil! "On second thoughts," I went on, "I agree! . . . You'll tell me the future, but as you'll have to stay on here, you'll pay dearly for any mistakes in your predictions. There's more. Before I let you unveil *tomorrow*, you'll have to tell me all about *yesterday* . . . Knowing about the future, you can't be ignorant of the past since that's the consequence, the logical connecting link with it . . . Yes! . . . First you'll tell me about the past, which, you'll admit, is fascinating in its own way? . . ."

My devil spluttered under the blow. Feigning increased excitement, I cried out again, violently: "The past, dear friend, the great mystery of the past! . . . That's what I want to fathom, the impenetrable night of the Past! . . . Not the immediate past, oh my short-sighted devil, not the number of days lived since my birth; I mean the past prior to that birth, all the pasts that make up the Past since *my existence*, all the existences that have led to my existence here and now! . . . You can begin with the fall of the rebel angels! . . ."

I waited. A formidable silence held sway in my room. Rhotomago breathed heavily. Feeling no pity, I viewed the bottle imp; he trembled like a lump of jelly and oily drops stood out all over his surface. No doubt about it, these were difficult moments for him.

"I'm listening! . . ." I spoke with imperturbable calm.

The silence thickened. The devil appeared to undergo agonies; under extreme pressure his head spun in all directions; his fabric broke out in cracks . . . I spoke again: "So, you aren't able to tell me about the Past? . . ."

Piteously he indicated no. And, deepening my voice for dramatic effect, I concluded: "Well then, you'll foretell the future, but not mine; you'll read your own! . . . A revelation of what's going to happen to you in the next five minutes, that's the least that can be expected! . . ."

So saying, I seized a bronze candelabrum from my fireplace. And I marched toward the fraud, growling, "I'm going to destroy you, and you haven't foreseen it! . . . Vain, ignorant devil! You're ridiculous, just like so many of my contemporaries, clever men, but vain and ignorant like you, swollen with nothing, with drafts of air! . . ."

The fatal blow didn't fall because, right before my eyes, something new occurred; expelling through his tubes and antennae the ozone that had inflated him, Rhotomago shrank second by second, in the same way as he had filled up but more rapidly. Pathetic deflation! . . . Soon my armchair was emptied of its occupant. And as I leaned over to grab the tiny glass bottle imp that the devil had once more become, the object slipped from under my hand and shot into space like a rocket. My eyes followed its trajectory and I saw that it was going to fall precisely into the jar, whose water was boiling . . .

The imp having made the most sensible decision, which was to return to his original condition, I abandoned all thoughts of revenge, contenting myself with carefully sealing the jar with its parchment membrane. I also did the most sensible thing, which was to abstain from any comment, so as not to imitate those detestable moralists, that pontificating tribe who take advantage of the most absurd incidents to dump the dung of their conclusions. And once more I took up my post in my philosopher's armchair.

I'm still there. The bottle imp is in his jar. And a supreme order reigns over the chaos of my room, my universe, where everything, where everyone is in its plaçe, ruled over by Mima the cat, an enigmatic divinity with mocking eyes . . .

Spells

For the great and much-loved Ensor,
these pages where, with deep nostalgic
delectation, a décor, a now vanished time
and world are evoked. After twenty-five
years of unswerving admiration.

The express train bounded toward the sea. Sometimes it rolled on infernal gridirons and howled, enveloped in fire; sometimes it rose up from the rails and seemed to soar in shrill clouds. Alone in the compartment and a prisoner of steel partitions, it made no difference to me whether the monstrous mechanism climbed to the dead moon or ended its terrible course extinguished at the bottom of the waves. I dozed, arduously cradled, and the throbbing metallic rhythm was as hypnotic as barbarian gongs. My thoughts rolled toward the sea, and the lacerated air, like the ground pounded by the train, evoked a great maritime movement from beyond the ages . . .

Twilight fell on the countryside. Landscapes fled by and horses fled in reverse across the landscape. I closed my eyes on the image of horses fleeing through smoke or through foam. I was fleeing too, and I tried to remember why. The police, a woman, an enemy, the demon? No, the drama was simpler than that; I was only fleeing myself. It happens to everyone at least once to get sick of himself, of meeting his own face in the mirror. A perilous moment, because so clear is the mirror and so frozen the face that the time to flee has come; for it can explode, that culminating moment, and blow to bits both the human head and the mirror that contains it.

I soliloquized, huddled in drowsiness: "Why bother fleeing, since I carry both body and brain with me? Life, or this living misery that arises from the want of a specific reason for living, having become unbearable in a certain place, near certain people who one suddenly needed to leave in order to avoid the worst, would it not become bearable if transferred else-where, immediately, through uprooting oneself?... All experience amounts to this, to know how to flee!... And why the sea? Because the mountains drive a man mad and don't confer peace. And because the sea is the world's end; we can't go any further; we can't embark on ships that travel beyond, to new worlds, afraid to abandon that which causes our misery... Better still, the sea was the balsamic abyss in which I would be able to annihilate myself, and it was also the very tall lighthouse, column of salt, carousel of the great maritime night..."

I'd fallen asleep. Rubbing my eyes, I saw, still far away, the lighthouse that had just uncased its yellow diamond. As the sea approached the ex-press slowed its pace. Standing up, I remained unsteady on my feet. Shouts and songs passed by each other in the carriage where I thought I was alone. Multicolored flames danced in the windows like stars. The express train seemed heavy and groaning, like a dragon entangled in chains. It would not lunge into the sea and would come prudently to a halt alongside ships—its enormous mass obedient to a minuscule gesture. Mockery of the most reck-less flights, you have to arrive! Still full of space and speed, I couldn't accept this, trying to collect thoughts that were turning round like the fragmented dreams that had fled contrariwise from my sleep. Reality! It was time it showed itself to me. It burst into the carriage corridor in the most unreal form possible, as a coarse, frighteningly ugly mask. This vermilion snout stared obstinately at me, throwing me into a daze identical to its own. A huge laughing mask was staring at me. I could see that it was worn by an obese individual, sewn into sacking. My movement of repulsion unleashed the clownish hulk's laughter and the mask yelled like a pig, provoking fur-ther incoherent yells in response. I was awake. But what was announced by this awakening, this apparition? I didn't want to know, and I jumped onto the platform, so intensely seized by sea air that I thought someone invisible was clasping me and suffocating me with a kiss.

How could I have foreseen when I set out that the little coastal city where the express train had thrown me would be in thrall to carnival, this little city closed in on itself in winter months, where one lives in sovereign solitude among shopkeepers and fishermen? No doubt I found it at the end of my road, the city, faithfully keeping its rendezvous, but how inclined, and harboring what designs? . . . Feeling vexed, I decided to avoid it and took a bypass, making my way toward the port situated on its northern flank from where I could reach the sea and the dikes. I only cast a brief glance over the twilight panorama presented by the city, silhouetted in black against the sunset, with its belfries and the spires of its cathedral; nevertheless I was astonished by the overhanging sky, deep-green, unhealthy and opaque, while a bluish halo emanating from the ground hovered at roof level. In this way the city seemed to me to be awaiting its nocturnal carnival, and this appeal, latent in the sickly air, made itself evident in a thousand details: flags and masts, echoes of music, distant streams of maskers surging up from everywhere . . . I knew it in all its smells, shocks, temperatures, this maritime carnival, at once brutal and refined, and it was through having succumbed to its contagion that I knew to keep my distance from it. The presence of the sea bestowed I don't know what enchantment of the infinite and the incomplete on this provincial orgy, and the form of the city itself, all backstreets and passages below the level of the dikes, made it a kind of closed arena from which the fun and games weren't easily escaped. Yes, ambiguity was in the air this evening; in the coming hours, in the absurdest of dreams or the most harrowing of nightmares, the city and its cargo of monsters would slowly descend under the waters in a universal drowning of soul and senses. I would have liked that, but I knew all too well how it felt to rise back up to the surface; I clung too strongly to that miserable glimmer of consciousness that made me so unhappy! . . . While walking I calculated that tonight was also the birth of springtime, the twenty-first of March. And the greenish sky, like a copper bell under which everything would become electric, looked yet more poisonous to me . . .

Taking the path of the loading dock, I strode along Fisherman's Wharf, the end of which opened onto emptiness and whose taverns, already glowing red, were flamboyantly loud. On my right, beyond the channel, the lighthouse inspired confidence; it whipped space ruthlessly with its igneous lashes, performing a mysterious expiation, or averting the bad angels wheeling about in this equinoctial night. Was one of these angels of the vernal witches' revels going to fall at my feet? A fishwife blocked my path, brandishing a bundle of peacock feathers, her face covered by a brown, menacingly beaked mask. The old woman shoved me against a harshly lit shop window inside which a hundred multicolored faces were gaping, macabre or joyful pasteboards, the entire garland of ecstasies and grimaces.

"Buy a face! . . ." the creature croaked . . . "It's well worth it sir, it's the right thing to do! . . ." I studied these faces thinking that I'd worn them all in my life, the lewd, the conceited, and the tragic, and I looked at myself in that window as though in the mirror of my detestable past, when I was nothing but a man . . . And I shook my head in refusal. "No," I murmured, "I no longer have the right to these lying faces and I no longer want to hide the one that life has made for me. It's taken me forty years to form my face; it's taken kisses and lecherous desires, friends spitting on me, spasms of disgust and even tears of shame to make this mask. It's unique, even if its impassive sorrow fails to please. I don't have the right to change it." But the street-seller wasn't listening to my soliloquy and showed me various hollow forms that she tried to sell me, insisting on a sort of obscene maw, the head of a satyr or a cop. There was no laughter in me. And I retreated toward the street, disturbed by those greedy eyes, those holes that stared at me, far more than by the fishwife's insistence.

"Sell me yours," I said.

Angrily, the old woman thrust her feathers at my craw, crying, "Spoilsport! You don't want to have fun! I'm not wearing a mask, it's my own face! You'll come to no good you know, no good, because the masks will take their revenge on you for rejecting them. Find a good place to hide! . . ."

I went away, irritated by this incident, not that the threats worried me but the curses she uttered echoed peculiarly in the silence of the wharf, a silence laden with ambiguities, pickled in brine, its limits nibbled by pianolas . . .

Once past the last buildings on the wharf I left behind on my left the ramp that led to the dike, from where the prospect of theatrical façades bathed in light seemed like a town of cardboard and canvas put up for an evening. Hearing the call of the infinite, I finally crossed over its threshold, stepping over the anchors and cables as though I'd already set foot in the perilous territory of my dreams, littered with traps. A little distance away the channel and its white jetties thrust out into the sea, suspended pathways that terminated, as I well knew, in the end, the absolute end of my flight. But before venturing onto the spongy boards I turned back to the city; it looked further off, as though drifting, still wreathed in nebulous blueness, from which emerged the spires of Saints Peter and Paul. How splendid and desirable it would have been had it not been for the sea, over which I was walking unburdened! . . . As I made my way forward over the jetty in the relative darkness I felt that I was vacating the ground and even the continent where I had been thrown by accident of birth; it seemed to me as though I was going toward a nameless fatherland, unknown and better . . . Yet I was turning my back on what was now a fairy city, magically illuminated, and where my fellow men, freed from their puritanical morality, abandoned themselves to sports that were, according to preference, angelic or bestial. Without pausing in my walk toward the infinite I turned my head toward that promised festival, the jetty being a long one that ended at a small lighthouse. Searchlights swept the zenith, their brushstrokes crisscrossing toward tethered weather balloons that resembled celestial buoys. And fireworks fell back down on the city, showering it with slowly descending stars, flowers, algae, and polyps. Once more I noted that the night, seemingly overcast, had darkened to violet, and that the intense green of twilight was spread on the sea like oil. It let itself be seen, the sea, retreating to the lowest reach of the shore, like a calm field swept by breezes. I wished it good evening, as to a fellow creature. Right now the city could go up in flames and collapse. I wouldn't spare it so much as a glance . . .

I was no longer a man in flight, I was a still figure, leaning on the parapet and contemplating the flow of water in the channel, under the protection of the fiery blades that the lighthouse held out over my head; a man who, having passed the threshold of the infinite, like that of a cathedral, leans forward, simplified, purified, under the nocturnal vaults. Nothing more remained of whatever had pursued me, except the weariness of the chase. I might also have thought myself on the bridge of a ship, for a swaying sensation, or rather a vibration, spread to my legs from the jetty's piles. But it really was a matter of departure, since I'd just arrived! . . . No alcohol provides the intoxication that I felt on inhaling the sea. I breathed in its perfume, as powerful as ether, and particles of brine, the damp dust of space, were absorbed into me, renewing my being, dehydrated by arid struggles. Never had the somber waters seemed more worthy of love, and it amazed me that a man could love anything other than the ocean and God, whose image it is. It mattered little to me just then that in the distance other lighthouses were pointing out possible routes and countries, that beyond the channel were the outlines of lunar hills where it would have been good to wander and sleep; I could see nothing but silky reflections on the amber water that licked at the pilasters, smacking its lips. One isn't more regally alone, without name or age, one isn't more primally happy than in such a moment, when able to believe oneself unburdened of destiny! . . . However I was surprised that the sea was so calm, on this equinoctial night, when the sap was boiling in ejaculatory spurts and nature raved like a bewitched old woman in the throes of orgasm . . .

This peak of happiness didn't last long, and apprehension seized me with an imminent and unavoidable sadness. An overriding desire haunted me; I desired this sea that poured out its euphoria for me like a wine reserved for its lovers alone, and I desired it absolutely, for my body wanted to possess it no less than my spirit did. And the torment that spread through my being was like what is felt on such a night by a man in a state of arousal who wants all the women of the world, can't get any, and runs breathlessly after shadows. I knew it to be multiple and ungraspable, this sea, but its nearness was so beneficial that I wanted to feel it still more immediately, not admitting to myself that in this darkness between sea and sky, there was nothing rational about such a plan. And the rationality that hinders our understanding of the essence of all things no doubt existed in me only in embryonic form, for it didn't stop me from going over to the gap where a landing point opened up at the side of the jetty. Moving with precision, I went down these rigid stairs that led to the water's surface, happy to be so free and so much in command of my movements while performing an act that the first comer would have found dangerous, if not mad. I descended through the internal scaffolding, between enormous, fragrant joists, the steps soft under my feet, carpeted with lichen. Soon I found myself on a level with the waves, within touching distance, and there was nothing more I needed, here in this wooden cage, unworried by feeling the water flowing everywhere or by seeing the stairway disappearing under it, but only by the thought that humans might find me in this position, in this place of refuge. Here was where my flight ended. In those depths, standing on a plank covered with wire mesh and caressed by the foam, it seemed to me that I was high above life and outside it; it seemed to me that in no other place in creation could I have felt that divine languor, that perfect disappearance of my poor, obsessive, and puerile personality. Not to be anything anymore, that was my supreme joy in that minute whose length I didn't measure, the time of centuries not being more measurable. And a vision came to me that, in the very beginning, before the world sprang up out of adversity, there must have been a powerfully fragrant sea like this one.

This vision wasn't the only one that haunted me. I also saw myself returning back through the ages, endowed with the faculty of living underwater, my blood become cold; I had been a fish, this was not just a biological dream. And so I ended up telling myself that throughout the oceans and in their bosom there must exist undefined creatures that eluded oceanographers but were known to sailors of long ago or ancient collections of legends. Alas! One should avoid imagining the Improbable which, like Fatality, is no sooner invoked than it ironically shows itself . . . A boat was sailing down the channel, heading toward the landing point. Half-submerged, traveling without lights and manned by beings I was unable to discern, its form unforeseen, this boat was in fact an old-fashioned, red-colored ferry. Neither the splash of oars nor the sound of a motor could be heard. "Only," I said to myself, "only fishermen arriving from a nearby port and en route to the carnival would dare to flout all the regulations by sailing up the channel in this way . . . But if they were drunk or overcome with excitement surely they wouldn't hold themselves so still, like pale statues? . . ." Although I was annoyed to see men again, I grew more curious as the ferry approached. There might have been a dozen insofar as I could make out. Men? Just then I wasn't sure. Maskers, no doubt. If the boat had been drifting I might have thought that a farce was involved, the kind that the rough-and-ready folk of the ports devise in their festivities, maritime farces incomprehensible to outsiders. But the boat cut obliquely across the current, well steered, and its appearance, sinister at first sight, ran counter to the idea of carnival revelry. There was no mistaking that it was sailing toward me. I could have climbed back onto the jetty, followed its progress from elsewhere, and waited from another spot for these strange passengers to disembark. Glued to the planking, I no longer had much willpower and there was no fear in my heart; I felt only a certain malaise, the result of waiting, and I also felt a foreboding that I wasn't merely to be a witness to that crossing, that something was going to happen that would concern me. The ferry approached, as though hesitant to dock. And I felt the urge to hail these beings, men or masks, I couldn't be sure; but the call stuck in my throat.

No, not in the engravings of hallucinated artists or the stories of lunatics have I ever seen anything so distressing and at the same time so pitiable as these seafarers now coming into view, and if, in all probability, the aspects of Beauty are limited, those of the Hideous are countless. And rather than thinking of saving myself—for such apparitions always imply danger—I philosophized methodically, surprising myself by not suffering agonies of inexplicable stupefaction. From my observation post I supported myself against a beam, craning my head above the water. I already knew that those who arrived like specters in some tragedy belonged neither to the human nor the animal species; nor were they simulacra, scarecrows set up on a piece of driftwood . . . Although average in size, they grew or shrank, floating, as though without bones, or fish-bones either, and inadequately filled with gas, not enough to rise in the air but enough to prevent them collapsing back in on themselves. Underwater flowers sway and tumble in just the same way, following the dictates of the current. At first I might have thought them covered by shrouds. They were naked, their grayish bodies barely sketched in. But their singularity derived from the thickness of their heads, as though too heavy for their bodies, the dilated heads of fetuses. These faces evoked jellyfish on account of their glaucous color and glassy sheen. From what rudimentary existences, concealed in the undertow, did the equinox confer on them a semblance of life? From what cosmic carnival had they been wrenched, these dregs of the abyss, these embryonic masks? . . . You would have to be demented to recognize these reminiscently human-looking membranes as men; but they really existed, able to move, and inexplicable though their presence might seem, they nevertheless approached the landing point. I shuddered at the idea that these things might, in the mirage and the confusion, be able to mingle with real people. And as the red ferry kept approaching, a true floating coffin, my panicked thoughts gave voice to old superstitions: "Couldn't these be souls from purgatory come to resurrect memories; couldn't they be ancient maskers roused from their aquatic sepulchers and come back to see the carnival?..." Pursuing my questions, I addressed the apparitions as though they had ears to hear: "You souls from purgatory or limbo, you drunken or distressed tadpoles, what do you want?... How is your humanity compatible with mine? But I'm better able than anyone else to understand you; whatever is abnormal or unnatural holds hardly any terrors for me... Have you brought a message?... Do you possess a sense of good and evil like members of my species, or the memory of having had it in previous times?..." The boat bumped against the joists of the landing. I pulled back. The monsters were upon me, and I felt the dread sensation that I would never again escape them. We were on the same level, and I only needed to stretch out my hand... The danger of my position was finally clear to me, but too late. Lost in my meditations and monologues I hadn't understood that if these phantasmagorical creations existed only in my eyes then I myself existed only in theirs, in their abominable dead eyes, deader than those of fish, mere traces in their gelatinous faces. Their sea journey had reached its destination. And the ferry foundered at my feet, overturning, hull in the air as though capsized by a force from beneath, and throwing its cargo of tadpoles into the water. There weren't a dozen of them, there were a hundred who, dilated, floated on the surface, frightful water lilies in bloom, or boils full of pus. Swarming round the piles and under the steps, these things surrounded me, sticking to the boards and rising with the tide, for the water rose, kneading my ankles, then legs, and the marine larvae rose with it. What help could I expect at the point I'd reached? Return to the top? I remained paralyzed, my lower limbs already under water, tied to the steps by secret seaweed. Yes, the horror of my situation became clear; water would cover me. But it wasn't drowning that I feared; I thought with dread that the tadpoles swam at the surface and would come toward my face, and that from them would come an unknown death, an unheard-of death whose recipe remained lost since prehistory, or was reserved for arrogant men of my stripe who sought to soar above Time only to see themselves condemned to a molluscular agony. In my mind I screamed "God, don't let that happen! . . . I can accept my body being eaten by crabs, but don't let my soul be tainted by these larvae, for they want me to become like them! Save me, God! . . ." I received a violent blow to the back of my skull when I finished this plea, and I thought that I was flung forward into the channel. I felt myself dying, caught in a dizzying spiral, my ears ringing like alarm bells sounding a shipwreck . . .

It's a proven fact that a man can die without his death finally occurring, and through a twist of Destiny he's thrown back into daily life. This is what happened to me. Had I been at the bottom of an abyss, and had the abyss catapulted me back to the surface? I don't know, I knew nothing, I didn't try to find out. I came back to my senses, the crystals in my brain gently lighting up again. The jetty steps were gone; better still, I found myself comfortably seated in an armchair against a scarlet velvet curtain at the far end of a brilliantly lit room. Although my eyes were still clouded I saw mirrors, flowers, goblets, and I also saw the astral light of chandeliers, active and intimate, dematerializing every object, their lilac-toned shadows making of this exquisitely enclosed room an ideal location, restful and utterly secure. However, silence wasn't to be found here. I seemed to hear flights of bees, the rustle of beetles' wings; then, too, a vast and harmonious sound came from beyond the room, proclaiming a ball and at the same time a procession. I accepted my new condition, one that could only be due to the Deity's timely intervention on hearing my plea, and it mattered little to me how the miracle was performed, knowing as I did that it was performed outside all commonsense logic. Neither did I feel any alarm when I saw coming toward me a slow and solemn personage, tall and movingly beautiful; a person conjured up no doubt by the place's lights and about whom I could make no presumptions save that I owed my safety to him alone. He looked at me with all the goodness of his splendid eyes, two mauve stars in a milk-white, hieratically molded face, a glowing countenance that can only be the attribute of archangels. A sort of helmet crowned that head of curly hair, and the mystically warrior-like aspect of the apparition was completed by a long and heavy brocade robe, belted with gems and falling in geometrical folds. Where had I glimpsed this magnificent stranger, in what theater or in what dream? From what museum or what century did he come to enchant me? Seeing so much graciousness I thought a superior type of woman was before me, such as we find in antique stained glass windows, but the virility of the apparition glowed in his warm, deep voice, for he spoke to me in a friendly tone and his voice seemed to awaken in the air the reverberations of an organ.

"It was the sea that you wanted to drink without knowing it, the whole sea . . . Take one of these cups and drink the juice of nepenthe, it's time you got drunk like the common mortal that you've never ceased to be."

I took the cup that lay within reach and drained it; warm satisfaction promptly flooded through me. And the magnificent being continued: "I know you, my friend, and you know me. I've been able to save you this time, but would I be able to do it again? You put yourself into danger so often . . . Why did you flee the heat of the carnival for the icy pit of suicide? Don't you know that folly is given to us as a support, and it isn't *always* shameful to fall? . . . My friend, you're guilty of the crime of solitude, and you deserved to be consumed by the sea. God allowed me to be in your orbit, to hear your utmost cry for help; will he always allow it? Without me you would have been the unidentified body that the tide unfailingly throws up, the carnival's drowned man, the one who, through a fatal tradition, is the 'not-masked,' as though some poor wretch was needed to pay a ransom for the sins of the festival . . ."

And the archangel burst into laughter, his mouth bright as the sun. Other laughter echoed in the room. It was only then that I saw that the room was peopled with bright maskers, pink, white, mauve, bristling with feathers and all intermingling as though for a dance. The archangel was the central figure and seemed to be their sovereign. They fell back at his gesture, these marvelous participants who certainly evoked the idea of Folly for me, but in the sense of the supernatural, the tutelary. With a further gesture he jerked open the curtain and said: "Carnival! Look at it and forget your cares . . ."

I let out a cry, astonishing myself, for I hadn't cried out like that, not with that surprised delight, since the magical days of my childhood.

Directly across from the balcony where I was seated as though in a theater box, I perceived the Place d'Armes lit up in purple and its town hall crackling with fiery sparks. The haze that hovered over the town had descended into the square and in its nebulous reverberation the fairground glory, the exultation of the carnival reached its peak. The illumination of the façades, the upheld torches and the swordplay of the spotlights going from one roof to another created an intensely combustible atmosphere in which tumbled the silhouettes of birds, flying fish, and a thousand fantastic forms, soon reduced to ashes. Dazzled, I sought to understand the spectacle offered to me by the archangel, who stood on the balcony with the hand of a demiurge, as though these rainbow-colored crowds and these fiery perspectives had arisen at his capricious command. But I remained seduced by this magician's hand, blazing with rubies and emeralds, seeming to bless the flocks of enthralled maskers. Was he the organizer of this delirious event, or was he absolving these innocents, so deep in their state of trance? I couldn't hear what he was saying, fanfares were belching out rough music from the eight approaches to the square, a cacophony that was nevertheless outdone by the loud shouts of the crowd—a din that evoked for me the anguish of a zoo engulfed in flames. However, thanks to its rhythms and colors, the vision remained carefree and fascinating to watch, and it didn't invoke the idea of calamity that is always summoned up by a gathering of the children of Demos. It was the people still, but rehabilitated by their attributes and their costumes as well as by their aboriginal simian grace, rediscovered in this great midnight of the instincts. This universal saltation was so pure that there was no call for sarcasm or rites of exorcism, and I approved the archangel's benediction. I thought I could read the words on his lips and was in no doubt that they said, "Remain pure both in suffering and in joy. This is the secret, the price of survival . . ." The unleashed uproar was necessary for me to take in such barely murmured statements! But at that moment I accepted everything marvelous, everything admirable as my due, and I felt no surprise at seeing beside me familiar features that I recognized from prints.

It was a nobleman in military costume, sash and ceremonial sword, and whose gauntleted hand was resting on my shoulder.

"Marquis," I cried, "Is it possible that you're haunting this city that you captured after a famous siege? No doubt you think that it's much uglier after being rebuilt! Even though the carnival transforms it to some extent. Have you found yourself here again since dedicating these ruins to the Archduke Albert?..."

The Marquis of Spinola grimaced wryly at the reference to his continuing renown and also at being reminded of how ancient he was. He pointed to the square, replying, "That's what I like! And what reminds me of better times..."

The crowd had been driven back by devils with tridents, freeing up a space in the center of the square, next to an iron stand full of people masked and disguised more sumptuously than the common crowd. Pyrotechnicians took to the field, bombarding the air and loosing off squibs that seemed to delight Spinola. What solemn ceremony, what interlude was being readied in the space cleared by the devils? I saw a big white effigy being erected, a kind of snow-white mannequin with lesser mannequins in hideous masks tied up at its feet, meant to symbolize the vices as well as the miseries of the season, its penury, its politics, and other current ills. Clearly we were waiting, to the sound of funeral marches, for the astronomical hour to be sounded, that of the birth of spring. And Theban trumpets proclaimed the hour. The multitude burst into increasingly ferocious applause as the fires climbed high; the flames formed an incandescent tulip at the heart of which the mannequins twisted about in the postures of actual torture victims. A splendid *auto-da-fé*, lacking only the smell of roasting flesh, for which the filthy cloud caused by the tireless pyrotechnicians was no substitute. Comets and spirals burst from the turret of the Town Hall. The entire square exploded, a multicolored volcano. And when the eruption relatively subsided a slender acrobat could be seen walking in the empty air above the rooftops, covered in leaves and as swift as a pink insect, waving the antennae of his pole. Springtime was passing overhead! Like everyone else, I applauded at my pleasure. But this pleasure was too intense, I choked, prelude to a swoon. My eyes misted over, retaining, however, the image of the archangel bent over me. His fingers touched my forehead. And I must have smiled at him as I slipped into metaphysical shadows, for his breath covered me like the first breath of spring itself.

One always comes back, from the most fervent festival, the most sovereign state of sleep, and even from death, since phantoms exist, sometimes benevolent ones, like those who had surrounded me in that fatal and poignant evening. I awoke without effort, finding myself in the armchair where I had fainted, in the hotel salon, the gray light of dawn filtering through the drapes. The festival must have reached its conclusion; not even the faintest sound of singing or shouting could be heard. And the friendly maskers had departed, returning me to the solitude in which they'd found me, departed not like unreliable drinking companions, but like the spiritual brethren that they'd shown themselves to be, grand, high-ranking individuals who knew how to live as well as how to survive. Was it the archangel who had drawn the curtains on the now closed balcony and covered me with a fur so that I wouldn't get cold, or was it Spinola, who knew the climate of this city, having experienced it during the siege? And the other maskers whom I couldn't recall so clearly, was it they who had left tasty snacks, cigarettes, alcohol, and some flowers close at hand, just what is needed for someone who sees a grim dawn of day after the festivities? "Such good manners show that I haven't been dealing with mortals," I thought. "One of my fellow men, even someone distinguished, would have abandoned me with a turd on my stomach by way of farewell. So whoever saved me and danced attendance on me couldn't have belonged to this world . . ." Convinced of this, I got up to open the curtains and rediscover the day, after a night that seemed to have begun far away in a confused past; to rediscover the day and, chronologically speaking, my contemporaries, all carnival now at an end, all ambiguity dissolved . . .

Alas! In the weak light and glazed by the drizzling rain, the remains of the décor on display in the Place d'Armes left me shivering. The Town Hall rematerialized and the bourgeois façades blew their noses in wet drapes as though suffering from head colds. In the center, near the forbidding iron stand, were the remains of the bonfire where the cardboard and straw heretics and witches had perished; charred stakes and poles bristled everywhere, bearing witness to the nocturnal conflagrations. Truly a dawn fit for executions, and so much remaining refuse to be disposed of before the city could be cleansed! . . . That disagreeable sensation affected me less than I feared, with order reigning in the salon and nothing there to remind me of the debased orgy; but my feet and legs were still damp, a reminder of the sea that had started to overcome me on the previous evening. "Know how to leave," I told myself. "Leave when the time is right . . . What is there for me to do in this place, on this floor where no one knows me? What is there for me to do in this provincial town, lapsed back into its hypocrisy and its speechlessness? It belongs to the street-cleaners . . ." And I looked for the staircase, not before taking a last look around that bourgeois salon, in the best of taste certainly, that had hosted such prestigious people, and me, the unworthy one, the leper at the banquet . . .

Coming out onto the ground floor, it was clear to me that the carnival's glitter was duly concluded. Tentatively, not yet fully awake, I opened doors, and more doors. One revealed toilets where a brown bear lay snoring righteously; a final door opened onto an English-style public house where all the light bulbs were still lit. In the foul air I made my way past overturned chairs toward a formally dressed waiter who remained upright, like a pilot in a tempest, arms widespread. On the benches some maskers still muttered confusedly, barely alive and as though groaning; shepherdesses with hair now lank and men about town suffering the horrors of the morning after. I thought that I was in a reeking cellar where sulfur could usefully have been burned. As I questioned the waiter, the wretched man looked up at me with the eyes of a sick dog. I gathered from his inebriated mumbling that he had no information about the people who had reserved the upper floor and balcony for the evening. He knew that these maskers had come in a cab shortly before nightfall, helping to support an acquaintance who seemed to be dead drunk . . . I couldn't help but smile and made my exit as the waiter's head suddenly collapsed into his serviette. There was vomit everywhere; maskers in a state of collapse were stuck to the walls by their puke. I would have liked to rescue them but I needed to breathe and all the formalin in the world couldn't disinfect that epidemic, resulting from the worst kind of retching. I leaped onto the pavement like a flea-infested man into cleansing water . . .

The day was dawning, not easily. Big clouds sped in low from the west. Springtime, pink acrobat who walks a tightrope in the city skies for us to marvel at, in which garret are you sleeping? And you, city, your leaden roofs ache, you huddle up in the harsh cold of the morning, your windows dead, your stones inimical, and your drains blocked, it's only natural . . . Late maskers were returning home, stooping, staggering, scared by the dawn and no longer able to recognize the scene of their exploits. And the nearby sea resumed its eternal conversation. Ascending the Rue de Flandre, I soon arrived at the terrace where, in a sullen and spiteful mood, I was able to confront it face to face. But its infinitude restored me to myself, and, voluptuously, I drank in the abundant air that surrounded me like a wave.

I strode along the strand toward the channel, on sands almost bereft of seashells and adorned only by beached jellyfish. The image of that sea and these jetties, in bringing back to mind the personal drama that had nearly occurred there, didn't upset me as I'd expected it to; I thought of those moments as a news bulletin concerning someone else. I felt no bitterness at the thought that I might at this moment have been rolling under the waves; the thought that I lived on by courtesy of a Higher Power thrilled me with no special joy. Sure of myself and certain that the value and quality of the miracle from which I had benefited would become apparent to me when I had gained some distance from it, I was still troubled by certain details of my adventure, petty-mindedly troubled, like a pleasure seeker who, after a night of dissipation, tries to piece together just what he did and how much he spent. And I asked myself obstinately: "Tadpoles, monstrous jellies, who were you? And what was your meaning, misshapen beings who wanted to drag me down? Souls from purgatory? From limbo? . . . As long as I don't know I'll never be able to get you out of my mind . . . Or if I'm not allowed to understand, could you let me know who you are? . . . A creation of my neurosis? I can't accept that . . ."

At that moment my foot slid, having stepped, as I thought, on a jellyfish. Leaning down over the sand I saw a sticky rubber membrane and the disgusting contact, besides making me shudder, suddenly and unexpectedly fired my brain. Whether through inspiration or simple association of ideas, the object that I'd just squashed underfoot told me the identity of the monsters. All over the strand I found these repulsive membranes, pitiful skins leaking their juice, mortal semen spread over sterile limestone . . . Everywhere the maskers, in flowers and in flames, had tangled with each other on this equinoctial night, male and female; everywhere they had sketched a venereal parody, being themselves nothing more than parodies . . . With every step I came across the instruments of that bad coitus, and I saw them in the advancing waves, bobbing in the foam; there they were, stuck to the dikes, on the planks of the jetty. There must have been enormous quantities in the channel, in the sewers, the chambers, the bilges. And I gave a bleak laugh at the thought of the seminal sacrifice offered up to the void, to this infinity, this sea that receives everything and contains everything, the primordial seed of all life . . .

Hungry seagulls flew around me and I was afraid that they would perch on the salty balloons. If I had bread . . . And the birds wailed, lamenting, mimicking sickly newborn infants, endlessly complaining, who we can neither console nor send to sleep; who complain of nothing if not of having been born and keeping their eyes glued shut . . . These screeches in a broken flight filled me with chagrin, and I'd have liked to chase away the nostalgic creatures for whom springtime was an empty word and who still lived the life of wintertime, close to men. My understanding was made complete by these inhuman cries, and I cried out, toward the sea, that traceless cemetery.

"You weren't souls; there's no limbo or purgatory for you, there's no possible prayer for you, since you were dead before having existed, unprocreated innocents and abandoned to the sheath, outside all knowledge and with less awareness than seaweed . . . Lacking destiny, lacking attachments, a secret attraction led you to me, who, like you, is possibly the offspring of rubber-coated loves, but who has fooled his shameless progenitors . . . Goodbye! . . ."

And I turned my back on the marine horizon, resuming my flight, this time in reverse . . .

I followed the quay in the direction of the station, still dissatisfied. The morning was progressing and the city would soon regain its everyday color and volume. That was of no interest to me. Not even the sea could hold me back. I took away nothing other than my nostalgia.

Who was that archangel? Why hadn't he left me with his name so that I could have spoken it in bleak moments when threatened by spells? The cathedral loomed on my right. But my eye probed its walls and towers in vain; no sign that my unreal protector had returned to his niche. He wasn't from here, no doubt about that. And what if, in the end, he'd been a human being like me? No. An apparition, on that I insisted . . . And yet again, since I needed some interpretation of the enduring mystery, I decided that the apparition could only be a sculpted figure, the prow of an old-fashioned vessel, come from Venice to founder in our waters several centuries ago; thrown up by the silt on a day when the universe was out of joint. What does it matter? He exists, my archangel. I've seen him, and if you dismiss me as a fraud it doesn't matter to me . . .

The express train was waiting. No sooner was I aboard than it whinnied and sped toward the country. I closed my eyes and truly gave no further thought to anything . . .

Stealing
from
Death

To the poet Willem Gijssels

"Death comes like a thief!" thundered the priest in the school chapel where, like sinners, we assembled in the evening. And we lowered our brows; a freezing wind scraped the nape of our necks and we were afraid of the chapel door opening, letting in someone invisible, come to carry one of us off. That phrase has stayed forever etched in my flesh, as deep as in a tombstone. The burning dust and corroding rain of the days of my life have never been able to efface it. Yes, the priest told the truth: Death comes like a thief, hypocritically, and for certain people, the liveliest and healthiest, he turns assassin and ambushes them, attacking and striking them down in the space of an instant. But poor unheeding creatures that we are, we can barely spare the time to think about him, who thinks about us; and it's to us that he comes in his shameful way to steal this thing—life—that we treat like dirt, and which seems priceless to us when we're about to lose it . . .

In those days I was at full physical strength and lived intensely through every sense, and in a state of perpetual restlessness. Like my colleagues who conducted their business at a frenzied pace, I squandered myself unsparingly, running around and thinking myself a man of action because, following their example, I made a noise in the world and was always feverishly busy. I no longer had the time to stop to look at a tree or a child, or read a book of poetry or listen to a symphony. My days roared past like engines. And when these labors were over I let myself collapse on the bench of a bar where I stayed to drink and argue stupidly with other people who were just like me and just as harassed as I was, and whom I only left, sometimes unsteadily, for an all too brief rest during which my thoughts continued racing in a loud ferment. I thought I was as strong as a rock, and I drove myself all the harder in the relentless daily battle to earn money that I didn't really need. However, I was aware of sudden fainting spells to which I paid no heed, and though I occasionally noticed the disappearance of someone or other from my circle, I would have thought it ridiculous to consult a doctor. Besides, my friends, or those to whom I gave that name, helped me to laugh off these weaknesses and told me about theirs, which they cured with renewed bouts of drinking.

Down here a man has friends when he goes to the bar every day, when he knows how to drink, how to pay for drinks, how to entertain those in his circle with a torrent of words, and above all, laughter. Friendship is something else, something exceptional: ordinarily it's nothing more than a word that's always on the tongue, a fine-tasting word when the mouth is on fire with alcohol, but spat out the following day along with the bile. So I had friends whom I trembled at the thought of losing, and it was a fraternal fraud from which everyone benefited.

Among my acquaintances, without whose habitual company I would have found life impossible, I singled out two who truly deserved the golden title of friend. The first was called Léonard, and there was no one who could match him in his attentions to me. I had a high opinion of this big, red-haired chap who was quick-witted, inexhaustibly voluble, and always in a sunny mood. The word friend was always on his lips and it was difficult not to acknowledge the sincere feeling shown me by this obliging companion. What's more, a smile was unfailingly fixed on his clear features. His multiple kindnesses as well as the care he took to entertain me with his amusing tales made him infinitely dear to me. The other was called Prosper and only rarely came to the nightly gatherings, for he lived midway between town and country. Swarthy and sturdy, he was no talker and not given to laughter. However, his handshake, like his upright character, gave me a good opinion of him. He sat off to the side and was content to listen to the others. Just as Léonard was well liked, so there were few who liked Prosper; he struck a jarring note in our concert and in these befuddled discussions his silences could even be awkward. Once he said to me, "I'm your friend too, but not in their sense of the word."

How different these two men were!... Léonard who had little school-learning but spoke eloquently and was sure of his own worth, who boasted of holding a position in business. In fact he had an undistinguished job as an insurance salesman. One day I asked him if it was true that his business activity consisted in torturing doorbells and going in through people's windows. I saw that the insult made him turn pale, but his smile never stopped beaming out from his face. As for Prosper, he was an old blacksmith who created works of art and sold paints and varnishes in a little house along the main road. In his spare time he relit his forge and made bronze flowers for his own pleasure. He read forgotten authors at a slow pace, absorbing the pith of their writing, and when he took part in a debate, we were surprised by his erudition. That learning made little impression on us then, and Léonard made fun of the old craftsman who was a target for his taunts.

Often, on leaving the tavern, I wondered what it consisted of, this friendship so noisily manifested; what they said about me, those who flattered me during those fraternal moments. Nathalie, the barmaid, who knew each and every one of us, told me all about it. It's in the nature of women that they don't talk psychology like we do but weigh us up infallibly on the basis of signs that we take no notice of; they look at us and listen. When I was on my own one afternoon Natalie talked about my friends. She confided to me that the red-haired one was a fraud who detested me. As for the other, the black man, she had clearly seen that he was honest. These statements chilled me. However, Léonard came along a little later and his geniality made me forget this impression; warmed by beer we felt more than ever that we were friends in this barroom where everyone was happy.

It was in this smoky and noisy barroom that one day Death made his entrance... An arctic breeze enfolded me like the wind from a wing. I felt unwell, suddenly overcome with shivering and dizziness. In a sudden silence, seeing everything in black and white, I felt a need for fresh air and went out on wobbling legs, refusing help from Léonard who must have thought I was drunk. In the street I felt the pavement slide from under my feet and was about to collapse when I was supported by a solid grasp. It was Nathalie, the barmaid, who, realizing the condition I was in, had left her post to come to my aid. She led me home, a few meters from the bar, and left me in the care of my concierge, taking it on herself to call the local doctor. I don't know what happened then. Partially recovering my faculties, I saw the doctor leaning over my bed. I knew this pleasant man, whom I found bluff and good humored, but who at the moment seemed altogether different, grave, even worried. He was dismantling a little silver syringe. A feeling of great tranquility engulfed me. The doctor asked me if I was ready to be taken to a nearby clinic where he had a practice and where I would be looked after better than in my own apartment. I realized that I was in danger and closed my eyes.

Who was it that tore me from the happy stupor into which the morphine had plunged me? I was floating between heaven and earth, or rather I was hovering over my bed as though levitating when I was pulled down from my miraculous situation by a scurrying voice. My eyes open again, I saw Léonard gesticulating and talking nonstop; above all I saw his face, like a laughing clown in spite of his attempts at feigning expressions of pity and alarm. It seemed to me that a flame of joy danced in my friend's eyes; yes, he looked delighted and regarded me with evident satisfaction. And a cataract of words fell from his lips. "You're my friend . . . I won't abandon you in your hour of need . . . It'll be me who looks after you . . . I foresaw this . . . I warned you . . . You'll get better . . . Tell me what you want . . ."

I motioned him away, but he came closer. Didn't he understand that I didn't need him and wanted to be left alone? He understood and that was why he carried on harassing me. My friend looked at me spitefully, I wasn't wrong about that, notwithstanding the lethargy engulfing me. And I was afraid. I was at this man's mercy. I believed that he was going take advantage of my breakdown to hit me or harm me. I wanted to cry out. He guessed my movement and turned away from my bed. So, what was he up to? I saw his back bent over my table where rare editions, papers, various coins were scattered in disorder. The priest's phrase lit up in the twilight of my brain. I was going to be robbed. I could no longer make out Léonard's ferreting hands.

"Death comes like a thief! . . ." At that moment I felt I was going to die and I closed my eyes once more.

However, I soon had to reopen them; a scene was being played out that I observed from afar, as in a theater. Prosper had come in and was addressing Léonard. The latter was incredibly pale; his voice burst out, aggressive and sharp.

"I'm his friend just like you are! . . ." the redhead yapped.

"Get out! . . ." the black man roared.

I thought that the two men were going to come to blows. It was Prosper who remained. His dark eyes dwelt on me. Save for a slight trembling in his big hands, nothing betrayed his emotion at finding me as weak as a child and unable to speak. If I already knew that Death had dealt me a fatal flick of his finger I also understood that Destiny had sent me this Good Samaritan. And I felt a sense of confidence that I hadn't felt with the doctor. The latter lost no time in coming back followed by a nurse, but it was Prosper who lifted me like a bit of straw and carried me to the ambulance. He too it was who put me to bed in a little room in the clinic.

I was relieved to find myself in this pink cubicle amid silent beings clothed in white, unaware of the meticulous and tragic spectacle that gathered all these beings around my bed. I also felt a measure of well-being thanks to the little syringes, delightful insects that bit me and poured euphoric venom into my blood. Prosper came over to me after the others had left and spoke in a rough voice: "You're going to sleep, eh? . . . We'll make sure you survive . . ."

Ah! How much I would have liked to thank him and call him my friend! . . . He'd turned his back on me already. Shadows conquered the little room whose pink partitions turned gray, to the point where I felt myself closed in a steel locker. And I saw Prosper rummaging among my clothes, which lay on a chair. He wrapped something in a newspaper. Then he sat down. Was he going to sleep in an adjoining cubicle? No, he got up and went out cautiously, carrying a package under his arm; he left like a thief. The blow now struck, was it Prosper or Death who went out? The terrible phrase lit up once more in my brain: "Death comes like . . ." This time the conviction remained; I was going to die. That was my last thought in the world that I thought I was leaving, softly, with no fear, but full of a sadness beyond words . . .

My decease was deferred for a long time, and for more than a month no one knew on which foot the macabre hurdy-gurdy player was going to make me dance. My friend put in only brief appearances, though, it's true, frequent ones. He thrust his black face into the opening of the pink door and called out, "Feeling better, eh? . . ."

Then the face disappeared without waiting for my reply. I learned too that the other one, the redhead, had sought by every possible means to reach me. Strict orders had barred his access. I remember very little about those longs weeks of sleep. The fat sister Euphrosine trod as lightly as a fairy. In my fever I called her Nathalie and ordered bocks. One morning she asked who the thief was that I spoke about in my fever. As my powers of reason were already much stronger, I was able to tell her that it was Death. The nun told me that I need no longer be afraid, my convalescence was well under way.

The day came when I left the clinic. Prosper showed up. He helped me to get dressed. It wasn't without sadness that I put on my civilian clothes. I had no option but to return to the shabby scenes of life and leave behind the immortal realm of dreams where I had wandered during my illness.

"Where are my shoes? . . ." I suddenly said.

They were missing. Prosper held out the package that he'd put down on entering.

"Here they are . . ."

I asked what this business with the shoes meant. Prosper proceeded to tell me.

"I stole them. Not from you, my poor friend, but from Death. He was coming. I knew it before the doctor told me; one more blackout and your heart would have failed. Now, I know how to stop Death from finishing his job. I've seen that in the country I come from. When Death comes he takes your shoes—and then it's all over for you. If someone takes your shoes before he does, and takes them away, Death is fooled and can go back empty-handed. I remembered that legend and I took your shoes, because I like you a lot and don't want you to die."

I looked at Prosper in bewilderment. He carried on imperturbably: "Obviously Death could chase after me and take his revenge; but I'm a fighting man, and back home I would have forged him iron boots, red hot boots, ha!..."

This time Prosper laughed, a pitch-black laugh. And the reflection of his forge flickered in his eyes. I was unable to speak. Tears flowed down my cheeks. I held out my gaunt hand to the smith who took it, without moving, as though he had held it for all eternity . . .

Nuestra
Señora de la
Soledad

Man is alone in life. He's alone in his cradle as he'll be alone on his death-bed; he's alone in love ... Solitude is a gift, a grace, or a disgrace brought by the gray-veiled fairy to the newborn infant while the good fairies vanish in a worldly hubbub. After that, the scorn and disgust that men declare when faced with solitude bear down on the solitary man so that he'll always be happier or unhappier than other men, superior or inferior. Within him lies the potential for both saint and monster.

Besides coming across others born to solitude, other souls destined to be encompassed by solitude, he sometimes journeys back toward the ances-tors, assembled shadows, becoming the mysterious keeper of their accounts. He meets living men who are already dead and dead men who still roam the earth. He bumps into angels, passes right through them, or feels them pass-ing through him, voluptuously fresh and cool. He sets himself to serve an animal, a dog whose human gaze he deciphers. He turns away from chil-dren of genius whose mothers don't see the signs, the dumbshows toward death. He's always hurrying toward some encounter only to halt in front of a mirror. What is he fleeing and who is he looking for? In fact he's seeking God. He'll search so hard, and where he ought not, that his legs will buckle under him and like the great penitents he'll end up on his knees. Some-times, in order to better seal the pact and confound the doctors of Law, God, when encountered, shines the troubling light of madness on the soli-tary man ...

As for you sir, friend or passerby (it makes no difference), who emerge from the crowd and grab hold of me in passing, taking face and name; as for you who fear being alone even for the space of a second and who, to escape this feeling of vertigo, address any words, no matter what, to anyone, no matter who, even to a leper; as for you who assume that my person is at your disposal, confident that I'll be charmed by your soft hand and glassy eye; as for you who call me "dear friend" while spitting on my shoes, I can only keep you at a proper distance, tell you that I have a pressing engagement that won't wait. And, ignominiously, the clown blurts: "A woman, eh?"

A smile suffices, that mute reply, sending the clown back to the crowd, to the nothingness to which he can't possibly avoid returning. This peril avoided I can go on to pay my respects, for I told no lie; my life centers on a woman. She's neither the practiced whore nor the tender mistress that you supposed, but neither is she a creature of my imagination. You can see her, dear friend, just like I see her, but you can neither comprehend nor love her. She too is a great lady who is also solitary. Better still, she's Solitude itself . . .

It's clear, isn't it? When you roam the streets the way I do, and when you make it your business to spend time with no one, you owe it to yourself to meet only people who are either infinitely noble or untouchable pariahs. She whom I visit so often and to whom the most dazzling of processions wouldn't prevent me from returning, I declare her to be in every respect superior to women, and she's illustrious beyond compare, though, judging from appearances, she's among the least of them. But, such as I untiringly see her, infallibly good and with a funereal aura, this is how she was in former times when the cohorts of Alvarez of Toledo moved silently toward the Low Countries, that army of ruthless and pitiless men, those lone men with no human ties, dragging behind them wagons full of baggage, but carrying in a forest of lances that great Lady, their mother and friend, princess of Soledad . . . Those bronzed assassins were thirsty for blood, and, more than blood, for glory, and, more than glory, for heaven, the highest of all glories in their eyes. Nothing remains of those armies but bones, rusted blades. However, their holy idol remained behind in the Low Countries, incomparably alone, an ascetic foreigner, under her black silks and the only one of her race remaining in our provinces from which the Spaniards departed when for them the sun set on Flanders . . .

Dona Maria? . . . Few people know that she remains in this decrepit old church against which the waves of the masses break, in a little chapel in the transept, ashamed and embarrassed among her cousins, the other virgins, radiant matrons, glorious, in full blossom, stiff in gilded cloth, besprinkled with rubies and fine pearls, all of them beatific, all wearing crowns. All these, the ones from Brabant, have good reason to rejoice, they have their baby, the Holy Child with varnished cheeks, and Calvary is still a long way off . . . But for Maria from Spain everything is consummated! . . . She wears mourning. Her olive tint, her bloodless lips, her dried-up hands, her cindered eyelids, all show her utter resignation, the limit reached by her sorrows, which are also evident from her posture, leaning over the void, ready to fall to the base of the altar. The angels are absent, they don't help to support her; there's no pageant surrounding her. But there remains the crucified corpse attached to the wall, pallid, a little swollen. That realistic presence isn't one on which the Madonna turns her back; it's a cadaver. One is alone with the dead. And Dona Maria remains alone, she from whom the faithful turn away as she herself turns from the dead man. In what way does she resemble the *Queen of Heaven* of the litanies? She can only declare herself Lady of Solitude, to whom only a few widows come to pray. It's very rare that a man stops for her, and it's always an old man. For these frail souls the Lady of Solitude represents the final sleep; this somber virgin sleeps upright; her Assumption has begun . . .

Dona Maria . . . It's she whom I visit early in the morning and sometimes in the evening. I sit down at the corner of her altar like one sits at the hearth. I greet her and I remain silent; I don't say anything to her or ask her for anything, don't confess anything to her. Her presence solaces me and I sense that mine is agreeable to her. She is the solitary woman who a solitary man comes to see, a man of few words . . . I could undoubtedly pray, as people do; there's no point; in these hours of mental tranquility, prayer bypasses words, pleas, complaints; it's nothing but a superior emanation of physical silence; it finds expression through the colors of the stained glass windows that replenish the dawn . . .

Dona Maria responds in the same way to my peculiar conversation, otherwise how could I go away feeling so rested and as though freed from a psychical burden? On departing I leave for her a token of my fidelity; a little light, a pauper's candle that I light from other candles. Fire, in truth, constitutes the wealth of the solitary man. Often in these timeless minutes I've attempted the impossible, to meet *her gaze*. But this gaze remains internal, goes out to no one. The boxwood eyelids will never open . . . Nevertheless, she recognizes whoever approaches her, the slope of her brows then becoming more prominent, humbly reverent; but she isn't one for miracles, on the contrary she rejects any hint of the miraculous . . .

However, there was a miracle one time, or something of the kind, for which I don't ask your belief. It was a sunlit Trinity Sunday, the church bathed in a violet haze. A procession of all the Virgins having exited to the sound of choral singing and fanfares, there remained only the unregarded Solitary One under naves empty of crowds and statues. She looked to me irremediably alone in this festival abandonment, distressed beyond all measure, to the point where I moved closer than usual to her altar, disregarding her apartness, gripped by a loving emotion. But her gaze nailed me to the spot, for she was *gazing at me*. The eyelids had opened in the twilight face. Dazzled, I stumbled. Then, on the steps, I felt myself magnetically transported. What anguish, that ascension toward the loved one! . . . And hissing between boxwood lips that didn't open, Our Lady spoke to me hastily, as though infringing a strict regulation.

"In all this time, you alone have never asked me for anything. Tell me quickly, what it is that you want. I'll grant it . . ."

"I don't want anything, Dona Maria . . ." I clearly remember having replied. "Or since you're so merciful, I ask you to keep me in solitude . . ."

When I returned to my very ordinary state of consciousness I was standing in front of the altar, on the memorial slabs. The countenance of the Virgin remained, impenetrably, that of a noble, pensive, and age-old statue. The sun had turned in the sky. The procession having returned, those accompanying it flowed in disorder toward the exits, while the organ's harmonious storms died away. The verger approached, swinging his keys; the doors were about to be closed . . .

Fog

Hearing ourselves distinctly and unexpectedly called by name is a common enough occurrence. Who among us hasn't felt a shock of this kind, on hearing himself named when alone and, in any event, far from people who might possibly have spoken to him? This phenomenon, common enough as I've said, has frequently happened to me. When I was a child I trembled every day at the sound of a voice calling, close by and at the same time far away; far away because it came from the limits of the real world, close by because while I myself remained silent it uttered my name very distinctly and in a way that was always unexpected. The phenomenon still occurs these days, though much more rarely. In fact this very thing has just happened to me, and in the oddest of circumstances that I want to tell you about now, but I'm not disposed to begin the story straightaway, preferring to explain myself more precisely. It's wise to treat these mysterious calls as nothing more than tricks of the senses that rational or healthy people do well to ignore. How many of those who have heard such voices have been worried by them? In the dispersal of sounds, the decay of harmonies or of fragments of music that go adrift, or in the space between the syllables, there must subsist particles of sound that are suddenly picked up by an oversensitive or exceptionally constituted ear, without these words or this music ever having any meaning, or being accepted as a signal, or as some kind of premonition. No, these aren't the voices of incorporeal beings calling you or warning you, though it wouldn't be mad to imagine so. What are they beseeching, what danger are they warning against, these voices of entreaty or threat? For a long time I indulged myself in finding a supernatural significance in these auditory hallucinations while knowing full well that they derive from nothing more than organic fatigue, neurosis. Now that I'm getting older and my sensibilities are a little duller I no longer attach any particular meaning to such rumblings of blood in the arteries. It's still the case, however, that if you watch me live my life you'll sometimes see me startled, though no one has uttered my name. I remain bewildered, as though a ghost has slapped me with an immaterial hand. Instinctively I reply, "What?..." I swear that someone is calling me and that I'm not dreaming; I distinctly heard my name ring out. I reply every time, deceived into thinking that a conversation is about to begin between my actual mouth and an unreal mouth that addresses me. The speaker doesn't persist, he was happy just to unnerve me. He has nothing to say to me, if, that is, he really does exist. However, very few people are as practiced in silence as I am and apt to perceive voices and music that could be straying through the air; I don't hesitate to write that there are very few people who live with silence as much as I do, or with a silence of such quality. But I swear that I've never heard anything other than my name uttered, distinctly and unexpectedly. And that hasn't failed to darken my temper.

It was last December, at that uncertain hour when, the short day not yet over, all the lamps of my neighborhood light up. Passersby slid on shiny ground as though on greasy mirrors, doubled by their shadows; and the atypical mildness of the weather at this onset of winter invited the crowds to a casual stroll. Coming back home from my office, and before confining myself to my austere rooms, I was in the habit of getting lost in that twilight crowd and letting myself be carried along on its slow tide, past the brightly lit shop windows and under the luminous cataract of commercial signs. A certain festive promise indicated that it was indeed December. It could be seen in the numbers of children that tired parents dragged toward the displays, or lifted above a sea of heads so that they could see a mechanical figure representing old St. Nicholas, clothed in ritual costume and bearded with cotton wool. I soon felt harassed by the pushing and shoving, and, freeing myself, I took the middle of the thoroughfare that passes through my neighborhood. Breathing more freely I resumed my walking pace, surprised by the mildness of the air, an air that was still and unmoving and full of a mist that announced some change in the weather. And indeed, I'd no sooner reached the point where the roadway widened out into the municipal square than I found myself caught in a fog that I hadn't seen coming to meet me.

Fog! What a hypocritical, malignant traveling companion! It knows that you're afraid of it, this plague-carrier, it has a thousand tricks to surprise you. You think you've outdistanced it and it finds a shortcut to catch you up again. Caught in its trap, I had no option but to move forward into it, multifarious, inexistent, and as tiring as a crowd. You can only escape this disagreeable companion by slamming a door in its face, the door through which it can't come with you. That's what I was thinking, hastening my footsteps and burying my head in my shoulders. The far end of the square opened onto a street whose point of entry I could sense, like a tunnel expelling bubbles of yellowish vapor, and that I knew would take me home more quickly. Usually I was fond of this old neighborhood street, on account of its antique name and its winding route, but this evening it was unrecognizable; entering it was like entering an unknown corridor with no guarantee of exit. Those who walk in fog often have the impression of moving in a dream, and that's how the fantasmal passersby whose paths I crossed must have felt. As for me, what I felt was more like the sensation of moving through water, or at the very least on ground saturated with water. The streetlights blinked like lifebuoys. It seemed to me that I was moving along a causeway, a quayside path, surrounded at every turn by dangerous gaps, sheer walls, and concealed pockets of water. This bizarre fancy of finding myself in a maritime zone soon acquired a hallucinatory dimension, for appearing before me I saw the riding lights of a boat that was moored somewhere; a red light and a green light. Was I going to come across some ship ready to sail and allow me to reach the sea for which I yearn every day, separated from it by cities and plains? That idea didn't seem at all absurd, and to escape the fog's clutches I'd have embarked without a second thought. But the illusion was already fading, the ship's lights, now that I saw them up close, being nothing but two illuminated glass jars in the window of a pharmacy. There's never been a time when I haven't known it, this laboratory and these colorful jars that light up at night, kindly signals for an ailing humanity. No, no ship will ever moor alongside the façades of the Rue Champ-des-Tulipes, a dry channel where nothing exists other than these two tutelary lanterns. A sad odor escaped from the pharmacy door, and the good tarry smell of quays and keels, momentarily evoked, was expelled from my brain by sulfuric ether. This perfume of misery, adding to the stench of the fog, had the effect of prejudicing me against the whole of creation, and my own self too. I had to get away from this stifling smell and find my room once more, that exclusive room where I could dismiss the universal distress, that extinguished lighthouse where I lived above and beyond Time and everything else. Weighed down by terrestrial clouds, I dashed toward the final section of the street.

I hadn't run more than three meters before I stopped, legs stinging. Someone had called out to me. Without a shadow of a doubt, my name had just echoed through the air. I peered into the shifting murk that enveloped me. Nobody to be seen, no passerby, or even the shadow of one; not a dog. I rubbed my wet ears and started running again. Once more, my name was called. Spinning round, I confronted that formal voice that sounded only in my head. Yet again, I saw no one, not even, insofar as my gaze could penetrate the fog, the hint, the outline of anyone. "Fine!" I said to myself, "I'm used to these untoward voices. This isn't a voice that belongs to a man or a woman, and it isn't a human voice calling. There's no need for me to worry about it! . . ." What was it really, the mouth that hailed me then, and why? I have no friends in this city. I owe debts or explanations to no one. Besides, no voice would have been able to resonate in this cloudy mass, no call could have carried beyond the lips that voiced it, and the mouths of men couldn't but help but resemble the mouths of fish, intermittently silent. Nevertheless I slowed my steps, feeling hesitant. I even stopped. My name no longer rang out.

I carried on my way, wanting to walk more rapidly but the fog grew still thicker, to the point where I had to tread carefully for fear of an accident. Nothing more to be seen. I brushed aside billows of smog, I steered with both arms, rowing in a sea of cotton wool. Façades were wet cardboard, and the paving stones were slippery, as though coated with foam. I didn't meet anyone. I felt like a blind man finding his way and counting his steps. Human life had vanished from this part of the world, this neighborhood where, somewhere, I divined, was my home, the magnetic site that drew me. I was so completely alone that I recovered my nerve and forgot about the troubling voice. My confidence was short lived. I wasn't alone. Once more, fear gripped me. I would arrive home, I no longer doubted that, but feared that I wouldn't arrive alone. Someone was following me. Had the fog become a person to whom I had already lent a voice? Someone was following me and my fear, growing with each step, was transformed into dread. And that dread didn't come from my feeling of being followed, but from being followed by someone impossible for me to see, a nonexistent being who, like the fog, was tyrannically present and whom I only heard as footsteps doubling my own, and only knew as an unidentifiable voice. Well might I tell myself that such creatures were merely illusions that owed their existence to the fog alone, but I had to recognize the evidence: someone was stalking me. Several times I turned abruptly round in order to unmask this phantom or this felon, for it might well be a thug whose designs on me were abetted by the fog. But no one was there; there could be no denying the evidence: there was no one but me in this pallid, yellow-streaked darkness. Besides I had no heroic aspirations, knowing that when confronted with any danger, whether real or not, visible or merely sensed, the best course is to emulate the wisdom of animals and flee. I was now on home ground. I could clearly hear that I was still being followed. My breath came in gasps; hot gusts passed over the nape of my neck, and at that moment I didn't think it could be the fever lit in me by this absurd chase. Unwell or not, it was vital that I gain shelter, for the pursuer's footsteps were sounding closer to mine. Finally, exhausted, I fell against the massive door that guards my home. But before hastening into the corridor, I tried to see the aggressor who, too late, was about to emerge; yes, before shutting the heavy door in the face of the fog and whoever was its accomplice I wanted to know what form the object of my terror took. No one came. And there was a splash of footsteps close by, drunken, irregular footsteps making the familiar noise of a dog's tongue lapping up water. In a mental flash, the image of a beast impressed itself on me. Hadn't I been chased by a big, determined dog? As I asked myself the question a shadow sped along the façades in a desperate flight. That was it, not a man but a beast, or a hybrid of beast and man. I didn't want to know any more and, jumping inside, I slammed the dark, heavy door with a crash that thundered through my dwelling. As far as my body was concerned, I was safe. My face and my hands were on fire. I waited until my breathing returned to a normal rhythm that eased my wheezing windpipe. Then I listened, ears glued to the door. But my door is so thick, no less than the door of a monastery, that a man or an animal could have panted or groaned or shouted aloud on the other side and I wouldn't have heard a thing. And if a rabid man or an unchained beast were to batter themselves against that obstacle, what did it matter to me now? What wound my anguish up to its highest pitch and left me shivering was the overwhelming silence into which I was suddenly plunged. It was on account of that silence that I heard a voice, the voice calling me for the third time. It rasped, heartrending and as though dying, perhaps coming from under the door, or, who knows, falling from the vaulted ceiling. It was so peculiar that I thought it was the sound of a child crying somewhere, on the upper floor, or nowhere, or no doubt from inside me. And an ice-cold hand slid down my burning spine. The fact is that I recognized it this time, this voice, and knew at last from what mouth it sprang. It was neither an old person nor a child, neither a woman nor a man, neither a person nor any living thing; it was the voice of a being who had disappeared twenty years ago, formally dead, and whose death only I here below could confirm, and in what degree. So a dead person was calling me? With that knowledge my dread evaporated and instead irritation burned right through me. Apparently I lost all reason, because I found myself yelling in response to that call from beyond life as one shouts in nightmares and nowhere else, "Go away! Go away!..." Yet they scarcely disturbed the silence, these words that I could only have mumbled while thinking that I was shouting. No, my lips didn't utter these words and they didn't become sounds; nevertheless imagining that I'd uttered them with such vehemence relieved me and returned me to my normal state of mind. Like a sick person feeling better after having spat out bad phlegm I hugged the walls and reached my apartment. The rooms were plunged in darkness and so, no less profoundly, was my demoralized soul. Collapsing on my bed, I was aware of having fought a terrifying combat, but one from which I hadn't returned in defeat.

That night, all of that interminable night, my body, a dead weight, remained stretched out where it had fallen. A cinder fire smoldered inside me and I was gently roasted by fever. I was atoning. The fog inflicted this febrile state on me, but my knowledge of morbid conditions ensured that my state of prostration didn't cause me too much concern. I waited patiently for the dawn, skirting round sleep and moving hourly in the shadows of its precipices. The fog and the voices lay far behind me, and still further the memories summoned from the great depths of the past by those voices. The intense combustion of the fever burned everything up. And I caught myself sighing while keeping my eyes open. At last, not unhappily, I saw the darkness of my room acquiring a feeble color, as though infiltrated by dawn. It was better than the first light of the morning, the dawn that arose before my warm eyelids and nowhere else; I was witnessing a vision. The space that was erected around me seemed made of glass, colored with the red and green reflections of hidden, continually moving lamps. The atmosphere had become milder, with, however, fresher gusts sweeping through it. This translucent space, this stained glass window enthralled me with its ruby and emerald highlights. "How precious . . ." I heard myself murmuring, "A window of sky! . . ." I felt no fear at having left the lower world behind, fever having granted me the privilege of thinking *outside* my body; and I observed infinity with the joy of a child awaiting the operation of a magic lantern. What I was able to see enraptured me. The stained glass window darkened, and mouths were revealed on its reflective surface, nothing but perfectly shaped mouths, succulent golden mouths, lips opening onto diamond teeth. Innumerable, these moving mouths, for they spoke slowly and solemnly; and as they also seemed to form kisses I thought they were speaking amorously. But I could hear nothing of their speech, and no doubt they were speaking from the end of the ages. "Archangels' mouths! . . . ," I imagined.

How long this supreme spectacle lasted I couldn't tell. Having spoken for a long time, the mouths gradually faded away and their disappearance left me with a nameless sadness, made from regret that I hadn't seen the faces of which these mouths were a part and had heard or understood nothing of their secrets, also that my desire to take eternal delight in contemplating them was unfulfilled. When infinity had died away I made no attempt to determine whether or not I had been sleeping, simply accepting this supernatural event. What did it matter to me whether I was dreaming in these moments or experiencing a real state of ecstasy! My thoughts focused on a fundamental question: these mouths, had they confided to me a message that I wasn't yet permitted to understand? I had the idea that the death of an archangel was disclosed to me, one of their own, or of some delicate creature who had been kin to me down the ages. During this respite I entertained many such speculations, and all the more easily in that I didn't have to deal with my usual rational self. Alas! No ecstasy goes without a reversal. The state of grace left me. And I felt myself in danger. Streams of lights climbed the walls, this time coming from down below, coarse reflections of nocturnal fairs lit up with opaque red and green smoke. What I saw could only be an invention of delirium: mouths once more, down at ground level and reaching toward me. A monstrous host surrounded me of which only the mouths were visible. Oh! Abject mucous membranes salivating and spitting, swallowing words that I sensed were sordid and that I congratulated myself on not understanding. Believe me, mouths like these can only be evoked in confessionals where sacrilegious words are spoken! The poisonous sermons that I had to suffer! What might these amphibian lips, these abominable fishes be disclosing? What could these leeches reveal if not the birth of one of their own, a demon? . . . I was abruptly galvanized by the image of a nearby hell over which I was cataleptically suspended. Thrusting myself back into my body from which I had psychically departed, I happily found myself once more in possession of my wits. And I saw the breaking dawn. I was saved, and not just from that hallucination, but from my fever too, just as I knew that the earth itself was freed from the fog. Discovering a clear, cold, frost-glazed sky, I wiped my brow and chased away the multiple buccal vision. But before throwing it into the nothingness where dreams are discarded I came to the conclusion that both the pure and the impure mouths had, in all probability, spoken to me about the same being, or the same thing.

Several days went by in complete tranquility. My neighborhood had recovered its wintertime timbre. One morning I bumped into an odd character who, like a journalistic hack or a concierge, always knew all the news. On seeing me the man assumed a priestly air and took hold of my hands.

"Do you know who's just died? He was your friend, wasn't he, or am I imagining things? . . ."

As one always does on such occasions I said how sorry I was, but I added that I wasn't unaware of the disappearance of a familiar face, having been informed of it. And I remembered the mouths. I now understood that those mouths were reciting some kind of funeral service, praying in a manner that was celestial or infernal and no doubt inviting me, in a unique moment, to pray like them. I was still puzzled to learn about the death of a dead man, of someone who, I'd decided some twenty years ago, no longer existed, and who, through a sustained act of will, was utterly dead to me. I frequently encountered his human semblance; he was truly a dead man walking and I circled round him without anger or disgust, a stranger, for all that I had to guard myself against his threatening gestures, or, worse still, his mute pleas. My resolve never faltered; he had just died a second time without my feeling the slightest of emotions, not even one of relief. What did this actual death matter to me, after the drama of his moral death, which, at that time, caused me to suffer, almost to die from it too! Who was this man? You'll have to be satisfied with knowing that in erasing him from the numbers of the living I forgave him, in this life and in all others, as is required by divine Charity. Beyond love and hate, is there a more perfect form of forgetting? . . .

A
Twilight

To the Master Engraver Jules de Bruyker

It had been raining since dawn. Damp had made my room as foul-smelling as a cave and its light was really that of a crypt where I was moldering, looking at tears streaming down the window and feeling that I was gradually swelling up with water absorbed through my pores. It seemed that this rain would last forever. I was surrounded by a pervasive odor of old scrapheaps and, since everything smelled, my body emitted the smell that tramps carry in their rags. My thoughts, like a bottle imp, slowly sank under the pressure of the opaque sky. And this inexorable descent into the void constituted a palpable but unspeakably horrible torture. Is it conceivable that a man in a room, unmoving and apparently impassive, could stand to feel his soul smothered without groaning, writhing, or praying?

As the day flowed by I sank lower and lower, my thoughts pulsing more and more feebly, but without obliterating themselves as I wished they would. And I was gripped by a premonition that this afternoon the world would come to an end, that the world could end in no other way. Our world wouldn't explode in a glorious detonation; it was becoming a ball of mud, peeling, rotting, hydropic, destroyed by water, a miserable humanity returning to its primordial marshlands where elementary life fermented, filthy living debris, deaf and blind . . . Such were my thoughts, creeping like long worms, until the moment when my consciousness was sucked down into a muddy sleep.

Emerging from that low stupor, it seemed to me I was climbing back up toward the mouth of a pit. The rain had stopped. And my window allowed a singularly strong and heavy light to unfurl in the interior, one whose brutal, almost material flow pushed everything aside. That intense luminosity astonished me. It was no longer day, but night could not have fallen yet, and the sunset sky, a shattered mirror, had to exist somewhere behind the fissured wall of the rain. This light seemed truly liquid, lacking vibrancy and as though everything it touched was left coated with glycerine. Worried by that shaft of light, I got up from my damp couch, managing my limbs with difficulty. I staggered, trying to gain my balance, and the fear of no longer finding anything solid in the three dimensions of my room redoubled my disquiet. Was the cave now transforming itself into an aquarium, and was I going to find myself incapable of useful action, deprived of part of my weight? This fear of being stripped of my humanity revived my instincts and I threw myself toward the door with the movements of a swimmer. I felt somewhat reassured on running down the stairs but only recovered adequate confidence when I made contact with the street pavement, with the terrestrial globe that my fantasy had imagined lost. And I moved forward along the walls in search of the city and those who lived in it.

Scarcely any living beings to be seen; the city still existed, a charcoal mass, all outcrops and passages, still streaming with water and drifting in the ashen atmosphere without a guiding light, like a piece of flotsam. It beggared belief that no one was doing anything to fight the encroaching darkness, that not one lamp had been lit, that not one window glowed anywhere . . . Thankfully the air was breathable and not chilly, though autumn was advancing; old heat still lingered, discharged from the ground. My body had been rescued and it wasn't long before I discovered what was pressing down on my soul. Coming out onto the level area that surrounds the church of St. Nicholas, where a hundred passageways and blind alleys come to discharge themselves as though into a vat, I surprised the secret of the deathly torpor, the lethargy that still suffused the city, similar in every respect to what I had suffered; just then the sky appeared to me, unexpectedly, like the sea discovered at the summit of a ramp; a bizarre, sunken sky, out of a prehistoric fantasia and made up of an accumulation of gaseous grottos. And these cloudy pockets seethed with light, a cold and slobbering light that you could have cut with a knife; a poisonously tinted light, slowly ejaculated . . . It looked to me like the invention of a possessed or mad painter. The discovery of this catastrophic sky awakened my sense of oppression and, simultaneously, my feeling that the Earth and the species pullulating on its crusts were threatened by an imminent calamity. I couldn't accept that I was witnessing a twilight at its moment of crisis, a luminous orgasm. My mind as much as my eyes questioned this impossible sky, because it was an inverted echo of the entrails and abominable fluxes of the globe, and also because this meteorological phenomenon seemed to me, if I dare write this, a monstrous error of nature . . . And I hid my inflamed eyes.

Freeing them after they had been rested, I saw that the aerial grottos had vanished and that the pallid twilit screen displayed a scene that was no less delirious; the clouds were outlined in relief and, in a sculpted frieze, depicted a pitiless scramble of cattle, ochre-, brown-, and blue-colored, a silent charge toward the gates of sunset. But everywhere the herds were surrounded by the darkness that had provoked the disaster, the panicked outlines drowned in black ink. Was I alone in contemplating these visions? Living souls sheltering in their dwellings obstinately persisted in leaving their lamps unlit. Did they reckon that the night wasn't yet at its darkest? The taverns that usually yawned open like so many outlets of hell round the grounds of the church, even they didn't send out their red glow! Nevertheless the city wasn't dead; it was in a deep sleep and would awaken late. The few shadows that stole by in the distance couldn't be those of passersby, rather of sleepers in search of matches. Was I going to remain petrified in the middle of this square where pools of mud surrounded me? The mud came out of the paving stones or else flowed like fetid lava from the hundred passageways, hypocritically filling the vat of St. Nicholas. And the danger posed by my solitude was heightened by banks of fog hovering as high as a man, where there was nothing to hold onto should the ground shift even more. A place of immediate refuge offered itself: the church, just like in the fearful days of wrath when people believed that the end of the world was nigh.

This decrepit church, so old and so shaken by the winds, was well qualified to awaken the idea of peril. Good people said that it constituted a perpetual miracle and a proof of Providence in action inasmuch as it never crumbled away, as in all logic it ought to have done on every day granted by God. Constructed in a quagmire, mistreated and set on fire a score of times, it persisted like an aged, decalcified body, all wounds and excrescences, standing thanks only to the crutches of its buttresses. Eroded by bad weather and dislocated by the water that swelled its porous walls, it endured only by the rights granted to phantoms, a shadow of a church that no archaeologist would have dared to touch for fear of seeing it collapse into debris. Nevertheless it regained its resilience and its primitive prestige in the darkness, and with its sheer walls and fortress-like central tower it appeared imperishable. I reached its porch, pushing at creaking partitions, stumbling on broken steps, believing myself descending, and descending in fact, for over the course of the ages the church had seen the ground rise around its walls, unless it happened to have sunk on its foundations. And I had the feeling of having fallen into a trap. I was in a grotto that was almost dark, but one where threatening, phosphorescent statues lay in ambush at various levels, where flights of columns formed frightening labyrinths. My eyes begged in vain for the illumination of a candle. From whence did all this fluorescence seep if not the stone itself? Or was it nothing but the glow emanating from the innumerable dead buried in the naves? I went down the axis of the chancel, advancing with outstretched arms, hypnotized by a distant tongue of purple fire licking at the void. The memorial slabs shifted under my feet. I breathed in funereal smells too, a latent decay added to which were rank odors, rancid incense. The mud of the city was no longer a threat, but didn't the flagstones of this religious charnel house themselves constitute a trap that was no less dreadful? Ah! If I were to sink down into the muck from which these enormous cryptogamous pillars had grown! . . . Who then would stretch out a hand to save me? There was no one in this church, and I repeated in a loud voice and without awakening any echo, "Is there nobody here? . . ."

There was someone, against whom I had just stumbled: a Christ collapsed against a column and regally offended under his crown of thorns; he confronted me with the horrifying face of a torture victim, his grimace intolerable, the contorted mouth of a man strangled with a garrote. I was truly in despair at having to disappear without remission for my sins, and, my voice failing me, only my lips continued to murmur their plea: "Miserere!" No, there was no one in this gigantic cavern, under these crumbling vaults; no one to bear witness to the despairing death that would be mine. At first I'd pretended to feel nothing, but the evidence was clear; the church was inexorably foundering and I was sinking down with it, sucked down by the depth, in an abyss of foul mud; the vessel was going down, broken apart, and even if my reason refused to admit it my feet and legs knew it. Had I cried too loudly to heaven that I was abandoned? God abruptly manifested Himself to reply to me that He was still there even if no one else was, infallibly above and beyond disasters; He threw me a lifeline . . . By a miracle I was able to seize a rope. It was salvation, or death postponed. I must have arrived under the central tower. With this cable I could reach the vault, the roofs of that crenellated tower where the errant bells were sleeping; with them I would be able to sound the alarm, but at what cost, of such a climb. Besides, I needed to awaken them to save myself and, at the same time, rouse the town from its torpor by means of this tocsin that hadn't sounded since the wars. How vigorously I grasped the rope, bending my knees like a gymnast, the better to jump. But at that moment a second miracle occurred: a golden tone broke out, solemnly, a voice of pure metal releasing a loud cry that spread out, undulating in the silence. That happened angelically, without my intervention. A gong sounded the hour of a mystery. Only a supernatural fist could have struck the golden hour over the abyss of Time . . . At this signal, the chancel filled up with an amber vapor, the pillars regained solidity and the naves unfolded harmoniously. The dislocated church remade itself geometrically, under the orders of an invisible architect that was nothing but light. Candles lit up like stars. The mortuary slabs once more steadied themselves. And with the advent of priests resembling bronzed birds, and who sought to exorcise the darkness with their gestures, I felt a fierce gratitude toward the magical Consciousness that prevented the world from perishing on this day of deluge. Everywhere human forms arose and went forward, like resurrected beings emerging from the walls and the pavements. These shades, were they singing, and were the organs expelling the opaque air of their lungs? This collective song might have been thought the voice of a crowd processing in the open air around the church; the song had barbaric overtones, though its inspiration seemed to be sacred. This vocal drone that I wasn't able to identify didn't fail to comfort me, just as the renewal of light had done, and it was without fear that I undertook to exit the church, climbing back up to the surface of the city without further difficulty.

Night had fallen, completely. Countless streetlights blazed, the façades wore their familiar faces. Living beings moved about in the reconsolidated city. And the precincts of St. Nicholas were swarming as in times of fairs and cavalcades. The church was encircled by herds. The cattle arrived in abundance, crossing the city from one end to the other, through the old passageways, with St. Nicholas as the cauldron that provided the terminus. It was the night of their holocaust. Their bellows fluctuated, melting together and making a deep pedal note that was counterpointed by sharp bleats and joyful barks. And the majestic cohorts were whipped on by mighty curses. I moved forward, squeezed between the oxen, lost in that flood of rumps and muzzles. The world hadn't come to an end; the world smelled carnally after the deluge. And, under the lunar searchlights, I went with the musical and so fatally beautiful herds, deported to the cruel abattoirs where the beasts are sacrificed, their blood flowing in torrents in order to appease, who knows which, the wrath of the gods or the hunger of men . . .

You
Were
Hanged

No doubt about it, Destiny played me a dirty trick in sending me for months, maybe years, to this little city in Flanders, this decrepit city avoided by tourists where, for Sunday entertainment, so the saying goes, citizens choose between eleven o'clock mass and watching the arrival of the twelve-fifteen train. Disembarking in the provincial town, I resolved to keep myself apart so as not to end up like the small-time shopkeepers and conceited petit bourgeoisie who populate this regional center. To tell the truth, I wasn't at all happy. Everyone knows from experience that there are uninhabitable cities that repel all sympathetic feeling; you pass through them so as never to return. But when you have to stay on it's a daily drama, with no way out other than flight, for there's no denying that our minds are as much governed by things as by people! So to escape the climate of mediocrity I single-mindedly buried myself in the city's history; it had been rich and powerful but was no longer much of anything. Meditating over musty archives and contemplating the remains of civic or religious architecture was, no doubt, a negligible pastime, but sufficient for my inner man who was as apt to take flight as to fall back to the ground. In addition to my studies, which involved nothing but sieges, riots, and plundering, I undertook to explore every corner of this old burgh where there's little to hold the attention of the archaeologist but which is preserved almost in its entirety and offers attractive views to the casual pedestrian: abandoned wharfs flanked by gables, ruined chapels, remains of an enclosed convent, everything so deserted and deteriorated that I saw in it the decline of Flanders itself. I thought that, helped by Time and the weather, I would acquire the color of these feeble walls, these stagnant waters, and these barren trees—becoming useless and without present-day meaning, like the old folks and dogs roaming in these faded neighborhoods where labor awoke no echo . . .

In the course of these melancholy walks I happened one particular morning, and for the first time, on the Saint-Jacques Plain, the last corner of the town left for me to discover; I swear I had never before visited this deserted marketplace on which I now set foot, and no book or print had ever informed me of its existence; my eyes took stock of this banal stretch of ground; and in contemplating this promenade, its trees, its buildings, like a fragment of town appearing in the course of a mirage, was I not suddenly warped out of real things, dropped into the middle of a dream? . . . This sensation of dreaming was so intense and prolonged that I had to start walking under the plane trees and to cross the whole extent of the plain before I could recover my usual objectivity. I knew it, this place that I'd never seen before, or rather, I recognized it; yes, I recognized this piece of ground that for a long time had been the market forum of the ancient city, traversed by a primitive roadway, with a pyramid-shaped public water-pump as its central ornament; I recognized the theatrical façade and absurd belfry of the Minorite Church that closed it off near the top end; I recognized the interminable black wall that formed a border all along one side, pierced with arched gothic windows; I recognized, completing its rectangle, these inns with monumental porches, all in a row, their signs jutting out. But how could I recognize a place where, in all my life, I had never set foot? This formal feeling of *déjà vu*, of *déja entendu*, or of *déjà vécu*, often happens and is so common that at times even the least sensitive of people have felt its influence. Do remembrances, traces of anterior lives persist in our memory? From that day on, the Saint-Jacques Plain held me in a particular grip and, whether I liked it or not, my daily walk always ended up in this lost corner. On various occasions I tried to avoid going there, but I was compelled by some power which no doubt was nothing but my own sense of disquiet. Yet the place could scarcely be said to possess any poetic prestige that would have justified such diligence, though its ensemble was composed of harmonious elements: old bricks, old surfaces, and timeworn resonances, with colors and sounds that varied according to the atmosphere and the sky. I found myself resenting the Saint-Jacques Plain, not so much for what it was in its simplicity as for the tyrannical fascination that it sought to exert on me, the secret of which I wasn't able to discover. My forefathers had never inhabited the town or the region, and I learned from the local archives that this area had never witnessed anything remarkable, that it was even the one spot that, uniquely, held nothing at all worth remembering. At best it retained its once considerable reputation as a cattle market. Disappointed, I persuaded myself that I might have once been a calf led to this market, and that I retained a vague and obscure memory of this sad previous incarnation . . . Eventually I stopped dwelling on a problem that was in danger of becoming an *idée fixe* and, habit taking effect, I was soon no more than a daily pedestrian, the little figure in the craquelured painting that was the Saint-Jacques Plain. I no longer sought to resist the mysterious attraction.

Since my walks had to end up somewhere, I became a client of one of the square's most venerable inns. The one in which I'd chosen to spend my time of an evening carried the sign of The Little Gibbet. The narrow glazed windows, the shadows that held constant sway under the beams of the low ceiling, the dilapidated furnishings, a silence filled with the ticking of clocks, and also the perfume of fermenting beer from the cellar, all made the barroom a restful place where my spirit idled and where the slightest sound carried an echo of the vestry. Like its neighbors, this hostelry survived thanks to the thirsty market-gardeners and porters who for centuries had kept faith with the old popular route; it opened early in the morning but after midday there was no longer anyone there. It was on account of this solitude that I liked to linger in The Little Gibbet where everything was maintained as it had been in bygone times, where there was nothing to remind me of the present day. The innkeeper was a little man with a pasty complexion, a lunatic with a disconcerting manner and confused speech. He lived on his own, passed his evenings drinking, sleeping on a chair and waiting for the first wagons of the morning. He spoke at great length in a stifled voice, not worrying whether anyone understood him or not. Toward dusk he lit an oil lamp and wound up the clocks. An odd character for sure.

He was called Jef. I found out that he was a compulsive collector, and that what he called "antiquities" consisted of indescribable debris that he accumulated in the cellars and the attics, rusted or corroded things that he found on demolition sites, delvings, or earthworks. He did me the honor of showing me his collections of junk where sometimes objects could be found that were worth a second look or a caress: church weathercocks, cast iron cannonballs, carved door fittings, gargoyles, bizarre keys or ironmongery, wooden angels or stone devils. No, this innkeeper wasn't a nonentity! I felt an instinctive and spontaneous sympathy with him. His inebriation left him elusive and unworldly, maintaining him in a kind of artificially prolonged dream. I suspected that this man, full of unspoken visions, was, like me, someone unsuited for the disenchantments of ordinary life and who moved in a world of imagination. Sometimes he sat at my table and retailed chapters of the town's history, whose thousand episodes, if he was to be credited, might have made for a fantastic and burlesque epic. And if by chance I asked the storyteller where he'd learned that mercenaries, during a siege, had found no one to rape but thirteen virgin maidens, Jef the chronicler replied imperturbably, "I saw it! . . ."

In his presence and on his premises I forgot about Time, Time that was scorned and disregarded by him, for in here clocks told mad time or stopped for no reason. Here a remarkable bird could also be seen, one I found somewhat disturbing, a mistress magpie of mature years who resided amid the pewterware on the bar. From time to time in the quiet of evening the bird happened to speak up, and always when you weren't listening; but if you observed her chattering, she obstinately closed her beak. No doubt this magpie uttered a thousand words for one, confusedly, like her owner. But usually she was satisfied with croaking banal phrases; "Good evening . . . Someone's there . . ." It was only that the piercing gaze of this chatterbox pursued me. I felt spied on by an attentive eye, rich in memories. This magpie too, like the innkeeper, was learned in shadows and light, on the margin of things reasonable.

And so I became a habitué of The Little Gibbet, which was far from being a place of punishment for me, idle onlooker that I was. With notable tact the innkeeper divined my frame of mind and, accordingly, either came and kept me company or left me to my twilight brooding. He was full of consideration and let me understand that, on account of my unqualified admiration for his antiquities, he regarded me as his equal. Disappearing like a gnome, he entrusted me, very disinterestedly, with the beer pump and the keys to the cellar. Where did he go? To dig the earth under the rear of the building, scavenging being his great passion! Was he searching for treasure? Only for underground passages, with which, on the faith of an old map, he knew the town was riddled. Sometimes he tapped the inn's stone floor with his heel.

"It's hollow, and underneath there's another hollow: skeletons, weapons, tombs, chests full of golden coins!"

It was a mystery and in Jef's eyes as, I confess, in mine too, there was nothing better than a mystery, not even all the gold of the hypothetical underground! One evening the innkeeper left me there on my own for so long that I thought he'd been caught in a subsidence. It had grown completely dark and I hadn't found the lamp. Some feeble lanterns glinted in the expanse of the Saint-Jacques Plain, which was now deserted. I was under the clear impression that I'd been in that place forever, and that my existence had never extended beyond that oblong square; "Who am I then, and what am I doing here? . . ." I murmured to myself, so low that that the phrase could only have been a thought. But I had nonetheless voiced my concern too loudly, for a mocking laugh rasped out from the depths of the room: the magpie was making senile fun of my perplexity.

"Good evening, pilgrim of Saint-Jacques!" said Jef, always ready to launch into hyperbole.

I was never at a loss for words, and that day I replied, "Good evening Mr. Gallows Bird! What an extraordinary idea, choosing that gruesome sign while your neighbors all have more pleasant names. The Three Kings, The Moor, The Mottled Cow! Was your tavern built on the site of a gallows, or have you got one of our ancestors' actual gallows in one of your collections? Something that wouldn't surprise me . . ."

The innkeeper pushed me toward the window and with his index finger pointed past the glass toward an indeterminate spot. Well might I rub my eyes, I could see nothing save for the long wall that extended all along the Plain, that time-honored wall, pierced with ogive windows and supported with buttresses, which seemed as though varnished by the late afternoon sun. But Jef grunted in triumph.

"You see it? Now you understand? . . ."

"Yes," I replied, "yes . . . It's all that's left of the covered market. And the gallows, won't you tell me? . . ."

The innkeeper didn't hear my question and started lecturing, waving his arms, spraying spittle, and with such an abundance of digressions that, sympathetic listener though I was, I felt dizzy and had the good sense to go sit down. It was his style, the good chap, and I knew that you ended up understanding what he wanted to explain, provided that you listened through to the end of his set piece. It concerned the gibbet. And, flushed with enthusiasm, my companion flew breakneck from high to low and back again. I resigned myself to his monologue, sure that my curiosity would be satisfied before nightfall. Except that I interrupted him from time to time, stealthily, with the insistent question, "And so Jef, these gallows? . . ."

While waiting, I learned from the innkeeper that he was a vehement advocate of the death penalty and regretted the passing of an era that was less sensitive but also less hypocritically humanitarian, when people of no account were publicly executed and sometimes people of high degree too. His harangue continued with an attack on democracy, which depersonalized the individual, and against compulsory education, which resulted in stupidity and encouraged vanity and disdain for the good old manual crafts. Then he railed against the utopia of Progress, and from that I could see that his speech was heading straight toward an apocalyptic description of the end of the world according the prediction of a Minorite father he knew.

I tried once more: "Of course . . . But, the gallows? . . ."

"I've shown it to you! . . ." Jef exclaimed with a hint of irritation. "Are you making fun of me? . . ."

"No!" I retorted. "This gallows that you're seeing, I can't see a trace of it. I swear! . . ."

Convinced of my sincerity, the innkeeper relented.

"You thought it was only my sign that showed it? It's still there, the gibbet. And if you think I'm seeing things, then go outside! . . . You can touch it, son of Doubting Thomas! . . ."

Perhaps he was a little vexed, for the lecture went no further. As for me, I still felt more or less in the dark. Having been invited by the innkeeper to go and look outside, I left the inn distractedly but without consenting to make my way to the wall, to the place where a gallows was supposedly located. I noticed that Jef was watching me from behind the window. A misunderstanding had arisen between us and I was sorry that the shadow of this gallows put a distance between us, however small. I cursed this damned gibbet that threatened to cause trouble between the two peaceful beer drinkers that we were, in the most welcoming tavern in the world . . .

The next day I returned to the Saint-Jacques Plain, where really I couldn't have failed to come, and I paced the length of the marketplace wall till I reached the point that Jef had indicated, but instead of the gallows I only found a simple bronze arm, a heraldic dexter arm, extended, plumbed into the wall at a height of three meters, and whose tarnished hand held a hook. Some kind of lantern post, I thought. Cursing my friend's overly fertile imagination, I went into his inn, determined to pour cold water on him. But Jef had seen my movements and was waiting for me with a gleam in his eye.

"You saw it this time, didn't you? . . . Who was it who spoke words of gold? . . ."

"You! But it was bronze you spoke, not gold! A gibbet, that iron stump, that piece of forged metal? You're having a laugh! Nothing but a perch for sparrows! . . ."

The innkeeper wasn't in an argumentative mood. So he set about enlightening me on the subject of the gibbet that he held so dear. I learned from him that what I'd called a perch for sparrows was nothing less than an engine of justice and that it would be wrong to question it or mock its prestige. It was in fact an auxiliary or reserve gallows, hence its description as "little"; at that time the big ones with wheels and other ominous scaffoldings were set up in a field *extra muros* known as Galgenveld. Capital punishments were traditionally carried out on the square of the Hôtel de Ville on a market day on the stroke of noon, with all the churches sounding the death knell. But the little gibbet happened to serve the purpose of quick or unpublicized hangings, summary justice executed at sunrise or sunset with no noise or witnesses; only very common game was hung there, small-time burglars, thieving gypsies, or armed vagabonds, just enough time for them to render up their ugly souls. Their carcasses didn't hang long enough to cure the meat, for after the "speedy procedure" the cart that had brought them took them away to the Galgenveld charnel-ground. Thus were judicial costs kept to a minimum and thus was satisfied Dame Jurisprudence, who understood that no execution could take place behind closed doors at night. Having happily explained all this, Jef concluded, "That's why my sign tells no lie! . . ."

These revelations left me lost in thought. I couldn't stop myself from gazing at the bronze arm that no one ever took any notice of, and I had a clear foreboding that from now on it would be impossible for me to ignore it. Did the secret of the Plain's fascination remain written in the sign of this arm, in this lethal gesture? And wasn't it to this instrument of torture that, unconsciously, I'd been coming to make my devotions? That left me in a troubled state of mind, and I turned my head nervously every possible way to tear myself away from the vision of the gibbet, above all from its hook from which henceforth dangled all my morbid thoughts. The innkeeper guessed my uneasiness and came to my aid.

"You can relax! . . ." he went on . . . "It was a long time ago . . . The last executions by rope took place toward the end of the *ancien régime*, at the time of the Austrians. The sans-culottes came to us, bringing Guillotin's machine. A new civilization brings its own innovations, and above all a new way of killing. As for me, I prefer, *even now . . .*"

I interrupted the critic of the democratic guillotine.

"Shut up Jef! . . . It's not as far back as you make out . . . What is it, a long century? . . . Maybe the great grandsons of the poor wretches who were hanged here at dusk are walking about in the neighborhood? . . ."

"It's quite likely," the innkeeper agreed, "but one thing's for sure, I can show you the hangman, I should say the last of the entire line of the city hangmen, still a sworn carpenter to this day, and the great grandson of the practitioner, the artist if you like, who presided over *our* little gibbet's last executions . . . He's never lived anywhere other than in the fine little red-fronted house at the end of the Plain, backing onto the Minorite's cemetery, his forefathers' home. You'll see him. He's one of my few evening customers. He'll seem reserved, even untalkative to you. No doubt about it, this simple and honest man suffers atavistically from having nothing "better" to do than make platforms for ceremonies or bandstands. Talk about nostalgia! I bet that the calling for a job like that must be passed on down, like a sailor's obsession with the sea! . . ."

This new revelation wasn't calculated to calm my nerves, much as I admired the association of images; starting from a gibbet, we'd arrived at the hangman. What next?

The innkeeper adopted a confidential tone. "He's called Blondeel, and he does me the honor of his custom. He's promised me for my collection the wonderful thing that he's inherited, the knot! Yes, the fatal cord, the rope! . . ."

The innkeeper's suddenly dilated pupils lost themselves in the clouds. What could he be seeing in his vision if not the gibbet fitted with its rope! Was I dealing with a lunatic, by nature peaceable but whose brain was in the grip of this terrible subject, this everyday and everlasting gibbet? I shivered and to break the ambiguous silence called out, "Hey, Jef . . . Won't this rope give you bad dreams? Won't you be the one taking part in a hanging sometimes? . . ."

The innkeeper seemed not to understand right away, but he'd heard my voice. His pale eyes settled calmly on me and fixed me with an undeviating gaze. Looking at me like this he carried on with his daydream. Was it me he was seeing adorned with his beloved rope, decorated with the hempen collar for high misdeeds? When that idea occurred to me I couldn't hold still any longer and started to pace around the room so as to feel the sane reality of the cold stone flooring under my feet. Jef emerged quite naturally from his reverie. He went over to the bar and pulled a beer. He seemed to be happy. A smile lit up his thin lips. There was a joyful little flame in his usually lackluster gaze. Being proved right gave him pleasure, no doubt about it. And for the first time I noticed that his gaze was identical to the magpie's; yes, at that moment the pupils of his eyes were the very same as the pupils of the sarcastic black bird.

On the days that followed there was no more talk of gibbet or rope though my head was full of it. Mercilessly, Fate led me back to this corner of the inn, beside the window from where I could see the dilapidated wall and its sinister bronze arm. I didn't look at the gibbet, or at least I forced myself not to look at it, and I avoided mentioning it. But I felt nonetheless that the innkeeper knew what I was thinking about, and that, hidden somewhere in the depths of the room, the magpie knew it too. Evening came and with the gloom I saw things that worried me. Were they products of end-of-day fatigue or the strong beers that I methodically consumed? Figments of my imagination for sure, or else the play of the wind shaking the trees of the Plain, swaying the new-lit lamps. The twilight gloom bred shadows, and more than once I saw these shadows gather together under the gibbet, I saw one shadow dancing, attached to the invisible bronze fist! I was afraid of these baleful visions, and yet I remained complacent, sure that they would soon be dissipated by the nocturnal air of the street.

On one occasion I arrived at the inn when the lamp was already lit. A man was leaning on the counter, his back to the entrance. He seemed old but robust, dressed in dark corduroy. He didn't turn to acknowledge my "good evening," but I'd recognized him. My blood froze. And as the innkeeper came over me to say hello, I could only mumble, "He's the hangman, isn't he? ..."

Jef seemed taken aback.

"That's right, it's our Blondeel. How could you have guessed, seeing as you've never laid eyes on him?"

I didn't reply and left in a hurry, feeling myself in danger. And I hastened through lanes that imprisoned me and wanted to keep me in their nets, promising myself at all costs to avoid the Saint-Jacques Plain and its inn just as I would avoid somewhere over which hangs an immemorial curse ...

A whole season flowed by, a fine summer during which I explored the surrounding countryside. The Saint-Jacques Plain sometimes happened to come to mind, but I was no longer haunted by it and I could go on my rambles without fear of being pulled once more into its magnetic field. I was amazed at having been the victim of such a feeble influence. And I felt so sure of myself and of my freedom of movement that I decided to pay the sinister site a visit someday soon, with the personal satisfaction that one feels in seeing a vanquished enemy. Meanwhile, autumn came on. The days growing shorter, I was obliged to return to the old city again.

Early one evening, and without having intended to, I came out on the Saint-Jacques Plain, immersed in a bluish haze and looking ghostly. The windows of the inns were already lit up and, one after another, the first lamps glinted meekly. A harsh little bell tolled obstinately in the Minorite belfry. Never had this corner of the dead city appeared so lugubrious. Shivering, I hurried over to the inn that had so often welcomed me. On entering I was greeted by an old woman's laugh: the magpie cackled at the sight of me and the hard flap of her wings sounded like ironic applause. How was this eccentric bird able to recognize me after an absence of several months, from the far end of the murky room where only the diffuse light of a neighboring streetlamp shone? In the half-light I found the innkeeper asleep on a chair near the counter, dead to the world. I was starting to regret having returned to the inn but rather than going back out to the damp and desolate streets I went and sat down in my usual place beside the window. I appreciated the satisfying warmth diffused through the barroom, and, above all, it was the silence, full of the breathing of clocks, that seduced me into that suspension of spirit, that beatific state of rest that's so necessary to me. The magpie kept quiet, and not even the devil would have known where she was lurking. Unmoving, like everything around me, I listened to Jef sleeping, to his regular breathing and the incoherent words he muttered from time to time. A deep lethargy crept up on me unawares. The fog seemed to have flowed into the barroom whose solid interior dissolved to the point of disappearing, melting into the lunar haze that enveloped the city. And this sleeping man near the counter, did he exist or was he nothing but a crayoned outline? And my own person, boneless and nerveless, was it worth the effort of asserting itself in this soporific ambience? I didn't fight the universal drowsiness that crept over everything and my thoughts drifted in the nocturnal Lethe, melting into the heart of this oblivion being the supremely wise thing to do.

For how many hours had I basked in this nonbeing, my consciousness keeping feeble watch under my lowered eyelids, an insignificant point of clarity in the vast night? However, my senses weren't entirely extinguished, for I heard the tolling of the Minorite bell at the end of the ages, an obstinate tolling that seemed destined for me alone, no doubt to stop me from sinking into total slumber. I also heard the approaching trundle of a cart, still far away, but so absolute was the calm that this gentle trundling soon echoed like a rumble of thunder close at hand. If a commonplace noise so far away caused such a din then the Plain must surely be keenly receptive to echoes! Soon, though, I reckoned that the cart must have arrived nearby and entered the square. Had I slept for so long that the first porters of the morning were arriving already? The trundling noise stopped. And the emphatic silence troubled me enough to make me open my eyes. It was still deep night, and profoundly hazy outside, with some yellowish halos and the ghostly gesticulations of the leafless trees. What time could it be? As the numerous lunatic clocks couldn't tell me, I would have to go outside to ask someone, for example those porters with red lanterns, those night owls who were at that moment busying themselves round a cart that *my ear* recognized across from the inn and on the other side of the Plain, alongside the wall of the covered market.

At precisely that moment I regained full consciousness. Terror, pitiless terror hit me on the chest with an iron bar. And I wanted to cry out— but my throat clenched shut and my mouth didn't release this irresistible cry; this lamentable cry, *my cry, I heard it sounding elsewhere*, on the square;

such a lamentable cry that I felt my flesh turn to ice. I was witness to an abject and terrible spectacle! The cart had arrived exactly at the little gibbet, under which shadows busied themselves in an elaborate dance of flickering lanterns. I wanted to get to my feet to escape the horrors of that vision but I remained paralyzed and I could only alert the innkeeper, the incorrigible sleeper, exclaiming to him, or rather articulating in my voicelessness, "Help! . . . They're going to hang someone! . . . The man cried out! . . . Quick! . . . The cart is moving! . . . And the man has been hung! . . . Too late! . . ."

Did the sleeper hear me? He didn't stir. And me, I stared at the execution as though an inexorable power had kept my head turned toward the spectacle, forcing me to watch it. Trembling with horror I looked on the victim's *danse macabre* at the end of the bronze arm as furious spasms convulsed him; I "physically" felt the agony of this poor wretch flung bodily out of life: the nape of my neck was on fire and my temples were swollen; my mouth filled with bitter liquid; I wanted to vomit; fire, like a fluid current, ran all through my body and shot into my stomach; whistling noises deafened me . . . What curses or pleas did I utter; to whom did I cry out, in heaven or in hell? . . . My sight gradually dimmed and I felt myself transported by a vertigo that was like the movement of the sea. But before my eyes conclusively closed I saw the hangman leap from the height of his cart in a lightning flash and grip the hanged man's shoulders, swaying with him in the void, a gigantic spider finishing off a meager insect at the end of a thread! I thought that my vertebrae would snap and that I would break in pieces, falling scattered in an abyss. The worst had come to pass . . .

When I reopened my eyes the cart was moving away in the fog, carrying the corpse. The Plain had again become a cloudy desert, beyond time and the world; but a man strode across it, his lock-keeper's lantern in his hand, a stocky man who, unhesitatingly, was approaching the inn where I was sitting. "The hangman!" I thought with a pang of fear, ". . . the hangman who's coming for a drink, his work done! . . ." Alas! I wasn't mistaken. The door opened and I saw no one, only a lantern that moved in the room. But the hangman had entered, I could hear his slow steps. Astonished at finding the barroom plunged in darkness he ranged his lantern over the tables without speaking. The light approached. I made myself small in my corner, my head shrunk back into my shoulders to escape the scrutiny of that alarming creature who had just now concluded a killing; but the hangman found me and his lantern came and whisked over my face. He stared at me fixedly, with boundless surprise. And his voice, a rumbling singsong, sounded almost affable:

"What's the story, little brother . . . Don't you know that I've just hung you by the neck? Or have you got a double? . . ." Blondeel started to laugh, a rich laugh, and shoved a black, greasy rope under my nose, the noose with which he'd dealt with the "other."

"Or if you're back from the dead so soon," he jeered, "I'll have to hang you again, eh?"

I coughed and ground my jaws in reply to this threat. Leaving me to my lot, the hangman was already moving away toward the bar. I collapsed back into the murk, and also in a sudden analgesia.

At length I recovered my senses. Every limb felt sore, my skull felt like lead. The inn was lit up now, full of a dim bronze light. Jef was behind the bar and serving beer. I heard the murmur of his muffled voice, for he was talking to someone standing in front of him, someone I could only see from behind. This man emptied his pint and went out, carrying his lamp with nothing more than an indifferent glance in my direction. But I'd recognized this customer: Blondeel, town carpenter. The innkeeper, however, bustled about as though gripped by emotion, babbling and gesticulating.

"What time might it be? . . ." I asked him.

It was scarcely later than nine in the evening. Jef looked unutterably happy and studied me maliciously. I wanted to smile at him but I couldn't shake off the agony I'd just undergone. I was about to explain to the innkeeper, but he forestalled me.

"I know . . . You were sleeping . . . I saw you come in, and I fell asleep just like you . . . Whoever sleeps, dreams, don't they? But you must have dreamed of something extraordinary, because you struggled, you cried out, then groaned . . . Anyway, I'm glad to see you here again after such a long time . . . I knew that you'd come back some evening . . . It's been a good day for me . . . I've found you again, and what's more, my neighbor Blondeel has kept his promise! . . . He's just brought me his ancestral legacy, the last hangman's rope . . . Here it is! . . ."

And Jef dangled the noose that he'd kept hidden behind his back, the tragic cord . . . His delight was innocent, so ingenuous that it won me over and I started to laugh in turn. And the innkeeper walked up and down in the room, looking for a nail from which to hang his priceless rope.

"We're going to have a drink under it! . . ." he exclaimed, and he disappeared through the bar-hatch. I thought it would be a good idea to drink a glass after that hallucination, and I got ready to clear my head, still laughing nervously, and laughing at myself, when there was a metallic clapping, and I felt a slight breeze on my face. With a flap of its wings, the magpie had just flown right across the room and perched on the table, taking advantage, so it seemed, of its master's absence. I was unnerved.

"Bird of ill-omen," I cried out heatedly, "why are you giving me such a sly look, and what do you want from me? . . . Perhaps you've got some age-old secret to tell me? . . ."

And in the silence a sardonic voice that could only have come from the magpie croaked distinctly and with unmistakable contempt:

"You were hanged! . . ."

The
Odor of
Pine

To the painter Florimond Bruneau

No! It's impossible, no one has ever received a visit like that. Besides, such things can only happen in my house—this old house, too big for the person clothed by its damp bricks—this solemn and clammy residence with its gloom, its stale smell of the kennel and the vestry; such incidents can only affect someone like me, emaciated, sallow, and, by the decree of God who's punishing me for old sins, lamentably, irrefragably asthmatic! Speaking of which, ah! it's got me in its grip again, ah! I warn you, ah! that the story isn't, uh! so very interesting, ah! but merely droll, ah! with, ah! its poison *in cauda*, ah! its moral, I should say. I'm better now, uh! I'm telling you this not to entertain you or scare you or educate you or make fun of you, because, reader, you're nothing to me; I'm spitting out this story for my own benefit, so there! Extraordinary gobs of spit exist, risen from the depths,— marble, metal, enamel, gems, holy ointment; all admirable, if only the sun would shine down on them. But me, being one of those types who belong to the race of old Job, Joshua's star turned its back on me long ago.

It was last Friday, better still, the thirteenth, and one of the most impenetrable mornings of this foggy December. The day obstinately refused to dawn. I can well understand why, seeing what its light has to uncover on our shameful planet. At nine o'clock I'd instructed my housemaid: "Mortal Sin? Light the lamp, the one that smokes! Then draw the curtains on this sodden garden, on all this dead wood and that big puddle! Last and not least, stop the pendulum on the tall clock that looks like a laughing coffin; you know, the one that times its ticking by my asthma! Answer me amen or answer me shit, but do as I tell you, because today my life is hanging by a thread . . ."

The horrendous redhead who bore this magnificent name had followed my instructions, against her will, it's true, and like she did everything, like she lived, with a groan: "Another fine day ahead . . ."

Infuriated by this comment (you've no idea of the insolence of the people whom you shelter, out of charity, and provide with a pittance, without regard, in exchange for their poor and disloyal services), I started to choke, ah! and to cough, uh! in the middle range, uh! uh! and the bottom, and, uh! the high notes, huh!—not a fine, romantic cough, huh! nor one of those cavernous echoes, those orchestral *tutti* that thunder out in hospital wards the moment a doctor makes his rounds, uh!—but a discordant and stifled yelp, like the gibbering of a hanged man, huh! . . .—but something like a dyspeptic senator's speech, huh! or the reverberating sermon of an octogenarian clergyman, huh! uh! huh! . . . The nooks and crannies of my room started to yelp with me, and my splendid chandelier, all crystal and spiderwebs, vibrated celestially on this miserable wretch down below. To cap it all, in the room next door, Mortal Sin, overcome by my chronic infirmity, started up in turn with a high-pitched yowling in the manner of an emphysemic clarinet, the slut, as though she'd swallowed a bundle of her red hair. She did it on purpose, in a spirit of mockery. Don't ever talk to me about women's compassion! They're she-monkeys who take their revenge as soon as we've stopped searching their hairy parts for lice. She did it on purpose, and did it badly, since I recognized it as a parody. Do you understand the name I've fitted her out with? Mortal Sin—her ugliness, the look on her face, the way she behaves—all irresistibly invoke the idea of mortal sin. As she herself admits, the creature has never known any other condition; it's her birthright, just like certain souls (one in a hundred thousand) are naturally in a state of grace. And, right from the start, as ugly as sin. And then, her baptism no doubt having been a mistake, she sinned like she breathed; the slightest gesture, the slightest word from her became sin. Her ugliness, her very presence: sin; she was sin made flesh! She sinned if she blew her nose in her fingers, sinned if she ate, sinned if she slept lying down or standing up; without counting the downright, deliberate sins she confessed to me in hideous, unsparing monologues; thoughts, actions, and sins of omission refined enough to dumbfound the most imaginative and overheated of demons! Why did I keep this thing of wonder in my employ? For the exceptional nature of the case, of course! For her white mask of a face topped by that astonishing mane of fibers. Didn't she scare away all possible visitors without even needing to utter a word, those hindrances who call themselves friends and acquaintances and try to come and observe my protracted agony? I kept her on the payroll as a specter or a scarecrow, even though she frightened me. Besides it didn't matter to her whether she was called Mortal Sin or Whore of Babylon, and she responded to her name no differently than if I'd tenderly called her Star Bright or Little Springtime Bumblebee. After a while the hag stopped coughing, having really choked at last, for which I gave thanks to the Almighty. My cough had also exhausted itself. But a black thought overtook me: that I'd have to give up the ghost under the pale gaze of that woman and that I wouldn't have the luck of an old dog that's left to gasp out its last on a sack that it's chosen for itself in the corner of the cellar! She dreamed about it and had a scheme ready and prepared, I was sure of it; she'd go and tell strangers, neighbors, a whole rabble picked up in the street, wearing false faces for the occasion, to watch for free the high-class spectacle of me about to croak. No, no, I'm ready to go into Hell's turbines, but without witnesses, alone in my damnation just like I've lived, miserably—alone! That was a thought that invaded the room. It made me see red. What a really fine Friday! It was then that the doorbell's rusty mouth shrieked frantically in the hallway like a danger signal. The din sent a chill down my spine. I sensed an impending drama.

"Don't go," I shouted. "I'm ill, nearly dead, Mortal Sin. Don't open the door!..."

But I was answered by a rapid pitter-patter of slippers, and the voice, all red: "Okay! I'll get it!..."

The doorbell choked, its tongue swollen, purple. It was too late...

◎

An endless length of time passed in agonizing silence. No voices to be heard. At last, the double doors opened as though for some distinguished visitor. Mortal Sin appeared, her complexion indescribable, green, blue, white, red, painted with surprise and fright. In an infantile voice she said, "Your Excellency, there's someone who . . ." (just so you know, the standing order is to title me "Excellency" when a stranger, by definition a dupe, is announced).

But I wasn't in a mood to dupe anyone, though it constituted my usual means of defense. I was too angry.

"Trollop! . . ." I yelled.

The baggage flew into the kitchen and shut herself in, leaving me alone, hypnotized by that door opening onto the void of the hallway. What is it you'd want to see emerging from that void? Ah well! Logically enough, it was an apparition suited to the time and place; nothing normal, or rather, nothing other than what passed for normal for that time and that place. Where had I seen him before? He stood like a rigid portrait, framed by the doorway, larger than life, dark and dismal. I recovered my sangfroid. In a lifetime of adventures what is there I haven't encountered? Kings, princes, cardinals, bandits, lunatics, saints; and wasn't I myself someone well worthy of consideration? So I addressed the visitor with composure:

"Come in, sir . . ."

Self-assured, completely at ease, the man closed the door and moved toward the lamp. Describe him to you, ah! Don't even think about it, huh! I choked on it, uh! put yourself in my place, huh! Gaunt, hands in pockets, arms glued to his body, no, to a flowing blue outfit that enclosed his carcass. On his spherical head, a navy officer's cap or something of the kind. Around his neck, a dirty scarf over a striped jersey. But it was his slab of a face that impressed me, no nose to speak of, hollow eye-sockets; a face made of putty, lipless and with exposed dentures, or rather, as though the lower jaw had been eaten away by some sort of lupus. Yes, a face ravaged by some sort of leprosy and cleverly simulated with cosmetics, made out of Roquefort cheese imitating flesh. It showed you powerful, yellow-encrusted teeth in a kind of perpetual grin. For the individual chewed on a plug of tobacco, his jaws incessantly ruminating. Add to this the smell, ho! Phenol seasoned with garlic. As the housemaid said, it was "someone." This individual couldn't have possessed any other name; he was called "Someone," which was enough to leave me dumbfounded. Admittedly I've often enough wanted to be rid of this mediocre life, but on my own terms, by my own choice, with no witnesses, without anyone looking on. And this someone's gaze didn't leave off scrutinizing me, and from what a height! What a gaze! Dead, the eye of a dead fish, without a glimmer in its gray gelatin. As a matter of fact the man smelled of tides, of slime. In this moment of peril I absolutely had to show a bold face. Now, left speechless, I couldn't find anything to say. And the man swayed back and forth on the spot, as though my floor was the bridge of a ship. He was waiting. Me too. He took a chair and sat down facing me, still swaying back and forth. Following his lead I swayed too, as though overcome with dizziness, but in the opposite direction. The ludicrous, excruciating situation! How long did this sideshow go on for? Long enough for me to locate a memory. One idea connecting with another, I saw myself again, one autumn, leaning on the crumbling quayside near the sinister Château des Comtes. It was a warm and humid evening full of mosquitoes. The oily water, brimming with eels, glistened under the rays of the dying sun with all the liquefied feces of the city. And what a fragrant aroma! What was I was waiting for? The gossiping little evening bells that harrowed my soul every time I heard them? Some swollen, drowned body floating joyfully to the surface? Yes, of course—ever since one time when I'd seen a naked woman resurface at the mouth of the nearby lock, the very first to see her, her stomach enormous, but thrilling too, worth a harpoon in her gas-filled belly. I don't know what I was waiting for, that's the truth. Then a silent barge arrived, gliding through the thick water, rectangular and without a bow stem, narrower at the prow than at the stern, with no mast or rudder, and painted black, like a gigantic coffin. And a wooden sailor on it, his movements automatic, slowly wielding his endlessly long gaff like a gigantic scepter. Nothing to be surprised at on these millennial waters, in this senile and decrepit and decaying city full of dotards—so many old people and so few children! At that moment I had the mad fancy that this coffer was coming to collect the anatomical remains lined up in the morgues of the age-old hospices and return with them to the plain, loaded to the point of sinking. It was this peculiar boatman who now stood before me, polluting both my room and my soul. I understood that the evil hour had arrived. Not at all as anticipated. Was I clinging onto life? No, but this last contact, which I knew was inevitable, filled me with horror. Resigned, I heaved an animal sigh, an old dog's sigh, come from the depths of the cellar, from my cavernous being. The lamp sputtered. My room, lit like this and inhabited like this, became a cask that sank down into the depths of the sea, of the centuries. Did the man sense my distress? He broke the silence and squelched out slimy words: "It gets boring, eh? Life, it goes on for such a long time . . ."

"You said it, captain," I replied, "a long time; a very long time . . ."

As though flattered, the stranger stopped rocking and came a little closer to my armchair. He continued, familiarly, "Come on now, you'll make a good end of it! Going along your street I realized that my visit to you would come as a pleasure . . ."

"True enough," I murmured, "true enough. Pleasure is the word . . ."

His eye of a dead fish lit up with a green gleam, then winked. "What a fine smell of pine . . ."

By God yes, it smelled of pine! No doubt I turned pale and sweat broke out on my brow. I had enough presence of mind to rise to the occasion: "Pine, exactly . . . You couldn't have put it better . . ."

It seemed to me that my teeth were starting to chatter. I was going to need immense effort of will, when my interlocutor proffered salvation in the form of a board. A board, yes, a square surface, and still better, made of pine, this pine whose presence he'd so clearly detected. There was nothing symbolic about his language, the rogue, and it was me who'd misunderstood, hearing a macabre ambiguity. See: the sailor had leaned over and was pulling toward the light my chessboard, which was propped against the wall. He seemed childishly pleased—need I add that his delight was infectious? I was safe, if only for the moment—because so long as the man was still in my room the peril remained, unspecified but definite. Clearly my partner was a devotee of the Noble Game and, wanting to share his pleasure, I started to jabber: "Pine, that's right . . . What a nose, Captain! What a nose you've got there, dare I say, even though it's tiny, nonexistent! Did you sniff it from the street?"

And as my audacity returned I went on giddily: "Pine, so humble; a preordained wood, sir, from which chessboards, and the boards of coffins are made—two objects that put you in touch with the infinite . . ."

The man started and gave me a hard look. Had I unfortunately happened to remind him of the "real object" of his visit, the game being nothing but an interlude, a delay? Once more, ice covered my brain, a skullcap of ice. But the chess enthusiast voiced none of the dark thoughts that my stupid outburst suggested to him. He placed the chessboard on our knees such that, up close to one another, I could breathe at leisure the stale smells emanating from his sordid person—garlic and formaldehyde, old tobacco, rancid herring—in point of fact, a very erudite and delicate mélange. Meanwhile, although the tragedy of my situation appeared in no way diminished, I felt I still had a chance, even if only to gain some time. And with my trembling right hand I mechanically caressed the sublime surface of sixty-four squares, infinity instantly evoked in black and white, as precise a trap, as formal as an instrument of torture. Taking advantage of my morose delectation, the man leaned down to the ground, rummaged in the shadows and, in the doubtful light, guided by the flair that I had praised, picked up a bag that he opened and emptied onto the board. The sound of the chessmen falling was the dry rattle of knucklebones. Reality, absolute reality, was reinstated. The game had to be played, and played properly. No, never have I undertaken a more fateful game! For once, against all the rules, there were stakes, and a stake like no other! I read my partner's face clearly, I read: "Take care! I'm the best player in the world, he who is never defeated. I never forfeit a single piece. The moment I say *check*, say your prayers . . . And when the *mate* follows, say goodbye to the world that you've cursed so often! . . ."

My brain, which I needed to keep exceptionally lucid in these culminating minutes, was still prey to confusion. I felt I had to negotiate.

"You'll excuse me, Captain. You're the absolute Master of masters. And me, I'm a pathetic practitioner of the seventy-seventh rank. A fantasist, see, an empiricist! Logic was never my strong point. This chessboard has never been anything for me but an excuse for dreaming, a springboard, a beach. I tackle a problem and my thinking goes up in smoke . . . So you'll soon have me on the run. Show some consideration please; with respect to the divine codes, the transcendental combinations, the high signs that regulate the universe, don't be in too much of a hurry . . ."

The man shook his head, a little impatient. I persisted.

"Bearing in mind my shortcomings, won't you give me the advantage of at least one piece, just a rook? Oh! You're implacable! I can see that! But if by some miracle I manage, say, a draw . . ."

"I only play one game, so in that case, I'll come back another time."

The lots were drawn, the lot that gave me black—a bad omen for sure. However, notwithstanding the imminent danger, I recovered my usual self-possession while I lined up the pieces—or else I was already in that state of abstraction that is the prerogative of adepts of the Noble Game. Better still, I became double. Was it the spirit of the great Philidor that surreptitiously possessed me? But confronted by a rapid attack, my play developed in good order, following rigorously orthodox rules, faultlessly and without flights of fancy. The man who played like he was in a café of chess novices, was that me? No, it had to be someone else altogether, a proven logician with tried and tested reflexes, devoid of nerves and emotions; a second self that came to supplement my febrile character, and coming from where? From the ether or my own marrow? As for me, I was, so to speak, the third party, the one who looks on, sees and criticizes, dominates the game, so that in my scant person I felt that I was *two* against one; I was a player doubled by his adviser, against another player, one who was remarkable and confident, astonishingly so, but prone to error like anyone else.

A fabulous silence prevailed—the silence proper to ritual events. I won't analyze the character of the game that emerged. It declared itself to be classical, severe, concise, nothing more. The psychological moment arriving when my opponent, his strategy well developed, planned a long-term and serious threat to my king, I castled in good time, indicating that I saw through that cruel geometry, and that I wasn't short-sighted—even that I enjoyed added insight. My man shrugged in vexation and, trying to appear unconcerned, forced some small exchanges on me. Then he launched a feint with his knights to draw out my pawns, to which I responded with treacherously diagonal moves by my bishops on his queen. But the game remained in a state of perfect equilibrium and it seemed that up to now we were equally matched; or rather that the being who sat alongside me and played for me—my double—was equally strong, equally vigilant and cunning. For how long? In my turn—my aim, as I've said, still being to win time rather than the game—I played my queen dangerously, with wicked, well-managed moves. It was then that the captain threw himself back in his chair and fell into silent thought. I could see that he was playing from my point of view. Mentally, I played from his. The silence intensified. An excessive silence that I wanted to shatter, as though we were both enclosed in a crystal sphere. There remained one way to avoid losing: interrupt my opponent's intimidating concentration. It's not playing fair, but it's only human when playing the one game that you know there's no way of escaping. A glimmer of inspiration came to me, or to be exact, came to him who wasn't playing, to my passive self.

"You'll take a dram, captain?"

"Gladly!"

"Strong stuff? Very strong?"

"As strong as you've got!"

"Mortal Sin?" I called, "Two bowls and the schnapps."

From that moment, the atmosphere changed. Mortal Sin kept us waiting, then came carrying two white cups and a full bottle of my best gin. Visibly terrified, she didn't dare approach, the poor woman. I had to gently entice her.

"What's the matter my dear? . . . Take the lampshade off and fill us to the brim!"

The redhead obeyed and the removal of the lampshade revealed her in all her ugliness, exacerbated by her dread. Hypocritically, she couldn't leave off ogling the visitor. And he, swiveling his fish eye, round as a monocle, measured her up, prudently distant, frozen like a shop-window dummy. Literally hypnotized, pupils dilated, the creature filled the cups as well as she was able and went out backwards in a trance. The captain looked at me carefully but didn't breathe a word. He took the cup and downed it in one. Then croaked: "To your health, Excellency!"

"My health?" I exclaimed. "Are you making fun of me? To yours, Captain! To your successful navigation of the Flanders marshes!"

The captain let out a hollow cackle. His gelatinous eye lit up. He'd just acknowledged me as "Excellency." A good sign. He smacked his lips and grimaced.

"Really strong stuff!" he ruminated. "It dries the paint nicely."

I immediately filled up his cup, which he drank—which already put two deciliters of rare alcohol into his vest. This, perhaps, was the moment to distract him. I started a conversation.

"I have a dozen liters put by. You know, I'm sorry to have to leave them to my good-for-nothing heirs. If you were to come to drink them, let's say whenever you drop into town? . . ."

"I'll drink them today," he replied and without asking my permission poured himself a third cup that he gulped straight down. But the respite I'd hoped for wasn't granted. My man rubbed the lupus that served as his mouth and cried forcefully: "On with the game!"

And he pushed toward me an innocent pawn that, if I'd taken it, would have cost me the king's rook and landed me on the chopping block in five moves. That blunder avoided, the captain castled in turn, moving his queen into line with mine. I hoped for the chance of an exchange, for then I'd be able to relax, endgames being my little specialty. A new attack emerged that I parried easily enough. But it seemed to me that the player no longer had the same self-assurance. He made useless moves, fiddled around, maybe to fluster me. No, the game had lost its initial style and intensity. The captain was distracted, his mind on something else. What was he chewing over? He suddenly burst out, "Damn!"

"I beg your pardon, captain?"

The chessboard wobbled on our knees. The man had become agitated. On account of the game? No, surely not, because he squinted toward the kitchen; then: "What is it, that bit of skirt?"

"My housemaid."

"Well I'll be damned!" He belched once more, then, calming down, he returned his gaze to the chessboard. All the same, his hand hesitated, toying with a pawn.

"J'adoube."

It was my turn to go on the attack and stupidly, unexpectedly, I captured a splendid knight that had been left unprotected. The captain didn't even seem to notice the coup, and leaned toward me: "So, tell me, her name is Mortal Sin, eh? Magnificent name; magnificent woman!"

"That's a fact," I replied. "A rare find that would be a real loss to me if anyone were to take her away. As magnificent as Sin itself!"

Now the captain was in a dream. The chess demon had abandoned him, making way for another demon, just as formidable, and that I won't give a name to. I had sense enough to hold my tongue and leave the creature to his erotic hallucinations. He'd just tossed back two cups, one after another. The bottle was three quarters empty. Grabbing hold of it the man from the sea considered it, shook it, then put the neck to his mouth and drained it without further ado. The game was coming along nicely, no doubt about it. I kept my head.

"Mortal Sin? Another bottle?"

Then, without pausing, in a toneless voice: "Check!"

The move was countered, mechanically. Distracted, inattentive, the captain played an elementary game, relying on his reflexes. My attack came into focus. Clearly he was no longer interested. Perhaps he'd also forgotten what the stakes were. Just then my housemaid came back with the bottle. I asked her to light the chandelier. The dusty crystals sparkled with electricity, throwing out a luxurious illumination that left the captain blinking like an owl. A sudden change was at work in him. His cheesy mask was suffused with poisonous blood. His cod's eyes were tinged with violet and stared hard at the housekeeper. Mortal Sin was in a tight spot, silently wringing her hands and miming who knows what entreaties. She'd turned crimson. Her swollen face under the flamboyant crown of her mane made me think of some jellyfish, or better still, some grotesque Romanesque carving come loose from a cathedral tympanum. I read a sort of ecstatic horror in her gaze, which never left the captain. The situation couldn't carry on like that.

I was afraid that the creature would suddenly swoon with fear. For his part, the captain, his face twitching, looked to be under pressure. The chessboard tilted dangerously on his knees. Some pieces slid off the board. I seized my chance, acting impulsively on a quick and treacherous inspiration: "Pick them up, Mortal Sin!"

After some hesitation, the maid plucked up the courage to approach and went down on all fours. Fumbling about like this on the carpet, she looked like a diabolical hound, some beast invented by Hieronymus Bosch. She exuded a powerful odor of perspiration—the invincible odor of redheads, offensive to my nose—and that thoroughly venereal odor assailed my companion's nostrils in the same way, since I saw him sniffing the air. For a moment, Mortal Sin was right up against me, paws brushing the floor, rump protruding below. I couldn't decipher the man's bizarre reaction, but I believe that he slipped his left hand into his pocket under the chessboard. Already the recovered pieces resumed their place on the board. But the game was left in a state of disarray; the contest had come to grief.

"Where were we?" I asked, feigning detachment.

To my great surprise the captain shoved the board aside; "I concede," he declared, through his chew of tobacco.

I betrayed no reaction and, after having put the game away, ceremoniously offered drinks. Two fresh bowls emptied, my opponent got up stiffly: "We'll play again one of these days. Traybian, Excellency. We'll smell the pine another time, believe me!"

He held out his hand, a bony grip, a bird of prey's claw, that I felt moist and burning. As I put on a show of wanting to usher him out he protested, "Stay there, your health isn't so good. Your nice housemaid . . ." (and he emphasized these words) "will see to it . . ."

A farewell tip of his cap and he was gone, swallowed up by the double door that Mortal Sin had just thrown wide open. The maid disappeared in his wake after having sent me a questioning look; but my index finger ordered her to accompany the unwanted visitor.

●

Saved? I could hope so. But nothing had been gained inasmuch as the captain (forsaking his phantom vessel, I would have sworn) hadn't left my chambers. I waited for a long time, heart beating fast. What if he took it into his head to come back, like one of those persistent drunks? No, I would have killed him as a preventive measure! In my panic I was looking around for a weapon, one of those rapiers from the Spanish epoch that I leave lying around on the furniture, when a noise of some kind came from the hallway; like a squabble, a shouting match. Then, some loud yells. The doors had been left wide open, allowing me to follow the dialogue. Mortal Sin didn't spare him her compliments: "Old goat! No, really! You're stinking!"

And the riposte, a rumbling of bowels, gulps, a bestial laugh: "Mortal Sin, whore-flesh, haul up, oho! Haul up!"

Then what? A scuffle? Murder? The woman screamed. He was strangling her for sure! Hand-to-hand combat. I didn't respond to the call for help, this cry that paralyzed me like a bolt of lightning—a blue, forked cry that left everything scorched and went straight to my guts. Ho! I heard alright, but, ah! what to do, ah! My lungs went wild, uh! and wouldn't it be better, ah, if she succumbed, ah! The horrible girl, ah, who had no soul, ah! this monstrous redhead, ah! Then, nothing more save floor tiles scraped by heels. And my ears, ah! strained wide to hear, ah! but what? Two voices that snorted, ah! from the void, ah! I swear. I was choking on it, ah! It was very far away at first, ah! These mute voices drew closer to each other, and then, uh! a prolonged cry from the jungle, hoh! the inflections of a wounded archangel in flight, hoh! the desperate and empurpled song of a virgin under the high priest's knife, ho! that hovers, rising, descending; then, dizzyingly, ascending so as to fall again with a fiery hiss, like a meteor, ho! And nothing more, nothing but the thunder of the heavy door that opened onto the outside world, and the din spreading, nearer and nearer. Hoh! The crime committed . . . A long time passed before I risked moving. At length I dared to venture out, lamp in fist, sure of finding a cadaver; a new object of fright added to all the others. But no! In the murky light of the hallway where a cloister-like calm held sway, Mortal Sin lay flat on the tiles, a big, broken, dislocated doll. No pools of red. On her back, arms spread cross-wise, the creature was sunk in a deep sleep. I read the bruising on her face, the tears collected on her closed eyelids, her cheeks glazed by a slimy tongue. Her torn blouse revealed a very white shoulder (I didn't know that the woman had a human body, made of flesh) and, jutting out, a dazzlingly youthful breast; but the seal of a violent bite-mark remained on her shoulder with drops of blood. Under the rucked up skirts I also saw the belly with its tawny tuft, the chalk white thighs, and, in their separation, the lubricated wound—no, the peculiar, gently salivating mollusk—from which arose that eternal aroma of seaweed that's so enticing. This vision filled me with an unspeakable emotion. I contemplated this slumber of a happy child with a pout on her lower lip. What might her sublime dream be? For, as I studied her, a supernatural light bathed the face of the creature infernally surrendered to passion. What supreme annihilation passed through her, like a warm river that snakes voluptuously toward the abyss?

"Mortal Sin?" I murmured, "from now on your name will be Sacrifice."

And I placed a fervent kiss on the forehead of that fallen statue.

Eliah
the
Painter

INTRODUCTORY NOTE

> The Jew becomes [. . .] this ambivalence, this border where the strict limits between same and other, subject and object, and beyond even these, inside and outside, disappear. Object, therefore, of fear and fascination. *Abjection itself.* He's abject, filthy, rotten. And as for me, who identifies with him, who desires a fraternal and mortal embrace with him, wherein I lose my limits, I find myself reduced to the same abjection.
>
> —Julia Kristeva, *Powers of Horror: An Essay on Abjection* (1980)

Out of print since 1941 on account of its anti-Semitism, "Eliah the Painter" requires separate comment. A work of concentrated intensity, it stands out as one of Ghelderode's best stories, but it's also an exercise in deliberate provocation and has paid a price by largely vanishing from view. Nevertheless, it's a significant document of its time, and possesses qualities that argue for its availability.

"Eliah" depicts a seedy petit bourgeois milieu in terms that are both realistic and expressionistic. The central figure of Eliah was based, so Roland Beyen tells us, on a Jewish artist, Mark Fuchs, with whom Ghelderode was acquainted in the 1920s, and one of whose paintings he owned; Fuchs committed suicide in 1934. Two other characters were even more closely drawn from life: "In Pollarch and Juwarec are the recognizable names, barely modified, of two old friends of Ghelderode's, a hairdresser and a grocer whom he had met in the army. . . . The fact that he showed no concern to conceal their names or professions indicates a clear desire to inflict hurt."[1]

Beyen established Ghelderode's anti-Semitism in his 1971 study and further explored it in a pungent later essay, "Michel de Ghelderode et l'Académie."[2] At times the writer believed that his creative endeavors were being blocked by a cabal of Jews in positions of influence.[3] He was initially sanguine about the 1940 invasion, in naïve admiration for "the Germanic gods, who love art as much as they love war,"[4] and also out of resentment for the Belgian establishment which, he felt, had disregarded his creative achievements. From 1941 to 1943 he gave a number of talks on Nazi-controlled Radio-Bruxelles. His subsequent defense was that the broadcasts only addressed topics of Belgian history and folklore and so were in the national interest, a claim that was supported by friends such as Franz Hellens, known to be anti-Nazi. However, Beyen points out that he vented his anti-Semitism in a broadcast on the legend of the Wandering Jew, when he pugnaciously invited Belgian Jews to clear out of the country. In the years immediately after the war, Ghelderode maintained his anti-Semitic views, though now keeping them more private. The absence of "Eliah" from the 1947 edition of *Sortilèges* went unnoticed, and the story and the suspect broadcast remained buried and forgotten until Beyen drew attention to them in 1971. Even so, his detailed exposé was greeted with silence; it was only with the publication in 1998 of volume 5 of Ghelderode's collected correspondence, covering the years 1942 to 1945, that the writer's anti-Semitism caused any degree of comment in Belgium.

The Ghelderode who emerges from Beyen's biographical research is both a great hater and a profoundly neurotic individual, given to rebarbative outbursts in letters to friends and acquaintances. Jews, it must be said, were only one of his targets, although a persistent one:

> Markedly paranoid, our dramatist was constantly seeking out scapegoats in order to give faces to his existential torments. The Jews were one of those faces. Others were politicians (present and past), the clergy, the Freemasons, the financiers. . . .[5]

> For the most part Ghelderode was endemically negative: anti-clerical, anti-Semitic, anti-Masonic, anti-Belgian, anti-Flemish-speaking, anti-French-speaking, anti-French, anti-American, anti-Russian, anti-communist, anti-rationalist, misogynist. . . .[6]

Beyen argues that, taken together, these were so many paranoid projections resulting from crippling frustrations, anxieties, and insecurities. Ghelderode falls well short of being another Louis-Ferdinand Céline. Chronically shy and reclusive, he was not a political animal, and not a fascist; he declared himself an anarchist and his contempt for politics and politicians extended to the extreme right. Beyen comments that his anti-Semitism was "irrational, without any basis in either theory or practice"; there was no given political or ideological agenda.[7] Evidence from later in life indicates a possible change of heart: in a 1961 letter he praised the new state of Israel and finally deplored the horror of the Holocaust.[8] But there was no mea culpa for his previous attitude.

Ghelderode remains a problematic figure, and "Eliah the Painter" is certainly his most problematic work. Whereas other "negative" narrators in *Spells* are voiced in parodic mode, the narrator of "Eliah" is intelligent and thoughtful in ways that liberal-minded readers can relate to. But in assuming the mask of a fascist thug, he becomes the thing itself, telling his story with chilling conviction. By the same token, Ghelderode, as writer, is responsible for a story whose political, historical, and cultural resonances render it unclean; it openly expresses anti-Semitism in a context of petit bourgeois fascism and further invokes the prospect of massacre. Written in April 1940 when the systematic persecution of the Jews in Germany was a well-known fact, "Eliah" must be counted as an early albeit minor symptom of the approaching Holocaust.

The indictment is damning, and yet the story isn't as straightforwardly anti-Semitic as might initially appear. In an era when negative Jewish stereotypes were rife, Eliah goes beyond mere caricature and becomes a compellingly human figure who readily engages the reader's sympathies. Meanwhile, the narrator's anti-Semitism is increasingly fueled by a claustrophobic drama played out between himself and Eliah. His fraught relationship with the Jewish artist involves both a psychical link and a significantly erotic element, suggesting that the latter is situated as his abject alter ego. Such is Jacqueline Blancart-Cassou's psychobiographical reading: "In choosing to give voice to the persecutor and in deliberately associating himself with his murderous hatred, Ghelderode violently rejects that part of himself that is Eliah."[9]

By a further twist, the story's power derives in part from the ambivalence it generates at the formal level. As the narrator's voice becomes steadily more inhumane it never ceases to be seductively intimate; add to that a hybrid narrative composed of anti-Semitism and the uncanny, and the net effect is one of transgression. Some readers will no doubt reject the whole thing as abhorrent; others, though, will recognize the fascination and force of the transgression. It's a troubling recognition.

These persistent ambiguities complicate our response to the story's profound incorrectness; "Eliah" cannot be dismissed as an instance of sheer prejudice in the way that the anti-Semitic letters can. Ghelderode the artist was working at a deeper level than Ghelderode the man. To say this is not to deny but to confirm that "Eliah" is a work of real darkness; for that same reason it should be treated not as this collection's dirty secret, but as its dark heart.

NOTES

1. Beyen, *Michel de Ghelderode ou la hantise*, pp. 417–418.
2. Beyen, "Michel de Ghelderode et l'Académie," http://www.arllfb.be/ebibliotheque/communi-cations/beyen040498.pdf.

3. "Michel de Ghelderode et l'Académie," p. 19: "When, in 1942, a friend unreliably informed him that one of his plays was rejected for performance owing to Jewish intervention, he responded angrily, 'You'll tell me that they're being chased away, that they're disappearing, that a new régime is slowly being established? I'm telling you that the Jews' occult rule over this unfortunate country carries on, in alliance with the Freemasons . . .'"

4. Letter of August 1940, ibid., p. 14.

5. Ibid., p. 18.

6. Ibid., p. 22.

7. Ibid., p. 20. Beyen shows that Ghelderode was always dismissive of Léon Degrelle's proto-fascist Rex party; see *Michel de Ghelderode ou la hantise*, pp. 304–305. Beyen also states that there was no connection between Ghelderode's pro-German (but not pro-Nazi) sentiments of 1940 and his anti-Semitism. See "Michel de Ghelderode et l'Académie," p. 22.

8. *Michel de Ghelderode ou la hantise*, pp. 422–423.

9. Blancart-Cassou, "Sortilèges, auto-portrait de Ghelderode," in *Michel de Ghelderode, dramaturge et conteur*, ed. Raymond Trousson (Brussels: Éditions de l'Université de Bruxelles, 1983), p. 142.

That certain beings can't exist without hating or feeling themselves hated, and can only live by placing themselves in an antagonistic posture outside society, that Nature fabricates sensibilities just as monstrous as anything she produces in the physiological order, these are things that no longer astonish anyone who has lived and observed life. So it is that I want to tell here the story of one of these disquieting men, or of the most unquiet man I have ever encountered. He was called Eliah, but he had another name, complicated and foreign-sounding. Where was it that I knew him? In the dreariest of outlying districts where the ill will of society has conspired to gather together everything whose existence pains the soul: gasometers, railway lines, hospitals, factories belching out their miasmal pollution, cemeteries, pits for incinerating waste; in sum, the dirty and hopeless canvas of the tree or lawn of the misery of the urban margins, of unrelenting labor, a corner of a false universe, its barely sketched outline already decaying. It was an accursed plain that you couldn't pass through without feeling contaminated and diminished. Such places exist, conceived and inhabited by men of these times, like damned souls building their own hell. It was the destiny of the man who was called Eliah to inhabit this depressing landscape, the subsidiary figure required by this suburban setting that he never sought to avoid, so much so that he seemed to have sprung up from these surroundings, produced by their tainted waters and infertile soil. It was said, nevertheless, that he had been born far from here, in Poland. But as far as I was concerned, this restless individual specifically stemmed from the outskirts, acquiring through mimicry the tints of the walls or the soil, like the toxic vegetation that is found nowhere else.

Now by a whim of that Nature that takes delight in the most frightening paradoxes, Eliah's ill-made frame contained an artistic sensibility and outlook. He painted. For some people he was none other than Eliah the painter, who could be found roaming the periphery, always looking behind him to check that he wasn't being followed, or abruptly moving his easel if someone appeared to be approaching him. For everyone else he was an anonymous business representative, trotting from the grocer to the wine shop, always obsequious, always in a hurry. He was mocked on account of his exaggerated politeness and also of his dislike of strong drink. He only drank water. And yet fate destined him to be employed by a brand of aperitif that he only talked about in a reluctant manner, denigrating the merchandise from which he made his living. I admired the courage of this poor wretch who was out on his travels from the early hours of the morning, always rebuffed or ridiculed, and who found the strength to go and paint, setting out toward the end of the working day to encounter the most desolate twilights, often in the rain, and carrying his equipment the way a penitent drags an expiatory cross.

The sight of him distressed me—not that I felt any sympathy for this creature who was like so many others passing on their way. But I couldn't begin to understand why he persisted in painting this repulsive region where everything spoke of inanition, or everything was an invitation to suicide. What longing for nonbeing, what vocation for misfortune incited him to this hopeless exercise, this dead-end career? No doubt he remained incapable of seeing and painting anything else and no doubt he could only feel himself living and suffering before this negative universe. People assured me that he didn't lack talent, though this talent looked labored. I longed to see this painting that dwelt only on thankless subjects. But the thin-skinned artist never took part in exhibitions and carefully hid his canvases if anyone came into his room.

Once, however, I had the opportunity of seeing the painter at work. It was an October day, very dark and rainy. I was wandering on the borders of the awful suburb, on the promontories that overlook the marshaling yard.

From the top of these embankments was to be found the most depressing panorama you would ever want to see: a lethal hollow glinting with brown pools of water where some wrecks of wagons were half-submerged, bristling with signals like gibbets; herds of black carriages were piled up on embankments; the horizon was blocked by the geometrical masses of gasometers and, further away, lines of hoists indicated the tail of the canal. You found emptiness below you, a lower depths where mysterious maneuvers were carried out in the absence of any human element; carriages that moved all by themselves, locomotives that sought each other out and, groaning, rubbed up against each other. And what a cataclysmic sky overhead, pressing down on this cauldron; all the dross of autumn! That's what Eliah, a few steps away from me, was painting in this sinister light . . .

He splashed about on the muddy ground, spellbound and agitated in front of his canvas that he abused with seemingly malicious little strokes; then he stepped back as though afraid of a counterthrust. The peculiar dance that the stoop-shouldered little man performed, the aggressive dumb show in front of the hostile landscape, on this clay proscenium! Although the time and place urged me to flee, I couldn't stop myself from approaching, drawn by the painter's antics, or rather those of the maniac who persisted in painting in these circumstances. I told myself that only a madman would push his absurd activity so unrelentingly, take his mania to such extremes! Yes, I was drawn, as one is to a morbid spectacle, and no less perhaps by the void that exercised its unhealthy power of attraction in this spot. I approached the painter cautiously, and I already had his canvas before my eyes, loaded with a thick color and plastered on with a knife, when the man sensed my approach and turned round all of a sudden; his eye shot a lightning bolt at me, then he flung himself on his equipment in an angry movement. But he missed his footing; he slid on the soaked ground and rolled down the slope of the embankment. It was a sorry sight certainly, but I had to make an effort not to burst out laughing. And I went to the edge of the embankment with the intention of helping the poor wretch whose fall I had unintentionally caused. He was already getting up, spattered with mud and breathing heavily. He refused the hand I held out and uttered an incomprehensible insult. His eye flared, jet-black with violet glints. He seized his gear and fled like a thief along the palings, so speedily there could be no question of catching up with him to apologize or to try to placate his resentment toward me. I vowed to avoid this unsociable creature, but it was written that I would see him again and more closely than I would have liked.

○

For how many years was it that on Sunday evenings I went to that cellar-kitchen under the shop run by a certain Pollarch? I can no longer tell . . . I don't know anywhere more degrading, but I ended up there as a matter of habit; habits, above all bad ones, form an envelope that keeps a man whole and prevents him from crumbling to pieces. In this rank interior littered with crates, bags, and conserves, I met with queer and detestable people who assembled there through their resemblance with one another, and who I must have resembled because I put up with their company. So, in this Sunday underground that we called "the crime scene," we made up a group of hybrid individuals, gathered uncongenially together to spit out the bile accumulated during a week's existence in the cruel city, and if anyone had stationed themselves over the trapdoor that gave access to the cellar and listened to the discussions escaping from that smoky cavern, they would have fled, thinking that that they'd witnessed an assembly of lunatics, some of them truly demented.

The tone was set by the owner of the establishment, the malnourished Pollarch who loved to declaim, regurgitating in spurts all the gutter political print he had ingested and digested between the two Sundays. Without intending to, he effected a striking parody of a spit and sawdust electoral demagogue, inflaming himself to the point of stumbling over his words, so pathetically that he cut his grotesque rhapsody short by yelling war cries: "Death to the bastards! . . . Everything is screwed up, long live corruption! . . ." and other imbecilities to which we responded in a ferocious chorus. It wasn't difficult to create that atmosphere of a padded cell, since no one who frequented the cellar had steady nerves or clear ideas. But Pollarch outstripped us all.

This little man, thirty years old, already gave an appearance of old age, his entire person proclaiming premature senility; he was bald and wrinkled; his teeth were spoiled. His gestures never agreed with his words. And his disordered utterances, his abortive tirades revealed a brain become cracked in the service of his monstrous vanity. That grocer detested me. He only valued his own personality and spoke readily about his genius as a reformer lacking a platform. He could barely read or write, but he quoted Jesus and Marx and undertook to enlighten us on the meaning of our destiny, in a language that wasn't far from pidgin French, that prompted the thought that he had salivated Yiddish before crippling the French language. He demonstrated to us, and with how much conceited self-indulgence, that his "*substlety had long ago measured the color of our egoicism*"! And we'd adopted his vocabulary to the point of taking all correct language as mistaken. We delightedly insisted on the "*substlety*" of the grocer and launched ourselves into tangled sentences stuffed with verbal clichés, like, "*In conformity with . . . It's an evident fact that . . .*" These games weren't always without upsets, for the grocer sometimes noticed our malice. Then anger made him horrible, though his feeble physique and natural cowardice prevented him from lashing out at us.

It was at that moment that the providential laughter of one of his allies, Juwarec the hairdresser, broke out. This narrow-chested monkey of a man used expensive perfumes and cosmetics to alleviate the pharmaceutical smells emanating from his rickets-ridden carcass. He too prided himself on being someone! Hadn't he scribbled some vaudeville ditties not so long ago?—"We others, the intellectuals . . ." he repeated at the drop of a hat. No doubt he was as deserving of contempt as the grocer, but Juwarec was treasured on account of his laugh, a surprising laugh; this hysterical spasm commenced with a series of yelps, then soared, fluctuating and reiterated, a long gurgle like the moan of a dog nosing death, to finish, after an eternity, in an explosion of coughing and choking.

No use in expecting it, it was a *coup de théâtre* every time; contagious laughter grabbed us by the throat, shaking us furiously, until tears came to our eyes; and nothing rang so tragically. The hairdresser was still choking like an epileptic while we got our second wind.—"Is he going to croak? . . ."

we wondered. The meeting terminated with this outburst and we escorted an exhausted and asthma-stricken Juwarec back to his home.

If there was one predestined location, one fitting milieu where you might meet Eliah the painter, it was just this damp cave. He came there one evening, fated to, and because it constituted a dark pole, an unhealthy sacristy where a certain kind of untypical individual was unfailingly bound to end up. Pollarch knew him from his shop where Eliah presented his tainted concoctions and he'd made it his duty to invite him to our reunions.

That Sunday the conversation languished. The grocer, whose bladder or kidneys were giving him trouble, was visibly annoyed, not caring to make speeches. The hairdresser too remained taciturn, and the others confined themselves to smoking and spitting. I kept my mouth obstinately shut to see how long these people would put up with keeping silent. Our assembly was literally crushed by silence.

"He won't come . . ." Pollarch muttered. And the grocer disappeared up the rigid stepladder that served as stairs to the top, to enquire after the painter who, he knew, was morbidly shy and capable of wandering around in the vicinity. In fact he was going to try to urinate. And the evening progressed, when footsteps danced on the ceiling. A ventriloquist's voice broke the silence.

"No! . . . I won't go down . . ." Muddy feet passed through the trapdoor, seeking the rungs. And two legs cavorted ridiculously.

"Eliah! . . ." one of us said. There was a gust of wind, a terrible fracas. The newcomer had missed the stepladder and fell among the crates and the conserves. We all stood up without a making a move toward the man who was lying on the ground. He must have split his skull! But the man got up, feeling his limbs and staring at us with a stupid expression. His black pupils were big with fear and, in the silence of the morgue, Eliah started to jabber.

"Excuse me . . . It wasn't my fault . . ." He bent his back and pulled in his rump as though fearing chastisement. His humility was so apparent that I felt an urge to spit in his face.

What an exasperating evening! In reaction we all started to speak loudly and all at the same time, surrounding Eliah, who shrank into his chair. His forehead was bathed in sweat. He remained very pale and his skewed gaze prefigured a syncope; however, he never stopped smiling effortfully at us. Then he recovered. And the malaise evaporated when Pollarch came back down, loaded with bandages and vials. The grocer was astonished, even disappointed not to find an injured man in his kitchen.

"Amazing!" he exclaimed. "That trapdoor and its ladder have already caused two deaths. It's true that the second casualty was drunk! . . ." With these words, someone asked for something to drink to settle his stomach. Alcohol, in fact, became indispensable. It was what was needed to expel that atmosphere of a quarantine ward, exacerbated by the hissing of a gas burner and the speechlessness of the painter, still dazed by his fall.

"You had a narrow escape," I said, to break the ice, "you might have been the third." The painter waggled his head by way of reply and from that moment on never left off examining me, yet lowering his eyes whenever I turned toward him. As for me, pretending to follow the conversations, I sought on the sly to study his person, so oddly assembled, without worrying myself about how much this ended up unsettling, then irritating, the artist. He certainly didn't elicit sympathy. His physical appearance was in no way repellent; but what contradictions in that body and that soul.

He gave the impression of illness, and yet he was robust; he seemed infirm, and there was nothing in his looks to confirm the claim; he had brief bouts of prostration, stammers and a trembling of the hands that might have classed him in the great family of degenerates, but a somber intelligence burned under the noble curve of his brow. I sought for the secret of such antinomies, of the singular feeling that was elicited by this expressive body in which there was nothing that was not enharmonic; you would have to make inquiries at the very point of origin, in the Eastern ghetto where this individual had been molded, out of what blood! Then, remembering that Eliah was a painter, my mind went in search of canvases or prints where I was bound to have already seen types of his kind; that overlarge head with unfinished features, like a carved turnip; the torso too powerful for the short little legs? Spanish school, yes! Eliah resembled those sturdy dwarves swarming in the perpetual shadows, those dwarves who have chanced to outgrow their native size. And like them, of course, a waif, an error, a botched thing, close to caricature but redeemed nevertheless by a magnificent gaze.

Finally the painter could no longer endure being observed and, with mouth open, turned brusquely toward me. He'd expected me to speak to him again. Faced with my reserve, it was he who took the initiative. At first I heard nothing, his words drowned out by the general hubbub. But he brought his chair close to mine and seizing me by the arm, shouted in my ear.

"Tell me, sir . . . Do you believe in God?"

For a moment I was taken aback by the impudence of the stranger and the presumptuousness of his question. However, I was quick to find the right response.

"Do you?"

Eliah was disconcerted and rocked his big head that seemed swollen under the pressure of burning ideas. It was my turn to go on the attack, wanting to teach him a lesson.

"You never get drunk, so I'm told?"

"Never!" He spoke emphatically. I seized one of the tumblers of white liquor that the grocer had placed on the table and swallowed it.

"You're wrong about that!" I burst out . . . "God drank! He was drunk the day he created the world. If you drank we could talk about Him! . . ." My outrageous comment crushed the painter, who pulled his chair back. He gave me a look that was both sad and contemptuous, then turned toward the gathering, having understood that I wanted no further dialogue with him. He didn't stop spying on me from time to time, but from then on I ignored him.

The brimming tumblers of cheap alcohol had quickly loosed the tongues of my cellar-mates, and even Pollarch managed to forget about his bladder and his kidneys. He ranted in the smoky fumes. I heard him talking about high finance and the Jewish threat, holding his own against hecklers who had sworn to make him lose his temper as usual. The debate grew warm, and as the volume increased so the levels in the bottles diminished. Juwarec the hairdresser got up and hugged the grocer, shouting at the top of his voice, "Pollarch is right! All our problems come from the Jews! Down with the Jews! ..."

His intervention was the signal for an uproar. Everyone else got up, and I caught their raucous yells: "Massacre them! ... No, hang them! ..."

It was then that the painter leaped toward the maniacs with a shrill yelp, fists clenched: "I'm Jewish! Me, I'm a Jew!" In all logic the fists of the others should have rained down on him, but his irruption into this committee of lunatics had the opposite effect; he was welcomed with a wave of laughter; offensive jokes knocked him back into his chair. He made the gestures of a man asleep, and, the only one to keep a cool head, I saw that his glittering eyes were filled with tears. Beneath ongoing laughter, his shoulders shaking, his heels knocking, groaning childishly, he grabbed hold of his skull. Pollarch went over and held the bottle of alcohol out to him. The painter seized the bottle and shattered it against the wall. The smash suddenly curtailed the uproar. And the only thing to be heard was Eliah's trembling voice, Eliah hiding his face behind his arms as though expecting blows. "I'm sorry ... Excuse me ..." I took advantage of the moment of calm to leave.

The night air was delicious after that pest-ridden cellar. The rain drizzled softly. I went away feeling at ease, looking back from time to time for fear of seeing the painter at my heels. My concern was justified, for there he came, in the distance, jogging from one pavement to the other, furtive like a rat. Without either slowing down or hurrying up I stealthily observed the maneuvers of my shadowy stalker. The painter strolled along in a bizarre manner that revealed his state of mind; his walk was full of hesitations, questions, second thoughts; a walking monologue. I was soon mingling with the Sunday evening crowd, without the pesterer having caught up with me.

All that night, as an insomnia induced by Pollarch's alcohol ran its course, I kept recalling that walk, that unaccountable meandering of a delirious dog, of a lunatic in the grip of his familiar demon ... Where was it that I had seen creatures moving like that, all arabesques? Of course! In circuses, in the ring. A clown! That's what Eliah was, with his overlong face and his misshapen buffoon's chin! That body and that thought attracted blows as though by decree of destiny; and whatever he did the man couldn't help but be wretched, seeking opportunities for so being. But why did he want to follow me and catch up with me after that gathering when I'd made clear my hostility to him? I didn't know . . . From then on, my hours were bathed in a dusty dream, the golden mist that hovers above the circus ring. I saw Eliah costumed as a comic butt and whirling endlessly round, distraught, searching for someone, for the fine clown, moon-colored and wearing a Roman mask, who, following tradition perhaps, whacks him on the head . . . The circus, the dream faded away. And on awakening I imagined that the perpetual anguish of the buffoon consisted in this, that he hadn't found his tormentor, that his appetite for suffering remained unappeased . . .

Following that evening I ran into Eliah daily, no matter where I went, as though accomplices dressed like him and imitating his actions had received instructions to mock me by planting themselves in my path; or was it only him, him alone moving so quickly, become ubiquitous? What's more, he didn't recognize me or didn't see me. He saw nobody and nothing besides his route, dragging a valise as big as himself and stopping in front of certain shops that he entered only after having performed an extravagant pantomime, as though arguing with his own image reflected in the shop window. This way of carrying on was amusing for a while, then I got used to these appearances until finally Eliah no more existed in my eyes than I existed in his. I happened to bump into him on street corners; he stammered, "Excuse me . . ." and carried on his way, quick and agile. Sometimes I undertook to follow him at the same pace; but he *sensed* my presence without having looked back and sped up until he was running, except when he suddenly escaped my gaze by springing into a department store. I deduced from this behavior that he retained an unpleasant memory of our meeting and didn't plan on maintaining ties with the disagreeable character I'd shown myself to be; on my side, I appreciated his attitude, not wanting to become friendly with this famished individual.

Then I didn't see him for several weeks. Had he gravitated to another part of the suburb? One morning I visited the grocer, and he hadn't seen the painter either. He talked about him at length, pleased to be able to show off his "*psychology*," as he put it, and described Eliah's personality to me; a volatile type whose mood changed with the breeze and who in one and the same hour went from the depths of despair to the heights of childish enthusiasm; in short, he was an awkward friend and a poor companion, if in fact it was possible to be friends at all with a creature of such extremes. He tried all patience, harassed the best of hosts, sowing confusion with his excessive agitation of body and mind. His taxing conversation usually tended toward opening gambits or interrogations: "Don't you think that ... ?" or, "Why do you say this? ... that? ..." His questions were in the imperative, not even listening to the reply, or if he listened to it he immediately went one better, pleased with himself if he was able to sour the temper of his crowd.

"We know the beast ..." Pollarch concluded ... "but if he's avoiding you its because he can see that he won't be able to fool you and you're able to turn the tables and overwhelm him with your own preposterous questions. He's guessed that you can be a ruthless joker when you want to be."

I thought that this was a wise policy on the part of the painter. "The city's swarming with nuisances like that," I replied to Pollarch, "and when they're Slavs or Jews into the bargain they end up clogging the traffic ... Whoever manages to avoid them or to break their hold can claim to have had an experience of life." As I left his shop Pollarch told me again that he was all the more puzzled by the painter's behavior toward me in that he'd previously shown a desire to get to know me.

In the street a surprise awaited me: Eliah was watching my exit from the shop! He reached me in three bounds, eyes shining, full of emotion.

"I saw you going in," he declared, "but I didn't want to follow you into the grocer's. You talked about me, didn't you? I really loathe that grocer, he's full of envy, he bad-mouths people ... He detests everyone, especially you and me. Will you tell me why you visit that cellar, with those people? ..." I freed my hand, which the painter was squeezing between his, deciding to upset the hothead, whose spontaneous sympathy I disliked.

"Why? I have a taste for the macabre. Oh! I repay those people's hatred a hundred times over, and I go to their meetings just like I'd go to a carnival, to look at repulsive things made of wax in the museum of horrors. The grocer, the hairdresser, the cellar's other mental defectives, I observe them as clinical cases, with their real or imaginary complaints; I secretly encourage their taste for these complaints and their fear of them too, telling them about death and actually waiting for them to give up the ghost. The grocer is syphilitic, but it's the hairdresser who'll cast off first; he's only got one lung and the second is pretty much in shreds. They can smell the coffin pine; it's the smell of pine that I go to inhale in their cellar. Ha ha!..."

The painter studied me fearfully, not knowing whether or not to believe me. A number of questions came to his lips, which I awaited, but he didn't dare utter them and stood there abashed. Finally, he made up his mind.

"Tell me, what about me, I go to that cellar. Do you see me as one of them?... How do you see me? What am I?..."

I didn't let him go any further.

"You, my dear sir? But I don't know you. You're nothing but a passerby... You're a matter of indifference to me."

The painter took several steps back, recoiling from the blow, only to suddenly come on again, disconcerted and shrill.

"You're lying!... You can't possibly not have an opinion of me. I don't leave you indifferent. I'm someone who doesn't leave anyone indifferent; I'm either despised or well thought of; above all, I'm despised. I don't care. At least say that you despise me, that you dislike me!... Indifference is monstrous, it's inhuman. You're an intelligent man and I expected to learn from you what I am in society!..."

I took my time and, speaking very deliberately, I replied.

"You're a neurotic, like we all are in that cellar, and even in this century... Get a grip on yourself. You enjoy debate, or at least ideas? When your nerves are settled and I feel that I'm ready, I'll debate with you. Then we might arrive at a good understanding, I'll keep an open mind about that. We'll discuss God, painting, Jews, and everything that stirs you up... But if you carry on in this frantic and high-handed way, I'll have to shove you back into the crowd and ignore you . . ."

Eliah rocked back and forth on the spot, his eyes lost. He gestured awkwardly as though to say: what's the use! And he looked at me without either timidity or pride, with a sincere simplicity and humility that I found almost moving, that would have moved me if only his gaze had persisted, this gaze of a mistreated and misunderstood animal. But the painter had already fled, returning to the backdrop of the street.

I was to see the painter often, in streets that rule over us, determining our steps and contriving encounters. Going round and about in the suburb— for one goes round even though the streets are straight—I often thought of a canvas by a Dutchman who died mad: *Prisoner's Round*. Whether wearing convicts' stripes or dull city suits it's as though in every respect—we're going round in circles. In my melancholic delectation I thought of carnival horses or clowns walking in single file round a ring of black earth as punishment. One image linked up with another and the figure of Eliah came unfailingly to mind, and, by way of a coincidence that I don't want to analyze or otherwise give a name to, it so happened that the painter, in that very minute, emerged at the end of the street, leaving a shop or turning a corner, as though the thought of him had conjured him from the void.

Depending on his mood he avoided me without seeming to do so, or abruptly switched direction, but more often than not he watched me coming, anticipating my greeting or stopping nonplussed as though I had dropped from the sky. In these situations we exchanged some banal phrases: how goes it with business? . . . and your painting? . . . More than once I was on the point of asking him if he knew the *Prisoner's Round*; but I refrained because that would have given the tormented and tormenting Eliah an opportunity to gabble on about the symbol that poor Van Gogh inscribed in his work, about himself, about painting, about the drama of life, about his own and everyone's, and God knows what else! . . .

Although we remained distrustful of each other and both on our guard, it seemed to me that on certain days the painter would have liked to break with convention, bridge the gap, and frankly, humanly, open himself up to me; I divined it on his lips that at that moment seemed in mute prayer, in his eyes that became moist, suddenly more glistening. Fearing these accesses of emotion I promptly fired off some wounding comment, with immediate effect: Eliah shriveled under the sting and went away without replying, even more bent and benighted, hugging the walls.

I regretted my action and on the next meeting forced myself to make amends to him by being cordial. This way of going on, this almost friendly invite, left the poor wretch confused, thinking that he was seeing a hitherto unknown aspect of my cruel character. In a strange reversal of the situation he turned refractory and threw out allusions meant to offend me. I let him carry on, pretending that I was increasingly irritated; but the painter wasn't fooled; he didn't finish his indictment and, leaving me on the spot, took to his heels without saying goodbye.

How childish and reminiscent of schoolboy quarrels, this charade that unfolded in two movements that never varied: if I wished my interlocutor well, he rejected me; if I sought to bully him he gave himself over to it unreservedly, body and soul . . . I considered the case, finding it simple: either Eliah consisted of nothing but instinct, a primitive, or else he possessed the complex sensibility of a woman; he didn't want a friend, or only wanted a friend who submitted to him; and if friendship proved impossible, he wanted its opposite, an enmity that shook him, scorched him, made him as quiveringly alive as a scarecrow in a blast of cold wind. I really did try to exchange some amiable words, some constructive conversations with this man who was so puerile or so perverse—it came to the same thing; a waste of time, with this deluded being who pursued his chimera from the break of day and who suffered every hour from being neither loved nor detested! He couldn't accept that the universe was indifferent to his crooked person, unable to understand, given his limited intelligence, that the universe in its entirety is nothing but indifference.

I soon had the chance of sounding the depths of that ulcerated soul, covered in sores. One threatening evening in November I'd ventured out to the farthest reach of the outskirts, near the last buildings and the beginnings of the open country. The rain didn't let up. Fleeing the downpour that had doubled in strength, I entered a little transport café bar where I found nobody besides the owner. I was feeling low, depressed to the point of wanting, calmly and coldly, to drink, in order to forget the suburb under this rain-laden sky and my own condition as a denizen of the outskirts whipped by the rain. The bar owner, who wasn't very joyful either, accepted a drink from me and after an hour we were chatting like old friends, already more cheerful and forgetting our solitariness as well as the deluge that was drowning the landscape.

"You'll be my only customer today! . . ." the bar owner said.

"No! . . ." I replied, "The weather will send you someone else . . ."

And the door opened, blown wide by a gust of wind. Was it the rain that came in, that soaked thing?

Eliah! He went and propped himself against the bar, out of breath and miserably spattered with mud. He saw me and stammered, "Oh, pardon me . . ." He made as though to retreat, but the bar owner had recognized him and held him back.

"I don't need anything," he said to the salesman, "but you've gotten soaked coming here. Put me down for six bottles of your purgative! . . ." And with a wink in my direction, he finished, "I wouldn't put a dog outside . . ." Eliah heard these words and stiffened, his face turning purple. This humiliating reception galvanized him. Defiantly he looked at the bar owner and looked at me, his hat tipped back. This behavior provoked me and, feeling inclined to be spiteful, I suggested that the bar owner offer a drink to this salesman who was so wanting in civility. Faced with the rudely expressed invitation to come and sit down at our table, Eliah made a gesture of downright refusal, something that unleashed the bar owner's anger.

"What? . . . This little Jew! . . ." he suddenly bawled. "They're all the same, they sell poison but they refuse to drink it! We have to give them a living, but they won't let anyone else make a living! . . . By God, you'll drink with us, and your own poisonous aperitif, or else I'll write to your firm . . ."

Eliah snorted derisively, now gone pale, his head buried in his shoulders. The bar owner grabbed him by the jacket and forced him to sit down, then he went to look for beer glasses and a bottle of the famous aperitif, the poison . . . The painter was resigned; he even pretended to drink. I was highly amused, watching the wretch's mime show, nervous in the extreme, but still self-controlled and expectant, his eyes watchful. Every atom of his being betrayed an intense animosity. However, the greater part of his rancor was reserved for me.

"Drink up!" I said to him. "Show us what a good businessman you are. If the drink doesn't agree with you I'll carry you home to bed . . ." Squeezed between the already seething bar owner and the ugly customer I'd shown myself to be, the painter seemed to understand that there was no way out and made an unexpected decision; he seized his glass furiously and emptied it, with great difficulty but without pausing for breath. We applauded this bravado all the more as the wretch, pale as he was, turned white. He shut his eyes and leaned forward as though he'd received a blow to the back of his neck.

"And the painting, Eliah? . . ." I asked. The painter didn't reply. Was he going to go to sleep, knocked out by the poison? I started in again. "And the Jews, Eliah? . . ."

Eliah stood up as though stung by the lash of a whip and flung his chair brutally across the bar. We looked at him in amazement, afraid that he'd fall back down; but the man who'd reacted so unexpectedly was seemingly transformed. He laughed wildly, ready for every comer, and for a second I felt that he was more fired up than I was. His laugh was provocative. The bar owner remained stunned. Were we dealing with a lunatic who was thrown into a frenzy by the least taste of tipple? I got to my feet to interrupt this false, insufferable laugh, putting my question again: "And the Jews? . . ."

This time the painter returned the sharp stone I'd flung at him. "The Jews . . . Pah! . . . Yes, the Jews. What are you waiting for, to hunt them down, massacre them? You, yes you! This is one of the last countries where the Jews live in peace . . ."

I moved toward him, replying in the same tone of voice, "No doubt about it, but you'll go so far that we'll set about it here too! Ever since the middle ages our princes have left you in peace, that's true; and that's lasted too long, hasn't it? Persecution—you're crying out for it, and you'll get it!

Peace is too simple for your kind, thinking of yourselves as born martyrs, and only fit for masochistic practices! . . ."

Jammed up against the counter, the painter clenched his teeth, but his wolfish gaze devoured me from top to bottom, and this look became steadily more intense, until I thought I read a black ecstasy there, a mysterious and infernal gleam. I stopped speaking, awaiting the insult. The rain hammered the windowpanes. And in the ever-growing darkness we remained like two dogs baring their fangs. Finally, the painter weakened, merging with the darkness that slowly absorbed him; he gave over, abandoning the field. His big head swayed, ready to drop. And his voice rose under the percussive rattle of the downpour, faltering and so aged, the voice of a prophet or a drunkard.

"Let me tell you . . . Everyone seeks pleasure and gets it; some seek suffering and are denied it, because it's precious and fruitful! . . . What to expect of men? Their goodwill? They're all capable of being good, to Jews and to dogs; being good, that's what pleases them . . . But absolute men, capable of not being good; men of consequence, where are they? . . ."

This rambling discourse lit the flame of my anger. I yelled, "Suffering? If it's denied you, it's because you don't deserve it! . . ."

I'd raised my hand to slap the puppet, whose arms flailed in the air. But the bar owner intervened, in a temper.

"That's enough for tonight."

He banged the door open and sent the painter sprawling into the street, into the nighttime deluge.

Relieved, we took to drinking uninhibitedly in the light of an oil lamp. The bar owner told stories about Jews. Drunkenness suited us fine and our hearts overflowed with a frank joviality. The bar owner laughed at the top of his voice, and this gross peasant laughter put me completely at ease. Then we sang soldiers' songs. I left the bar toward midnight. The downpour had ceased. Guiding myself along embankments and unfinished roads by means of the infrequent lamps, I returned to the city, staggering in the dense shadows. My head was full of songs. At a certain point, something came and fell in front of my feet, no doubt another drunkard, rolling in the mire with his skin full of bile. I couldn't avoid the obstacle and kicked this filthy thing or being several times, eliciting sickly groans. And I continued on my way. I felt happy and powerful, more powerful than the suburb whose malign spell I'd exorcised.

○

A few days later I received an anonymous letter, a greasy paper full of incoherent phrases that could only have been concocted in the grocer's cellar and at the behest of the painter; I detected Pollarch's hand, while certain references to the drinking bout betrayed Eliah; what's more, the paper carried the insipid smell that characterized the monkey Juwarec. It was to be expected that these people would get together to spray me with their venom, and I knew plenty about the conduct of these vermin whom I was under no obligation to keep on seeing. I didn't even consider revenge, knowing from experience that life usually takes care of a job like that, and in style! But I couldn't bring myself to forget the Jew—I no longer called him anything else!—and his image haunted me more often than was called for. No doubt he lost nothing by waiting, this scum to whom, I promised myself, I would, circumstances permitting, mete out the punishment that he seemed to crave. At that moment I detested him with such dogged determination that I believed I hated him; but these outbursts of anger that his name ignited in my blood can't be called hatred. Moreover, wouldn't that have been a kind of victory for him, exacting from me the hatred that he tried so hard to earn? In this case, the best revenge consisted in maintaining a disdainful silence, with the painter unable to do anything other than live in expectation of abuse at my hands. I soon acquired proof of this. Every time chance brought us face to face in the labyrinth of the suburb the Jew stopped short and, turning on his heels, fled without further ado. Wanting him to imagine the worst, and to aggravate his torment, I assumed a threatening air as soon as I saw him appear; I waved my fists and charged forward like a man gripped by a ghastly fury. The trick worked every time, so well I ended up fooling myself, so that the sight of the Jew made me really angry, even if only superficially so. Of course, no sooner was he out of sight than I forgot about him.

This loathing ended up exhausting itself, until I reached the point of finding myself a few feet away from Eliah without remembering the infuriated role I was supposed to be playing. But then, seeing me for the preoccupied passerby that I was, the Jew resumed his offensive behavior and, driven by a taste for danger, came close, almost under my nose, to provoke me by pulling a face; then he took to his heels as fast as he could, looking back to see if I was chasing him. Most times I lengthened my steps, trailing him through the streets till the moment when, almost within reach, he jumped onto a moving tram. Once he mistimed his jump and, amidst shouts and curses from passengers, barely escaped being crushed to a pulp, helped up by strong arms. That incident procured for me a strong thrill that I hoped to savor again.

This pleasure was given to me, and sooner than I'd hoped. One day at lunchtime I came across Eliah wandering along the road. He was wearing a raincoat that reached down to his shoes and on his head a felt hat wedged down to his ears; he was pushing a baby's pram covered with a waxed cloth. Outfitted like this he looked so comical that I decided, once and for all, to make him into a laughing stock and I rushed over, shouting, "Dirty louse, I've got you! . . . The letter! . . . your anonymous letter, I'm going to make you eat it! . . ." People stopped. But the Jew had executed a half turn and was fleeing, his pram bouncing along the pavement. I could easily have caught him up, but I took my time, enjoying the public spectacle. The joke was a huge success. Children scampered after him. A barking dog provided an escort and hung at his breeches. Passersby called to each other, "What's going on? . . ." Right up to the moment when a stout woman emerged from a house, shouting, "He's stolen a child! . . ."

"Must be a pervert! . . ." I replied.

There was a mad pursuit. The hunted Jew ran faster and faster, keeping his vehicle from tipping over, and so adept at bypassing obstacles that he seemed to be performing an acrobatic stunt. But I was the only one laughing. And the catastrophe occurred: a policeman blocked the path. The vehicle overturned. And bottles smashed on the pavement while a bloody sea spread in the street: the aperitif! The mass of pursuers gathered in a circle. The policemen held Eliah by the collar and bellowed, "Why were you running away? . . . Who are you? . . ." The Jew, his wits scattered, didn't reply and threw desperate glances at the threatening or jeering on-lookers. I had hypocritically threaded my way through to the front row. The Jew recognized me. He blasphemed and would, I'm sure, have throttled me if people hadn't held him back.

The shout went up, "A lunatic! . . . A straitjacket!" The ambulance soon arrived. Amidst the clamor of the excited crowd the miserable wretch was thrown inside like a parcel.

I remained in place, crushing glass under the soles of my shoes. A fine heat radiated through me at the same time as a cool shiver ran down my spine. I told myself that Eliah must have found what for him defined happiness: he was persecuted. For that he was in my debt and I could expect him to thank me for it. But no, I saw his wild gaze once more, the gaze of a murderer. This man, not unreasonably, would end up killing me; unless, foreseeing that, I got the blow in first.

○

Kill my fellow man? Like anyone else, I felt capable of it, though repudiating such an easy action; but the idea of the possible crime gave me a queer inner thrill. Kill Eliah, preemptively and, if I dare say so, as a kind of legitimate, anticipatory defense? Why not! On condition that I wouldn't have to lay hands on the patient and that the crime would be executed solely through the force of my willpower, beyond the ken of the legal code . . .

My "victim" must have become aware at a distance of my perverse intention, for I no longer crossed paths with him. On the other hand, I had news of him from Pollarch, whom I providentially bumped into one evening. The grocer turned pale on seeing me, no doubt thinking that I was going to pull the anonymous letter from my pocket and demand explanations. I did nothing of the kind and seeing my air of distracted politeness he grew bold enough to ask me why I had abandoned the Sunday reunions. And me by way of retort: "Because your cellar smells . . . and you all smell too . . . Of what? Corpses! . . ."

The grocer agreed. "You're right. The place isn't cheerful . . . and my friends are dogged by bad luck . . . Juwarec has had to go to the hospital . . . And as for the painter, he's living in a state of terror . . ."

I put on an innocent look, concealing the pleasure this revelation gave me.

"Who or what from? Is his brain in working order? . . ."

Pollarch didn't dare say any more and stared at me mistrustfully. I finished by saying, "That man will come to a bad end . . ."

"That's my impression too . . ." the grocer replied. And we went our separate ways with a banal good evening.

Inwardly I felt an equivocal satisfaction in knowing that my enemy was possessed by the angel of fear, and that thought alone gratified me for several days. The crime, after all, was merely an end point, a formality. And if I wanted nothing less than the person's disappearance, I put a high value on what must be his prior daily feeling of mental torment. But how best to manage or maintain his anguish? The Jew no doubt knew the times of my comings and goings, and I no longer encountered him at all. Or else his maneuvers were so adroit that I credited him with all kinds of disguises, even as far as seeing him in an old woman or perched on a bicycle. These burlesque fancies added spice to my initial satisfaction, which consisted in imagining him prowling through the suburb sick to the pit of his stomach.

Meanwhile, in solitude, I toyed with the idea of the crime that I wouldn't deign to commit, fine-tuning the plan, perfecting it, just like one plots a detective novel. I dismissed all the easy situations and relied on Time, which ripens all things, fruit, works of art, cancer. This pursuit, moreover, lacked any tragic signification. And how absorbing I found it, this progressive premeditation; how necessary it was to me, this preoccupation with the crime that I was preparing, refining, improving, without high fever or red lights. My head was so full of this murder that I frequently ended up dreaming about it, and each time I awoke in a transport of intense though incomplete bliss. At length my desire for the crime was transformed into a desire to dream about it, and I believed that, through these imaginary actions, these mental expeditions, I would end up ridding myself of the obsession; in a completed dream, with murder as its conclusion.

The thing came about on a Sunday night when I went to bed tired and earlier than usual. I had a nightmare, the nightmare that I'd hoped for, but that, each evening, I feared to undergo, knowing what monsters arise from the dark sleep of reason. I was en route through the suburb, seeking the Jew. And no Jew to be found in the streets. Nevertheless I needed at all costs to come to grips with him, that night being the last one available, and once this fixed time had passed I would, thanks to a sinister reversal of roles, become the hunted man. Despairing of the outcome, I stopped in front of a house where, I remembered, his lodgings were. I read his name on the buzzer: Eliah, business representative. I pressed the button. High above, a window lit up; the other windows remained dark. No one in the street. The door stayed shut. I buzzed again. At long last the door opened. Eliah stood before me in shirtsleeves, mouth agape. I pushed the door to get in. The Jew wanted to close the door. And both of us silently pushed. My effort carried the day. Very calmly, I entered the corridor while the Jew, still without uttering a word or a call for help, reached the landing, waiting for me. And I started to climb the steps. The Jew was no longer waiting for me and, in several bounds, reached the second floor. I reached the second floor in turn, completely relaxed. Already the Jew, spellbound, was clinging to the banisters above me. And I reached the third floor. There were more steps. And I found myself on the final landing. The staircase ended but I saw an open door. The Jew must have disappeared through this door. I went in. And the lights suddenly went out, all over the house. I felt my way forward into the room. And not a word, not a sound. I bumped into furniture, an easel. Then I entered another room, where cold air seized me.

"Eliah?..." I breathed... "Where are you?... I've come to kill you..."

How calm it was in these deserted rooms! Was the Jew hiding or had he reached the rooftops? I didn't worry about it. I didn't even think of striking a match. Forgetful of what I had come to do, I told myself that I needn't remain in this stranger's house and that it would be better to go home to bed. Still feeling my way, and in no hurry, I went back down, step by step.

The door had remained open and I closed it again, gently. And I went back home to my bed, where I found myself at dawn.

But this quite simple dream, that I'm wrong to call a nightmare, left me thoroughly unsettled. Unfolding as it did, I hadn't in fact committed the crime. Nonetheless I felt a real sense of relief and I understood that Eliah had departed from my thoughts this night, once and for all. But how tiring I had found that ascent of the staircase! I went back to sleep, for long hours, like a man sleeping off the effects of drink, or who has enjoyed a violent orgasm . . .

○

Toward the middle of the week I visited the home of Eliah the painter, having learned that he'd died. A cobbler occupied the lower floor, a decent individual who was still upset by the drama he'd witnessed. He told me about it.

"A reliable chap, he never touched a drop, never received any visitors. On Sunday evening I was reading my newspaper in the kitchen. The sound of someone rushing down the stairs alerted me. All the other tenants were out so I went to check . . . Eliah had left the street door open and was groaning, climbing up as fast as he could, you'd have said he was like a man out of his wits. "Monsieur Eliah? . . ." I called. He kept on climbing. Then I went out to the street, see if anyone was there. Not even a cat. I was worried and I climbed up to the fourth floor to find out what was going on, in case my lodger might have had an accident . . . He wasn't there anymore, monsieur, I mean to say that he was already down below . . . Bang! . . . in the skylight glass . . . from the fourth floor."

I interrupted the cobbler, who was sweating profusely: "Was it a suicide? . . ."

The gentleman was indignant. "Certainly not! An accident! The examining magistrate declared it . . ."

"What time was it on Sunday evening that the accident happened? . . ." I asked again.

"Between half past nine and ten o'clock . . ." the cobbler replied, questioningly.

I knew what I'd wanted to know.

"Oh, nothing . . ." I said . . . "You see I had the idea . . . I thought I'd met up with him at that time . . . I was sleeping so it's not possible."

"Was he a friend? . . ." the gentleman asked as I went to leave.

"A friend would be putting it too strongly . . ." I finished. "An acquaintance, one among so many . . ."

NOTES ON THE STORIES

This translation follows the text of 1947 edition, with additional material taken from the 1941 edition.

In 1947 Ghelderode undertook a light stylistic revision of some of the stories. As part of this process he edited out a few minor but not necessarily insignificant points of detail. In three instances, identified below, I've seen fit to restore wording omitted from the 1947 edition.

THE DEVIL IN LONDON

> But the very worst boredom with which I had to contend was the English boredom that for several months I breathed in like a treacherous gas with the London air, *the boredom that is apt to be emitted by a moralizing nation—if not a moral one— and the most moralizing of all nations.* (p. 19)

The italicized phrase above is omitted from 1947 edition.

THE SICK GARDEN

Ghelderode's best-known story, it was included in Jean-Baptiste Baronian's anthology *La Belgique fantastique*, and has been the subject of a eulogistic essay by Thomas Owen and of critical analyses by, respectively, Ana Gonzalez Salvador and Philippe Met. In 1943 it was published separately in a limited edition under the title *L'Hôtel de Ruescas*, illustrated with lithographs by Jacques Gorus (included with this translation). For the 1947 edition, Ghelderode revised it more extensively than any of his other stories, making numerous stylistic amendments.

In *The Ostend Interviews* Ghelderode chronicled the events of 1917 that, so he claimed, inspired the story. Roland Beyen, in his account of Ghelderode in that year, makes no reference to the episode; presumably he found no corroborating evidence and his silence may indicate skepticism. Certainly, Ghelderode had a talent for mystification and can't be relied on for truthfulness.

NB: "The Sick Garden" yields its revelations gradually; readers should take care not to read the following extract from the *Interviews*—effectively a summary—before the story itself.

Is it a lived story?

Yes, but what does that matter? *The Sick Garden* represents a rather odd period of my youth, a time of black and white. I'd gone seeking solitude in one of those very old buildings due for demolition, of which there were quite a few in Brussels at the start of the century, and of which nothing remains today but rubble and dust.

I'd gotten free lodging in an old mansion reduced to total disrepair and with an enormous and neglected garden adjacent to it, and I thought that I was utterly alone and absolute ruler of a population of rats. But this solitude was deceptive. After some time I eventually became aware of that, in the wake of troubling noises. Groans came from the ceilings and walls. I thought that the mansion was haunted, and I was pleased with the thought that the mansion was haunted, for, like all children, I knew that fear is precious. And at that time, in 1917, while I was already a man, thrown into life prematurely, I remained a grown-up child, more so than someone with the benefit of experience. As a result I watched out for these ghosts that only manifested themselves aurally. And my nights were romantically disturbed by that! Furthermore there was this unmanageable and indecipherable garden, very disturbing, full of mysterious beasts and just as invisible as my ghosts; but as I had my dog close by me—a dog to which I was attached by a pact of that sublime friendship of which very few humans are capable—I was reassured, I was never alone in the face of the mystery. And it's then that this drama ensued: I'd discovered the existence of a frightening little girl in this ruined house, a ruined creature that someone seemed to be hiding. Finally there was an elusive woman who might have been the guardian and nurse of this deformed child and who hid herself too, as a precaution, for I only succeeded in glimpsing her at dawn, when early masses were performed.

And then the drama took shape. This child invalid went down into my garden, which was unwell, too, and became attached to the dog, became the dog's comrade; and then I discovered the horrendous condition of the damaged little girl, epileptic no doubt, with dead hands and nightmare eyes, and who wandered in the menacing garden.

It's all true. The cat that you see in the story, it's true too, the horrible, pellagrous cat that looked to me like it emerged from the pages of a hellish bestiary. It crept on the wall like a spy, and I saw it as a menace. And the drama unfolded, as in the story, on a torridly hot day. But of course I don't tell all in the story, since the reality by far surpasses what a writer dares to imagine, at the limits . . .

And then once more a sepulchral silence fell, and I found myself all alone in that house from which I was evicted by jeering workmen, come to demolish it and its dying garden. You won't be surprised if I reveal to you that the bewitching power of this tale, and therefore its success, consists less in narrating meticulously and carefully, with consistent truthfulness, a banal happening—an item of news— taking place in an extraordinary place and décor, than in a certain art of not telling, or not telling everything. (*Les entretiens*, pp. 51–52)

THE COLLECTOR OF RELICS

The figure of the antique dealer Ladouce is derived from Julien Deladoès, a significant and influential companion of Ghelderode's early manhood; Beyen gives a detailed account of their relationship (see *Michel de Ghelderode ou la hantise*, pp. 125–140). Ghelderode eventually broke with Deladoès in 1932, believing him to be responsible for anonymous abusive mailings he received. This incident probably inspired the anonymous letter episode in "Eliah the Painter."

"a beautifully worked vermilion ciborium of Mosan origin" (p. 74)—i.e., from the Meuse Valley.

RHOTOMAGO

In a late autobiographical fragment, Ghelderode relates that, when he was a boy at Catholic school, a priest examined the contents of his desk:

> "Above all there was an old book [. . .] *The Secret of Grand Albert, Master of Wizards and Witches—with spells for love and for levitating in the air at night and passing invisibly through walls* . . . This book [. . .], among other things, contained a spell for invoking the apparition of the devil Rhotomago who knew the future." (Beyen, *Michel de Ghelderode ou la hantise*, p. 92.)

SPELLS

Set in Ostend, home of Ensor, with whom Ghelderode was acquainted, having met him in 1925. The brief 1941 dedication "to James Ensor" was expanded in 1947 to a fulsome tribute.

"Spells" includes less obvious allusions to Ensor. The story invokes the historical Marquis of Spinola, immortalized by Velazquez in his "Surrender of Breda." The siege of Ostend (1603–1604), conducted by Spinola for the Spaniards, had left the old city in ruins. Ghelderode knew that Ensor was greatly interested in the siege and when, in 1933, the artist wrote a tribute to the dramatist, Ghelderode responded gratefully by writing a major puppet play, *Le siège d'Ostende*. At one point he hoped that Ensor would provide designs for it.

> "And the nearby sea resumed its eternal conversation. Ascending the Rue de Flandre, I soon arrived at the terrace where, in a sullen and spiteful mood, I was able to confront it face to face." (p. 108)

As Ghelderode well knew, Ensor was living on Rue de Flandre at the time the story was written—he had probably visited the artist there. From 1880 onward, Ensor's attic studio overlooked this street; then, "from 1917 on Ensor lived in a house inherited from his uncle . . . located at number 17 (that is today number 27), Rue de Flandre, which, terminating in a ramp, opens directly onto the sea and seems to ascend toward the sky" (Jacques Janssens, *James Ensor* [Bonfini Press, 1978]). Ensor's bird's-eye view of the street from his studio is commemorated in both canvases and lithographs, most strikingly in a lithograph of 1890, "Musique rue de Flandre" (recreated in the following year as an oil painting).

> "Why bother fleeing, since I carry both body and brain with me? Life, or this living misery that arises from the want of a specific reason for living, having become unbearable in a certain place, near certain people who one suddenly needed to leave *in order to avoid the worst, would it not become bearable if transferred* elsewhere, immediately, through uprooting oneself? . . . All experience amounts to this, to know how to flee! . . ." (p. 93–94)

The italicized phrase above is omitted from the 1947 edition. This is not a deliberate edit but rather a typographical error involving the omission of a line of print. The error is carried forward to the Marabout and Jacques Antoine editions, but smoothed over as "people who one suddenly needed to leave for elsewhere."

I saw a big white effigy being erected, a kind of snow-white mannequin with lesser mannequins in hideous masks tied up at its feet, meant to symbolize the vices as well as the miseries of *the season, its penury, its politics, and other current ills. Clearly we were waiting, to the sound of funeral marches, for the astronomical hour to be sounded, that of the birth of* spring. Theban trumpets sounded the hour. (p. 105)

The italicized passage from the 1941 edition is omitted from later editions.

NUESTRA SEÑORA DE LA SOLEDAD

A carved Madonna in l'église de la Chapelle, Brussels; it also features in a short treatise Ghelderode wrote in 1943, *Mes Statues*.

YOU WERE HANGED

Set in Bruges. Ghelderode's comment on the setting of his play *Mademoiselle Jaire* applies equally well to this story: "I discovered this décor in Bruges, this corner of the Parish of Saint-Jacques, that appeared to me as a theater, an empty theater awaiting actors, awaiting a potential drama. What drama? I didn't know, but the décor was there, available, and I understood that it belonged to me" (*Les entretiens*, pp. 152–153).

In the 1941 edition, the final paragraph of the story includes an extra phrase, "jusqu'à sept fois de suite":

And in the silence, a sardonic voice that could only have come from the magpie croaked distinctly and with unmistakable contempt, no less than seven times in succession: "You were hanged! . . ." (p. 163)

THE ODOR OF PINE

This story, written in 1942, was originally intended for a subsequent, unrealized collection, *Le dormeur de Bruges* (The sleeping man of Bruges), but was included in the 1947 edition, replacing "Eliah the Painter." For details of the original Mortal Sin, see the introduction.

Roland Beyen, in a chapter of his 1971 study that explores the vein of misogyny running through Ghelderode's work, does not discuss "The Odor of Pine," but he quotes a brief extract from *Mes statues* that bears directly on its apparently redemptive conclusion. The context is a conversation between Ghelderode and Franz Hellens in the Parc de Bruxelles:

> "The fact is, women frighten me," Franz sighed.
> "Me too," I acknowledged, "that's why I love statues."

Ghelderode discussed the story in *The Ostend Interviews*:

Do you have a personal memory at the origin of this story, even, let's say, an experience?

At the origin of all my works! There's always an incident that provoked them, a shock!

The story that you refer to, "The Odor of Pine," was written after a serious illness in the course of which I had a premonition of deadly danger. I'm not concerned to reconstruct the ups and downs of that adventure, our suffering and torments are devoid of interest unless treated and transmuted with a view to the work of art. I can tell you that I found the elements of this bitter tale, which could well be an allegory [. . .] in the shadows and lights where I was foundering then. (*Les entretiens*, pp. 48–49)

On a point of information, "J'adoube" (p. 177) is a specialized gaming term, used by chess players when they toy with a piece or pick it up but decide not to move it.

SELECTED BIBLIOGRAPHY

Beyen, Roland. *Michel de Ghelderode ou la hantise du masque: Essai de biographie critique.* Brussels: Palais des Académies, 1971.

Beyen, Roland. *Michel de Ghelderode ou la comédie des apparences*, catalogue redigé par Roland Beyen. Paris: Centre Georges Pompidou; Brussels: Bibliothèque royal Albert, 1980.

Beyen, Roland. "Michel de Ghelderode et l'Académie." http://www.arllfb.be/ebibliotheque/communications/beyen040498.pdf, 1998. Accessed 24 September 2016.

Blancart-Cassou, Jacqueline. "Sortilèges, auto-portrait de Ghelderode." In *Michel de Ghelderode, dramaturge et conteur*, ed. R. Trousson. Brussels: Éditions de l'Université de Bruxelles, 1983.

Ghelderode, Michel de. *Les entretiens de Ostende.* Edited by Roger Iglésis and Alain Trutat. Toulouse: L'Ether Vague, 1992.

Ghelderode, Michel de. *Seven Plays.* Translated and introduced by George Hauger. New York: Hill & Wang, 1960. (Includes translated extracts from *The Ostend Interviews.*)

Ghelderode, Michel de. *Sortilèges.*
1941, Paris-Brussels, L'Essor.
1947, Liège-Paris, Maréchal ("édition définitive").
1982, Brussels, Jacques Antoine.

Ghelderode, Michel de. *Sortilèges et autres contes crépusculaires.* Verviers: Presses de Gérard (Marabout), 1962.

The editions of *Spells* listed above are those consulted for this translation. No two are the same in point of detail; all include minor textual variants and typographical errors. The 1947 text is the most reliable and also provides a template for subsequent editions, including those, most recently, of Labor (2002) and Gallimard (2008). The Marabout pocketbook edition, which enjoyed a number of reprints and became widely available, adds a subtitle—*Spells and Other Twilight Tales*. This was the initiative of market-minded Marabout editors; however, Ghelderode may well have agreed to it—he saw the proofs before his death. Any trace of Franz Hellens disappears from the Marabout edition, probably at Ghelderode's behest (in later life he seems to have fallen out with his old friend) and the Hellens preface to the 1947 edition is replaced by one by Henri Vernes.

FURTHER READING

IN ENGLISH

In addition to the volume of George Hauger translations listed above, a number of Ghelderode's plays are available in English, including a further volume from Hauger. The ambitious, full-length puppet play, *The Siege of Ostend*, is available in David Willinger's translation (Host, 1990). André de Vries's *Flanders, A Cultural History* (Oxford University Press, 2007) includes a brief overview of Ghelderode.

IN FRENCH

Philippe Met's academic study of fantastic literature, *La lettre tue* (Presses Universitaires du Septentrion, 2009), includes a chapter on *Spells*, with detailed analyses of "The Public Scribe" and "The Sick Garden." Arnaud Huftier's scholarly essay on *Spells* (in *De l'écrit à l'écran*, ed. Jacques Migozzi, Presses Universitaires de Limoges, 2000) focuses on its generic status.